KEEPING PRIVATE IDAHO

Rick Just

Keeping Private Idaho
By Rick Just

Published by:
Cedar Creek Press
3380 Terra Drive
Boise ID 83709

Publisher's Cataloging-in-Publication Data (Prepared by Quality Books Inc.)

Just, Rick Keeping Private Idaho / Rick Just.
p. em. ISBN 978-0-9910790-9-4
1. Idaho--Fiction. 2. Tourist trade--Idaho--Fiction.
1. Title.
PS3560.U78K446 1996 813'.54 QBI96-40179

Acknowledgments

I am most grateful to those who critiqued the early drafts of Keeping Private Idaho, Glenn Selander, Roberta Rene', Orvis Burmaster, Lisa VanDercar, Deborah Long, Connie Vaughn and Mont Short. Special thanks to Carl Wilgus and Georgia Smith, without whose understanding the book would not have been possible. For keeping me straight and laughing in all the right places, I am indebted to Rosemary Hardin. For keeping the weak words out, my thanks to editor Mary Kelly McColl. And, for his terrific cover art for this edition, my thanks go to Ward Hooper.

For Tom Trusky

Idahoan Extraordinaire

PROLOGUE, 1995

The Undiscovered America

"Damn! How the hell do you find Idaho?" Mark Angel drove hunched over the steering wheel, getting as close to his destination as possible without actually leaving the car.

"I don't know, dear," said Rita. "It can't be far, though." She held an Idaho road map, fuzzy along its folds from being creased and decreased in a variety of innovative ways.

"Like, who gives a flying ..."

"Todd, don't even think it." Mark shot his best warning glare into the mirror.

"It's not Todd. It's John. Todd's a little-kid name." As soon as his dad took his eyes off the mirror, John Todd Angel stuck out his tongue.

"Really attractive, Toad. Catch many flies with that?" Heather asked.

"Stick it!"

"Hey guys, let's not have any fighting. Your dad needs our help. He's lost."

"I'm not lost." He hesitated. "I just don't know exactly where I am. We should have crossed the Jordan River by now."

"Creek," said Rita. "It's just a creek."

"You sure?"

"Yes, I'm sure. Look." She tapped one perfect nail on the map. "The town is Jordan Valley and it's Jordan Creek. It's on Highway 95."

"Whatever. Hey, there's a sign. We're coming into Vale. See if you can find Vale on the map."

"Just a second." Rita looked over the top of her sunglasses at the Idaho index on the bottom of the map.

"Did you say 95? The sign said this is Highway 20 or 26," Heather said, rolling her eyes. "Like, they couldn't make up their minds which, right?"

"Shh," Mark said. "Your mother is concentrating."

"There's no Vale in Idaho. There's a Victor, a Viola and a Virginia." "How about Ontario? That's coming up too." "Ontario? That's in Canada, Dad, geez!" John Todd said.

"Let's see. No. No Ontario, either. Are you sure it didn't say Orofino? There's an Orofino. Oh, look! There's a town called Paris."

"In Idaho?" Heather wrinkled her nose like she'd just tripped over the carcass of a badger.

John Todd said," If we'd just followed the dumb moving van we wouldn't be in Canada, I bet."

Mark caught his son's eye in the mirror. The look he gave Todd nearly made the glass frost over. The "follow the moving van" suggestion had been brought up before and was holding less and less favor with Mr. Angel as the miles rolled past them.

They traveled on for the next few minutes in silence, reaching the outskirts of Ontario which, much to Mark's relief, didn't have any road signs in French. But where had they gone wrong? That Nevada gas station, maybe. The attendant had said this was the way to Jordan Valley. It was Nevada where that couple and the baby got lost in the winter. They were looking for Idaho. They were from California, too. Was there a conspiracy going on? Mark was beginning to believe it until he saw a red, white and blue sign for Interstate 84.

"Hey, that's it!" He switched lanes without looking and roared up the ramp.

"Mark, be careful! Where are you going?"

"To Idaho, just like I promised." And within 30 seconds they saw it, a big billboard that said "Celebrate Idaho," with the governor's signature in the right-hand corner.

"This is the Snake River, guys, I saw the sign. Get ready to give a big cheer. When we're halfway across, we're in Idaho! Ready? We're he-re, everybody say hooray!"

Rita joined him in the hooray, while John Todd said, "BFD" and Heather added a lethargic "yippy-skippy."

The Beamer bounced as it went across an expansion joint in the bridge. The movement was enough to dislodge a lemon-sized chunk of coagulated oil and road grunge from the undercarriage that had been building up over the past few months. It dropped, ricocheted off the pavement, and miraculously wedged itself between the floorboards and the catalytic converter, where it turned into a science experiment, changing from a solid to a liquid, to a gas.

"Look," Mark pointed, "there's a visitor center on the hill. It can be our first stop in Idaho!"

They took the short road up to the rest area and obediently followed the sign to the cars side of the parking lot. The idea was not unique. As they drove slowly in, it appeared that every spot in the lot was taken.

"Shoot. Where are we supposed to park?" Mark checked his rearview mirror and spotted a car backing out two spaces back. "Bingo!" He threw the lever to R. As it happened, the driver directly behind him was also from California, and so had razor sharp reactions. She threw her car in reverse, too. That move was not anticipated by the Idaho driver behind her. Used to taking two, maybe three nanoseconds to make decisions, the Idaho driver froze. The resulting crunch was accompanied staccato by a similar sound coming from the rear of the Idaho car.

"Hey, there's a better one!" John Todd pointed to a station wagon backing out several steps closer to the front doors of the building. Mark clicked to D and slid into the slot like he was born to park there. Meanwhile, the oil glob on the catalytic converter had converted into a blue mist that wafted up on both sides of the car. All four doors flew open and the Angels got out.

"This is it, guys," said Mark. "We're home at last." He closed his eyes and filled his lungs. "Smell that air."

Heather sniffed experimentally. "I can't smell anything."

"That's my point. It's clean!"

Mark took Rita's hand and they buoyantly made for the visitor center. Heather shuffled along behind. John Todd was the only one who noticed the commotion at the far end of the parking lot. Traffic was backed up to the rest area entrance behind three drivers who were gesticulating angrily. "Bozos," he said, and turned toward the center.

Inside the restroom stall Heather took the time to use her nail file to neatly scratch "Idaho Sucks!" into the paint on the metal door. At the same time John Todd was engraving in his own stall, though not as neatly: "LA Rules!"

Eager for a fresh road map, Mark waited patiently at the information counter behind a frazzled-looking man who was trying to find Ontario, Oregon. The patient woman at the counter explained with a smile that he had just passed Ontario two miles back and would have to go two miles further down the road to the next exit to turn around.

When it was his turn, Mark shook his head in sympathy to the IdaHost and said, "Tourists."

She sighed and clicked her hand-held people counter, laying it down next to a stack of maps. "We get that all the time. People just don't pay attention." The woman reinstalled her smile and said, "Welcome to Idaho. Where are you from?"

"Oh, me? I'm from Boise," Mark said, winking at Rita who had walked up. "I just thought I'd stop by and pick up a new map."

"Sure thing," the woman said. "Here you go."

Mark started digging in his pocket. "How much?"

"Oh, no charge. They're free."

"Free?" Rita sounded insulted. "How can you give them away for free? In California they charge two dollars for them."

"That was at a gas station, Mom," Heather said as she walked up.

"Well, it doesn't matter, sweetie. They could sell the maps and then the taxpayers wouldn't have to pay for them." Rita turned back to the woman and said, "Really, you should look into it. I'm just sure California does it that way."

The woman continued to smile broadly, perhaps a little stiffly. "Thank you," she said, without moving her lips. She picked up the people counter and clicked it twice.

John Todd, fascinated by every brochure in the center, was grabbing three or four of each. "Let's go, Todd," Mark called, as the rest of the family headed for the door.

Quietly the boy told the brochures, "It's not Todd." Several stacks of flyers were lined up on the information counter. He took handfuls of each while the IdaHost helped her next customer. Click. Another customer. Click. Hey, John Todd thought, that's cool. He worked his way across the counter- Click-to the maps. Click. The woman put her clicker down to show a customer the best route to Yellowstone. Todd grabbed a map, then another, then the clicker and headed for the door.

Outside the center he saw his parents and sister getting into the car, his dad waving impatiently. All right already, he thought, I'm coming. His hands were full of brochures. Too full. They were getting to be a pain, and besides, he was more interested in the clicker. He pitched the brochures in the general direction of a garbage can. Click, click, click. Three trees. Click, click, click, click. Four cars. Cool. He could count anything. Click, click, click, click, click, click. Six tourists getting out of a van.

"'Todd, hurry up."

"All right, all right," he said. "I'm here already."

CHAPTER ONE

Discovered

In which our players notice something new.

With no concept of how long he had been asleep, Coyote let out a shuddering breath. He flexed his fingers. The movement was hesitant, tentative. As if learning their limits he stretched and curled them, stretched and curled, making a fist then relaxing it. Worn out from the exertion, he stopped for a time. Then, languidly, he moved his index finger back and forth in a beckoning motion. That, too, stopped.

He had been having a dream about helping maidens across the water when something woke him up. A strong thing made him open his eyes. Usually it took a strong thing, like Magpie pecking at Coyote's eyebrow fat. Or vengeance. It was so dark. Was he in the belly of the Monster again?

***

She had her speed up, cruising the greenbelt with an easy, practiced rhythm, swoosh, swoosh, swoosh, leaning from side to side in a sine wave cadence, stretching out her strides. The trees on the island filtered the light and strobed it, giving a red flash to the edges of her vision. The slightly fishy smell of the river and the perfume of the cottonwoods gave her a heady feeling of energy. Faster now, she skated around a gentle curve, tucked up across a wooden footbridge, then pushed off perfectly to catch the next corner without losing speed. Had to watch for roots breaking through the pavement along here. They could catch a wheel and put you on your face. On her right a few half-million-dollar houses wearing cedar roofs and distressed brick peeked through the trees. Then they were behind her, and she was the only person in Idaho. She broke into a thirty-foot-long clearing, then back into a tunnel of trees. There was a corner coming up she could not yet see. Her memory had it placed. At just the right moment she'd let her left skate drift out, step into the corner with her right, then repeat to get the perfect line through it. In a moment she...

A scream cut through the morning air. She lost her balance, caught it again with a clunk of her skate, then, back in control, skidded her right skate around and stopped, facing back along the path. She stood in the middle of the deserted path feeling awkward and vulnerable on her skinny wheels. Her breath came fast, her heart pounded. What the hell was that? She listened hard. Nothing. Even the air was quiet. It had sounded like a woman. No, not a woman. A child, maybe, or an animal. And it really wasn't a sound at all, was it? More like the echo of a sound, like an eagle heard across Hells Canyon.

Best move on, slowly. Maybe it was metal against metal. Some huge, grinding. She shook her head. It was gone. The memory of it was fading. Impossible to describe now, she almost knew exactly what it was the second after it happened.

She'd worked up a bigger sweat than she thought. Careful not to rub it into her eyes, she started to brush the moisture off her cheeks. She straightened and stopped striding, rolling along slowly, stiffly. She was crying. Why the hell was she crying?

***

Sunshine came streaming in through the glass, bouncing brightly off the orange tables and yellow chairs. The day was so sunny it reflected off the customers. Every one of them smiled and chatted and laughed. As for Blaine Stope, flipping burgers behind the grill, the light hurt his eyes. You practically needed sunglasses to work in here for god sakes. Not that it was real work. His muscles, bulging out from a rolled up t-shirt, felt flabby. They wobbled like jelly when he slid the spatula under the ground beef. Lifting a quarter pound at a time didn't keep them in shape.

"Order up!" he shouted, tossing a red plastic basket on the shelf beneath the little merry-go-round of fluttering order slips. He squinted at the next one in line. Damn bright light. Two burgers, two fries. Hold the onions on one. He was about to call out to Cyndy to lower the damn blinds when he felt it. Stope grabbed a counter with one hand and a knob on the front of the grill with the other. He stepped back to brace himself against it. Wow. A big one. He hadn't felt one like that since. . . The customers still chatted. Cyndy served a pair of monster Cokes to a couple of teenagers in the corner. The white plastic globe lights hung straight down from the ceiling like plumb bobs. Blaine looked around. His water glass, perched on the edge of the shelf to his right, was full nearly to the rim. The kitchen spoons hung perfectly still on the wall.

Cyndy, who navigated through tables like they were cones on a road course, stood now in front of the order window. "You okay, Mr. Stope?"

"Huh?"

"You look a little pale."

"No, I'm fine. Just fine." He looked around one more time, half-expecting to catch something swaying. "Hey, did you feel anything just now?"

Cyndy raised her right eyebrow. "Like what?"

"Uh, just something unusual."

"Like me getting a tip bigger'n a quarter?"

Blaine laughed with her and dismissed it. She picked up the order and careened back into the restaurant. I'll be danged, he thought. That sure felt like... something.

***

The crack of thunder made Frank Thompson whip around, spilling a bucket of oats. Funny, there wasn't a cloud in the sky.

***

When a tree starts to fall there is a feeling in the air, like time has been called off. That feeling came to Jake like an old-growth cedar was coming down. He looked over each shoulder, then did a 360. Damn strange.

***

Debbie Bennett Anderson caught a smell that made her shudder. It was gone as fast as it came, a wild, coppery scent like something fresh killed. She tightened up on Skid's reins, expecting him to go ballistic. He plodded along.

***

The light started over the Owyhees to the southwest, instantly traced across the ridges like an EKG gone wild and flashed in a straight line east along the Nevada border like a sheet of Mylar snapping across the horizon.

"Holy Jesus!" Bill Clark had been looking through his lens when the edge of the earth became a daytime silhouette. His hand clenched the camera, finger jammed down tight on the shutter. I wonder if I got it, he thought.

CHAPTER TWO

I was here first!

In which Jo Beth takes her space, Bill is amazed at how wrong he can be, Blaine gives a mine tour, Farmer Frank thinks about the good old hay days, Bill names The Place, Shoshone Falls are misplaced, and something goes bump in the dark.

Traffic on Park Center Boulevard got heavier every day. It used to be theirs was the last development on the road. When they first moved in, he didn't even have to look left when pulling out of the subdivision. Then, they added phase II, then phase III. After that a shopping center went in across the road and down a couple blocks. Other subdivisions and phases grew, splitting off the first, then splitting again like a cell. Not a cancerous cell. Just a cell. His wife was in real estate, after all.

Bill Clark sat through three lights before he could get onto Broadway. He left early for this? While he waited, he twisted the mirror for a quick check. Once or twice he'd forgotten to shave in the morning. Shaving was for work. He grew stubble on weekends and a short beard on vacations. This morning his cheeks were smooth. His hair was more-or-less combed. It was still red. You could count on some things in life.

Ha! A break. Bill gunned the Explorer and turned right on red in front of a Volvo that had lagged back a couple of spaces creating a hole. It came up fast on his bumper and blasted its horn. He scowled into his mirror and saw the guy give him the finger. Bill smiled back widely at him and waved, knowing it would irritate the jerk more than the expected digital salute. A Volvo with Idaho plates. Ten to one the guy was from California. Most native Idahoans didn't even know where their horn button was.

He wheeled into the parking garage behind a Toyota four-by-four and started to spiral up the floors. The Toyota's roll bar sported a set of five high-power lights tacked across the top, each covered with insipid vinyl smiley faces. The rig was spotless. The guy probably never took it off-road. There were getting to be so many like that—people who bought the lifestyle image, but not the lifestyle. The parking garage roof hung so low on the corners Clark kept hoping to hear a crunch as the concrete stripped the lights clean. The Toyota made it around three turns unscathed and found an empty spot. Bill went on by, dreading the thought of going all the way to the uncovered fourth floor. Two more turns without an empty then, on the third, a spot came up on his left. He'd gone right by without noticing. He threw the shifter forward and started to back up. A red Miata came rolling out of nowhere and shot into the slot like a pinball flipped into the 500 hole.

"I'll be go to..." He let his rig roll back ten feet so he could be in a good position to share his mind with the driver. "Hey, I was here first!" he shouted as the door to the Miata swung open.

Deja vu. That had been his older brother's favorite line. Bill was Billy then and John was Johnny. Whenever they competed for anything of value from ice cream to TV time, Johnny claimed the superiority of his birth. If Billy beat him to whatever it was by ten minutes the answer was always the same, "I was here first." Johnny did not claim dibs case by case. He was always the first. He was the oldest.

"Tough cookies, Clark," the woman said, peeking around the soft top. "You snooze, you lose."

The fuzzy, platinum blond hair was the first clue he had pressed the wrong button on life's calculator. He should have recognized the car; should have noticed the personalized plate: TOURISM. Jo Beth Crowder was his boss.

He grinned at her. "Just kidding, Jo Beth. In fact, I saved that one for you."

She unfolded herself from the sports car, smoothed her suit and said, "Charmer. You ready for today's meeting?"

"Sure, as ready as I'll ever be."

Jo Beth pulled out her briefcase and slammed the car door. Her heels made a harsh, hollow echo in the concrete garage. She leaned one arm on his door and tapped her fingernail on the glass. Bill rarely noticed perfume. His wife said it was a genetic defect. No one could miss Jo Beth's trademark scent. It had a subtle undercurrent like something you savor and never quite get enough of. Maybe amaretto. Another fragrance wove through it more like a memory than a smell. It reminded him of sea air and sunshine. Pleasant as those elements were, the unforgettable component was an overpowering odor of citrus. It was too much to take for more than a few seconds.

"Have you got all your ammo ready?"

"I didn't know this was a war."

She gave him a tight little smile. "Not a war, just a battle. You know how important this is to me."

Someone in a junky, pale blue Health and Welfare sedan stopped behind him and revved the engine.

"I know it's a big deal. You can count on me," Bill said, then pulled away from her.

As he feared, the only spot left was in the paint-fading sunshine. A couple of years and a few hundred bureaucrats ago he didn't know the roof of the parking garage even existed. When he shut his door, a trickle of Owyhee Desert dust drifted down onto the concrete.

Ignoring the elevator Bill bounded down the stairs to the tunnel that connected the buildings in the Capitol Mall. Inside he joined a crowd of bureaucrats on their way to another day of filing forms, processing words, and making decisions Idahoans wouldn't learn about for six or eight months. Fifty feet in front of him Jo Beth Crowder drove her heels into the smooth concrete of the tunnel floor like pitons into granite. No one watching her walk would ever think she was out for a stroll. Her legs pistoned with purpose.

Clark smiled to himself and shook his head. He could probably catch her if he trotted. Or maybe he'd have a chance with his Rollerblades. He rarely took the tunnel without thinking how it cried to be skated, with all that broad, flat concrete as smooth as polished metal. Maybe some weekend he'd work up the courage to break the rules.

At his desk on the second floor of the flashcube building everyone called the Hall of Mirrors, he listened to half a dozen voice-mail messages, clicked through his e-mail, dated and initialed and coded a couple of bills for payment. The meeting began at 9:00 a.m.

Bill was in his chair five minutes early. Film Bureau Chief Clayton Beck showed up on time. Jo Beth, who was sharing herself between two meetings as usual, slipped in about ten after. "Not here yet?" she asked.

"Not yet," Beck said. "Do you think we should call?"

"She'll show up eventually." Jo Beth shrugged. "Indian time, you know." She darted out the door.

Bill asked, "What does she mean Indian time?"

"Oh Hell, Clark, you know. Indians don't pay a hell of a lot of attention to clocks."

"Yeah, I know what Indian time is. What's it got to do with..."

"Hi. Is this the place?" Bill turned to the door. He had heard the name Mary Lewis a couple of times. Based solely on the simple old fashioned sound of it, he had assigned the woman plain, frumpy looks. He was constantly amazed how wrong he could be.

Mary Lewis, dressed in a tasteful charcoal business suit and a red blouse with a high buttoned collar, strode forward and offered him her hand. "I don't think we've met. I'm Mary." She was about five six or seven. Her face had the high cheekbones of a model, without the harsh, chiseled look. Soft was the word that came to mind.

"Pleased to meet you, Mary. Bill Clark." He gestured to one of the executive conference chairs. "Please have a seat."

Warm. Warm was another word to describe her, he thought. Where did that come from? They had exchanged only a dozen words. Maybe it was her skin. Just as black rarely came close to the actual hue of an African-American's skin, red missed describing hers. She looked like she was shaped by an artist from almond-colored wood. Sanded and smoothed, not carved. Her eyes were such a deep, dark brown you might have called them black, if they were not framed by the jet of her hair. Had it ever seen scissors? It cascaded across her shoulders and down her back like a black waterfall caught in a beautiful blur by a slow shutter speed, and ended just past her waist.

She put her briefcase on the table, snapped it open and sat down. "Hi Clay. Sorry, I'm late. I'm not used to Boise traffic yet, I guess."

Beck gave her a tight little smile and a nod.

Bill said, "So, you're new to Boise? Where are you from?"

"Idaho," she said. For a moment he thought she would leave it at that. Then she added, "I've worked at a couple of parks, most recently Ponderosa. I was a ranger there when this job came open at headquarters."

"A ranger, really? What made you decide to become an information officer?" She flipped a few stray strands of hair over her shoulder.

"The big bucks, life in the spotlight. You know, the usual."

"So, do you like it?"

"Boise?"

"Yeah, and being an information officer."

"Boise's great, for a city." She laughed lightly. "Information officer is okay, too, for a job."

Idaho's administrator of travel and tourism popped her head in the door. "Hi Mary. Good to see you. No, no, don't get up." Jo Beth had her public face on, which came equipped with a wide smile Clark always imagined as propped up by poles. "Are these two guys treating you all right?"

"Just fine, thanks."

"Well, don't let them bully you. If they try it, you know where my office is." Crowder gave her a measured wink. "I've got to be in another meeting, but I'm sure the three of you can work this out just fine. Bill will be representing me, and I'll drop back in to see how things are going."

When Jo Beth left, Mary Lewis wrinkled her nose and touched her forefinger to it demurely, as if stifling a sneeze. Clark wondered if she'd gotten a blast of perfume. He'd caught the edge of it even across the table.

Bill was glad Jo Beth was tied up in her usual meeting knots. The woman from Parks looked a little dainty to be tossed to the lions so early in her career.

"Well, let's get started," Bill said. "Mary, I think Clayton sent you a fax yesterday of the latest proposal for the travel writers' tour."

"Yes," she said, digging into her briefcase and pulling out a manila folder. "Jim and I talked about it last night." Jim Casper was the director of the Idaho Department of Parks and Recreation.

"Great. What did he think about it?"

"Well, he thought it was interesting," she said. "But he had some concerns. As Clay probably told you, our park manager is dead set against it."

Beck's lips tightened. He and the Lewis woman had been trying to come to terms for over a week. That was why Bill was suddenly involved. He interjected before Beck could say something stupid. "What are his objections? We want everyone to be comfortable with this."

"We'll be happy to host the writers and give them all the information about the park they need. Gary Preuit isn't ever going to be comfortable allowing ATVs on his sand dunes."

"His dunes?" Beck said. "I thought they were Idaho's dunes."

Mary doodled on her legal pad. Bill could make out five or six shapes penned across the binding on the top. One of them gave him a momentary start. Then he realized it wasn't what it appeared to be. She had drawn a simple silhouette shape of a bird in flight. From where he sat, viewing it upside down, he'd at first taken it for a chevron.

"They are Idaho's dunes. Of course. Protecting a park is a manager's job. Sometimes they get a little possessive."

"Arrogant is more like it," Beck said. "Can't Casper just overrule him?"

"He could." She put her pen down and let the words hang for a few seconds. "But he won't. He trusts the judgment of his people."

"Oh for..." Beck folded his arms and looked away.

"Mary, help me out here," Bill said. "I don't see what harm running a few ATVs across the sand just once would do."

She gave him a quick smile. "In the first place, it wouldn't be just once. The minute you let one group bend the rules, another group will want to do the same thing. Before long, the ATVers will be lobbying for set-aside areas where they can ride. Then they'd want bigger areas. Eventually you'd have nothing but a noise park out there."

"You make it sound like there are people on motorcycles waiting at the gate with their engines revved up," Beck said.

"They practically are. This is North America's tallest single-structured sand dune. We're under pressure constantly from off-road groups."

"Let's put it in perspective," Bill said. "We're just talking about taking a few people back there to shoot some pictures of the dunes at sunrise."

"Fine. We're not against them taking pictures. Why can't they walk like everyone else?"

The sleeves of his blazer rode up on his arms as Beck leaned across the table. "Because they're not Everyone Else. These are travel writers. The cream of the crop. They're used to being pampered and catered to, and for damn good reason. They have the power to bring thousands of tourists into Idaho. And—do I have to say it?—millions of dollars."

Landing the World Travel Writers Association annual convention was the biggest coup of Jo Beth's career. It was like quadrupling the tourism advertising budget without spending an extra dime. Better. First-person travel stories had far more credibility than ads. The side trip to Bruneau Dunes State Park on the last day of the convention was a small part of the package—a part Jo Beth had already promised.

Lewis locked eyes with Beck. "We're aware of the economic potential. But at Parks, our first duty is to the resource."

"What resource?" Beck asked, raising his voice a notch. "It's sand, for Christ sakes. The wind never lets up out there. Ten minutes after we're out of the park the tracks will be gone."

"We're not worried about the tracks. It's the precedent that concerns us. Besides, there's more than just sand. There's the sand lily and the tiger beetle to worry about."

Beck threw up his arms. "We'll drive around the damn lilies. That's a no-brainer. If you'd like, you can skip merrily along in front of us shooing the miserable beetles out of the way."

The woman from Parks gave Beck a look that would wither ants. "Whoa, whoa," Bill said. "Let's keep it friendly." He asked Mary, "Is there a way we can avoid doing any damage?"

Before answering, she picked up her pen. "Deserts are fragile environments." She drew a careful circle around the tiny Idaho on her pad. "They look indestructible because they're so rugged."

The opposite of you, Bill thought. He had been wrong, again. She could hold her own with Jo Beth any day. "I respect that," he said. "I spend a lot of time taking pictures at Bruneau myself. The desert is crawling with life."

"Bugs!" Beck might have been aiming the word at a corner spittoon.

Lewis did not look up. She continued her doodle, retracing the circle. "Clay, you've made your disdain for the ecosystem abundantly clear," she said.

Bill thought he saw her draw something across the circle. Mary continued, "Which is why I cannot recommend that we waive park rules for you. If the travel writers want to take pictures of the dunes, they can. We'll let them in the park for free. We'll provide a ranger to guide them back to the best shooting locations. That's it." She tossed her pad and pen in her briefcase and snapped it shut. Bill tried to get one last look at her meeting art. It was gone before he could confirm it.

Automatically, Bill stood and took her hand when it was offered. "Nice meeting you, Mr. Clark. I'm sorry we weren't able to work it out to your satisfaction. Please let me know what we can do for you within the bounds of our regulations."

She was gone before he could form a response. "See what I've been telling you," Beck said. "She's a bitch with a capital B."

Bill shook his head. If he were looking for a B word to capitalize, Beautiful would sooner come to mind.

"You're mad because she won't roll over and play dead."

"The woman's a bitch. She's the one who killed the film shoot at Harriman."

"Really? The one where the production company wanted to close the park to the public for six weeks during the heavy use season?"

"It was a two million dollar shoot!"

"They wanted to move one of the historic ranch buildings, didn't they? And wasn't there some problem with helicopter shots?"

Beck shrugged. "They wanted some aerials. The park manager was afraid it would scare off the fucking swans."

"It was a bad proposal, Clay."

"It would have pushed us over ten million from films statewide for the first time."

Jo Beth came breezing into the room. "How did it go, guys? Did you charm Hiawatha out of her pants?"

"Oh yeah," Beck said. "Good thing you didn't come in a few minutes sooner. You would have caught us making love on the table."

"Not so good," Bill said. "She wouldn't go for ATVs on the dunes. They want us to hike them back in."

"Hike them?" Jo Beth looked like she'd bit into a lemon. "After they've been drinking till two in the morning she expects us to drive them for an hour and a half then make them walk for twenty minutes to catch the sunrise?"

"It's an optional tour," Bill said. "We might suggest they get a little earlier start on sleep the night before if they want to go."

"No good. We want as many of them out there as possible. Everything we do has to be first class."

"We're already giving them a catered champagne breakfast."

"That's fine, but we're not going to make them trudge through the sand at 5:30 in the morning. No way. Would it help if I called Casper?"

"You could try it. I think he'd stand behind her decision, though."

"Screw it, then. I'll talk to the Guv."

Problem solved. Jo Beth rushed back to her other meeting. Beck scooped up his tablet and quickly followed. Bill sighed heavily, got up and slowly headed for his cubicle. He liked working in the Travel and Tourism Division of the Department of Commerce. He was starting to tire of the insatiable appetite for numbers. Dollars here, visitor days there, housing starts across the way. They sold Idaho's quality of life as if it were as eternal as the Sawtooths. Someday they might wake up and find the product gone.

***

"Oh, yes, it takes a lot of wood. Most people never think of that." Blaine Stope was in high gear. "There were times when the mines around here were using six million board feet of timber every year."

He loved the look on their faces when he threw out figures like that. Their eyes got big around and sometimes their mouths really did drop open, or form air-sucking Os like whitefish out of water. Now one of them, a young guy with wire rim glasses, had a question. "What kind of trees did they use?"

"Douglas fir and larch, mostly."

"Well, where'd they get them?" Glasses asked. "There isn't much of anything growing in this valley." There were a few giggles of agreement.

Sometimes you got an idiot. Actually, most times you were talking to idiots.

"Well, sir, that's exactly why there aren't a lot of trees around here. Big ones, anyway," Stope said. "They cut them down to hold up the ceilings in the mines. Bunker Hill had its own sawmill for sixty-six years. You can cut a hell of a... Sorry, folks. You can process a heck of a lot of timber in that time." Stope gave them a silver medal smile and said, "I haven't counted lately, but at one time there was more timber underground in this valley than there was above ground in the whole Coeur d'Alene National Forest." That one always brought out the fish mouths.

"Sir?" A little boy about nine held up his hand. "What did you used to do in the mines?"

"Well, son," Stope sucked in a chestful of air, "I did a lot of things. I ran a drill for years. Drilled holes in the rock so we could put charges in and," he bent over so he was inches away from the boy's face, "boom! We'd blow up the rock so we could get the silver out of it."

The kid gave a satisfying jump when Blaine boomed. He tousled the boy's hair and straightened up. "I also ran a skip for a while. That's like an elevator that takes you down in the mines. We'll see it later on. I even worked at the concentrator for a few months. That's where they crush and process the ore. A lot of people call it a mill. Nothing I liked better than horsing that drill, though." He made an easy fist and bent back his arm to show off a bicep tattooed with the outline of Idaho superimposed by a miner's pick. "Makes a man out of you."

The boy had the mouth and he had silver dollar eyes. He looked up at the young woman who had her fingers touching his shoulders protectively. "Mom! I'm going to be a miner when I grow up!" The group laughed politely.

Blaine Stope did not laugh. He looked at the excited little boy and saw another boy in another time. He knew this one would change his mind a hundred times before he finally became a fireman or an accountant or a computer programmer. That other boy had never wanted to be anything else. Never ever.

***

He could have hired this done. He sometimes did, if he was too busy with other things. There was probably nothing he liked better than watching that rich green alfalfa, standing thigh high and thick as rabbit fur, feed into the blades. One minute it was there and the next it was gone, like somebody had come along with shears and shaved it off. And that's about what swathing was. In front of the swather grew a forest of stems and leaves rippling in the breeze. Behind it, the field—30 inches shorter—took on a pale green with dusty streaks of ground showing through, except where the machine laid the harvest down neatly in a windrow.

His swather was twenty years old and still seemed like a miracle to Frank Thompson. He remembered the days when this was a two-step process. First, you'd cut the hay with a sickle bar mower that attached to the back of your tractor. The bar lifted in the air like a mailbox flag when not in use, and dropped down to extend behind and to the right side of the tractor when you were cutting. The power take-off shaft at the back of the tractor ran the serrated blades back and forth through the arm. Long, pointed metal fingers fed the alfalfa into the blades, which sliced it off clean and dropped it flat. Sometimes, you'd catch something you didn't want to catch in that bar. A cat maybe, or more often a pheasant. The birds liked to hunker down in the hay, hoping invisibility would save them from the mechanical monster coming their way. At the last second they might decide to fly, or if they were just chicks, run. Frank remembered dozens of times getting off the tractor to put a pheasant, who found itself suddenly without legs, out of its misery.

The second step, in those days, was to come along with a hay rake pulled behind a tractor that gathered up the downed alfalfa and combed it into a row for the baler to pick up. Hiram Thompson, Frank's dad, rest his soul, had been about convinced his son would never get the hang of raking hay. There was a little trick to getting the pattern right, raking along one edge of the field, then moving out a hundred feet or so to the first irrigation dike to make your pass back. Then, you'd catch the inside of your first pass, and the outside of your second pass, working your way across the field one section at a time. Frank got that part all right, but he always seemed to end up laying down a swath right on top of the dike where the baler couldn't pick it up. His dad would never get angry with him. Since he was Brother Thompson, too, he would certainly never swear. He just got so disappointed Frank liked to about melt.

It seemed lately he was thinking more and more about when he was a kid. About the old times. Especially when he worked this field.

It was a little piece of ground. At twenty acres, it was almost too much trouble to operate anymore. It was too small to go to the expense of setting up sprinklers, so it still had the old-fashioned dikes running the length of the field. It was also five miles from the house, so he had to drive the swather on the highway, with that silly pyramid sign dangling from the back.

Keeping the land didn't make any economic sense. Frank still kept it. It was the only piece left of his granddad's original homestead. He didn't know how many times his kids, Levi, Joseph Brigham, Mary Ellen, Lehi, Denton, Spencer and Margaret, had tried to talk him into selling off the land. Those blessed kids didn't care a thing for tradition; all they could see was the money.

Oh, they were good kids. Who could blame them? Farming didn't really pay anymore, and you had to make a living. Levi and J.B. were already working at Idaho Supreme, processing spuds. Mary Ellen was planning to go to BYU, as soon as she graduated from Ricks. She wanted to teach home economics. The rest were still in high school. Not all of them knew what they wanted to do with their lives. Every one of them knew farming wasn't it.

He could sell the land real easy. Houses were going up on two sides of it while he made hay. There were already people living in homes along the far end of the field, their fences right up against his ditch. Every time he made a pass down that way the backyard dogs went nuts.

Frank shook his head. Barking at him on his own land. What a crazy world this was getting to be.

***

Traffic was moderate this afternoon. Which was to say too damn heavy. If he thought about it too much it made him angry. So Bill always concentrated on something else to take his mind off it. He thought about a place and time so far removed from State Street it might have been on another planet. Not just any place. The Place.

One memory always came back first. It was the memory of a cottonwood tree that had fallen across the little gully near the river on The Place. That tree was many things, while it lasted, suspended over the deepest canyon on earth.

It could be a ship, a jungle, a bridge, a fort, a rocket. Mostly it was an airplane. He was the dashing young pilot. It was in that broken cottonwood he decided 24 would be the perfect age—not too old, not too young. He wanted to be 24 forever when he was nine. He did not remember how old he wanted to be when he finally reached 24. At 44 he wanted to be nine.

That time in the gully tree when he could be whatever he wanted to be was a time aside; a time that could never be touched by now. Nothing changed the gully tree. Or the "jungle" or the rope swing or the corral poles. Or The Place. They were as constant and incorruptible as the sun.

Bill did not know when The Place took on its capital letters. Some farms or ranches gained names that pleased their owners, names that reflected local features or history or ambition. No such pretension attended the naming of The Place. The Clark family had a home. On the rare occasions they were away from it, in town to buy seed, for instance or attend the state fair, the family had to call it something. Calling it "Our 320 acres on the Blackfoot River" would be awkward. Without giving it any thought, they began calling it the place. Their neighbors probably called their places, "the place," too, though Bill never noticed. The capital letters came along sometime after they moved into town, he thought. Maybe the moment they moved.

When he became a city boy—a derogatory term his cousins used for anyone who lived within shouting distance of anyone else—they talked about The Place a lot. The ranch was still there, virtually unchanged. It was not a place his mother or Johnny or Billy could call home. Perhaps instantly, perhaps slowly over the years, the letters grew until they were tall and sturdy. The Place.

***

The Toyota wagon pulled up to the curb and a blond woman in her mid-thirties rolled down the passenger window. "Excuse me. Could you tell us how to find Shoshone Falls?"

Ed Wilkie brightened. He had received his Private Idaho membership card just that morning, so this would be his first official act.

"You bet. You folks tourists?"

"Yes, we are. You have such a beautiful state."

"Thanks. We like it. Let's see. Shoshone Falls, huh? Well you keep on going down Blue Lakes to the third light, then you take a right."

"Ed, that's ..."

"Now, Maria, it's confusing to folks to have two people try to give directions. You just let me take care of it."

"But ..."

"Like I said, you take a right at the third light. That'll have you going west."

"Okay," the blond said. "A right at the third light. Got that honey?"

"Got it," the driver said.

"Then you go west six miles and take a left. I don't remember the name of the road, but its six miles." Maria started to say something again. Ed gave her foot a little kick. "Once you're there, just keep on heading south until you run into the falls. Can't miss 'em."

"Six miles, then turn left. That sounds simple enough."

"Can't miss 'em," Ed said.

"Thank you. Appreciate your help."

Ed gave them a friendly wave as they pulled away.

"What has gotten into you?" Marie asked. "That'll no more get them to Shoshone Falls than the man in the moon."

"Oh, be quiet. I was just having a little fun with them."

"Fun? They'll be lost for hours with those directions. They'll probably end up in Nevada."

Ed chuckled. "Yep, probably so."

"How'd you feel if they gave you directions like that when you were on vacation in their home town?"

"Never gonna happen," Ed said, grinning at his wife. "Ain't never going to California."

CHAPTER THREE

Used to be is now

In which we meet Pauline and Nick, Jake sculpts a fender, Bill meets Mary on a Boise bridge, Debbie gets a special delivery, and someone has a private moment.

"Hey, Bill," the man called. "How was work?"

Bill closed the door of his Explorer and walked out onto his driveway. Nick Hawthorne stood across the street spraying water on a corner box of petunias that grew up around his mailbox. "Same ol', same ol'," Bill answered. "How about you?"

"Oh, just another day of making miracles," said Nick. He was an engineer at Micron. Nick did some inexplicable magic that made computers run faster.

Bill strolled over to watch him drown flowers. "How's the house?"

"Oh, great. Just great," Nick said. "It's everything I expected it to be."

"Glad to hear it."

Hawthorne nodded toward Bill's half-empty garage. "Sure don't see as much of Pauline as I used to."

Bill laughed. "Me neither." Pauline sold Nick his house a couple of months earlier. "She's deep into this Eagle Rock development. That keeps her going to meetings, and when she's not at a meeting she's showing a house to some Californian." He drew out that last word as if it tasted bad.

It was Nick's turn to laugh. "Still bitter, huh?"

"Well, you know us natives don't cotton to you fur-iners. You come in and clog up the roads and drive up the prices and probably even steal some of the local women." This last, Bill thought, was almost a certainty. Hawthorne looked like a surfer, drove a new Porsche and made something over six figures.

"Yeah, right. But you'll take our money, won't you?"

"Every dang chance I get."

Hawthorne dropped his hose on the lawn and walked back up to the house to turn the water off. He unhooked the hose and began following it back to the street, making loops with it over his arm as he went.

"Hey, I see you hitting the greenbelt once in a while with your skates."

"Yeah," Bill said. "I like to unwind after work."

The last wrap of hose flipped a string of water spots down the left leg of Bill's slacks. "Oops. Sorry, man."

Nick folded his arms with the coiled hose still hanging in the crook of his elbow. The late afternoon sun turned the blond hair on his forearms golden, accenting his deep tan. "I'll have to dig my blades out and go with you sometime. They're packed away in a box somewhere."

Before Bill could comment, a car honked. They both turned to see Pauline wave at them as she wheeled her BMW into the driveway. She plugged it in next to the Explorer and got out the instant it stopped rolling.

"Hi guys!" she called. "Nice day, isn't it?"

"Beautiful," Nick answered.

"Hate to be rude, but I can't stop to chat. I've just got time to change clothes before I show a couple of houses. Bye!" She waved again, and disappeared into the house.

The Beamer's cooling engine popped and creaked. Not that it would get very cool. The car was less than a year old and already had over 30,000 miles on it. Bill shook his head and said, "Who was that woman?"

***

It was like following a god damn billboard. The RV must have been 40 feet long, and as if that wasn't enough, it was towing one of those prissy little minivans all the Yuppies had fallen in love with.

Jake Burrell pulled out into the oncoming lane to see if there really was a road in front of him. The RV drove around a curve at the same moment, swinging its big butt end around so he couldn't see a damn thing. Jake pounded on the steering wheel once with his fist, making it bong.

"Inconsiderate sons a bitches," he said, addressing his windshield. If the road wasn't so damn twisty he'd take a chance and shoot around them. He wasn't in a hurry, really. Jake hated not being able to see ahead of him. It made him feel like a damn sled dog two dogs back from the lead. Following nothing but an asshole, you understand.

The RV was covered with bumper stickers. They were plastered all over the back of it like patches on a quilt. Jake could have closed his eyes and gotten 90 percent of them right, he figured. "If its rockin' don't bother knockin'." "Tiltin' Hilton." "Foxy Grandma." There would be a sappy Good Sam sticker, showing that cartoon guy with a halo. Probably they had a dozen or so proclaiming they'd been in the Black Hills, stopped at Wall Drug, wintered in Quartzite, seen Yellowstone, discovered some mystery spot and driven through the towering redwoods. The one that was always there—swear to god they must slap them on at the factory: "We're spending our kid's inheritance." Jake would advise those kids to shoot the parents dead, sell the RV and use the money to defend themselves. Justifiable homicide, as far as he was concerned.

And would they pull over to let traffic pass? Nooooo. They proved that a few years back when those people from Back East were towing a car that caught fire. Happened not ten miles from where he was right now. They drove on and on, cars honking at them, people waving and flashing their lights, semis blasting their air horns. Never mind they didn't notice they were towing a damn fireball, they didn't notice everybody trying to tell them they were towing a damn fireball. Jake twisted his fists around the wheel thinking about it. Hell, they actually did notice the people honking. That was the worst. The driver saw people flashing and waving and honking. He thought they were trying to get him to pull over and people did that all the time. No shit, Sherlock! Maybe it's because you're in their damn way, did you ever think of that? Did you ever think people might not all have wads of money in their pockets and be gawking at the scenery at ten miles per hour? Nooooo.

Jake wasn't sure what pissed him off more, the attitude those Easterners had about owning the damn road, or the fact they'd dragged that little piece of junk foreign car for miles while it burned and sent little flaming comets into the trees alongside of the road. They burned the damn forest! He could have cut trees until he'd dropped dead from old age, but they burned the damn forest! And when the State tried to get them to pay for it, the whole damn country felt sorry for the RVers. Could you believe it? If they'd done the same damn thing in Malibu, or one of those other California snot-nose subdivisions that were always catching fire, people would be up in arms. Hang 'em, they'd say. Except, they didn't burn down houses, they burned the damn forest. Which put him out of work most of the time, now. The environmentalist wackos were just as much to blame, of course. But this wasn't an environmentalist. It was a damn RV.

He saw a flash of road ahead. There was a car coming. If he hurried, he could make it. Jake dropped it into third and stomped on the accelerator. The 390 Ford engine started to roar. He loved the sound of that four-barrel sucking air.

Jake pulled out and let it wind to the nuts, then caught fourth just as he went by the driver's window. He didn't have time to finger the guy. He was busy trying not to hit that car coming head on. He swerved, cutting the pass short. The jerk in the motorhome, who looked like he was about a hundred and fifty, tapped his brakes and swerved behind him. Then the guy honked. Honked! Could you believe it? Like Jake had been the one doing something wrong.

He let the speedometer climb to 80, then backed it on down to 50 for a corner. The Payette crashed over boulders twenty feet away. He didn't want to spend the rest of the afternoon sitting on the roof of his pickup waiting for a raft to come by.

When he came around the corner, he saw it. Another damn RV. His blood, already on simmer, started to boil big. He wanted to jam it down and go around this one too. Not enough time. He wouldn't be able to make it around and slow down in time for his turn off. Damn. That meant he had to crawl along behind it for a quarter of a mile. Which made him madder. Which is why he went into the parking lot of his chainsaw art shop too fast, which is why his tires skidded a little on the gravel, which is why he cut the corner a little wide pulling into his spot, which is why the front left bumper of his rig—the bumper he had put together himself from 3/4 inch diamond plate steel so little trees wouldn't hurt it any— caught the minivan parked there just behind the sliding door, putting a gash in it three feet long. Damn!

Jake got out of his pickup and slammed the door, making the whole rig rock. He kicked a bootful of gravel toward the river and cursed. Meanwhile, the driver of the minivan, who had been getting ready to back out, opened his door. Jake turned and caught his eye. It was a Yuppie-type wearing one of those alligator shirts. A pink one! His hair was perfect, like he'd just had it styled and still smelled like perfume. Jake felt his lip curl thinking about having to apologize to the jerk. Then the funniest thing happened. The Yuppie suddenly looked like a spotlighted deer. He stared at Jake with those big doe eyes then, like somebody pulled a switch, he came to life. The guy turned, hit the transmission lever with the heel of his hand and gunned the minivan. He sprayed rocks backing up, then spit them out the other direction when he'd swung it around, heading out of the parking lot and onto the highway.

Stunned, Jake stood there watching the little creep go. He watched as the van, now sporting a very deep racing stripe, sped on down the road and around the bend. Then Jake began to laugh, slowly at first, then building until he was laughing harder than he had ever laughed. He laughed until tears rolled down his cheeks and trickled into his beard.

Charlene Burrell stared out at him from behind her change box, wondering what the heck her crazy husband was up to now.

***

There was nothing more invigorating after fighting traffic for 15 minutes than to strap on in-line skates and go for a fast sprint on the greenbelt. Living a hundred feet away from the riverside path was the biggest advantage to owning a house—more precisely the mortgage on a house—in River Run. Neighbors sometimes complained about the riffraff the greenbelt brought in. Bill Clark felt lucky to have his own easy on-ramp.

When he got his stride going, nothing could touch him. The traffic could snarl all it wanted a few blocks away. He heard none of it. The pressures of work blew off in the breeze behind him like an aspen losing leaves. The exertion of skating never caught up with him until he was done with his run. He only felt lighter, faster, stronger as he glided along. When the skate ended, his hard breathing always surprised him. It felt like stopping caused it.

Clark agreed with his neighbors that the greenbelt got too much use. He could do well without the obstacles of walkers, joggers and bicycle riders. Even other bladers brought only a begrudging nod of camaraderie. He could lose the lot of them, save for the occasional tank-topped female biker coming his way, scooping air between her breasts. Obstacles like that were tolerable.

This evening he spotted an interesting girl—or, as his wife would insist, a woman—about a block ahead of him. He had seen her several times lately, never up close. She was easy to spot because of her long, black hair and her apparent love for all things black. She wore black Spandex shorts and a black tank top. Her skates were black, and so was her helmet. None of those things was unusual in itself. Together they were striking.

Bill increased his speed, only to find she was moving out faster than he thought. She dodged pedestrians better too. Maybe she was just more aggressive. Bill didn't trust walkers. You could call out "on your left" until you were hoarse and they still wouldn't know you were about to skate by. Some of them understood, then fell into confusion about which side was their left. Twice he had collided with Sunday strollers who decided to step in front of him to get out of his way. Now he always cut his speed to pass.

Bill gained on the straightaway; lost ground on the corners and obstacles. Closer now, he admired her technique. She called out to walkers and bikers, too, announcing her presence. If she slowed he didn't see it. The woman set her wheels right along the edge of the blacktop when she passed, cutting closer than Bill dared. If anything, she sped up for the curves, pressing tightly into them and using her drift to set the attack. With her last thrust out of a curve, she shot off like a Frisbee snapped from a wrist. Must have been hard on her mother, Bill thought, bearing a child wearing skates.

He was a couple seconds back. They came up under the Broadway Bridge and onto the service road that doubled as a section of bike path behind Boise State University. With the wider pavement she started throwing her arms out rhythmically, extending her strides. Passing pedestrians was no trick here, or she might have out distanced him.

He was close enough to overtake her now, if he wanted. Did he want to? It seemed a little macho to come striding up beside her and say howdy. And where was he going with this, anyway? He wanted to get a good look at her. Better look. His eyes were already enjoying the view of her buns pumping in front of him. He watched her thigh muscles knot and release, knot and release. Same with her calves, though that was somehow not as sexy, even though they were bare. The Spandex made her seem more than nude. Her hair gave a constant show, swinging with the rhythm, swaying back and forth across her hips and flying in smaller strands with the wind. This was an outdoor girl—woman. Her skin reflected many hours spent in the sun. His own skin, protected by prudish dollops of sunblock, was white as a carp's belly. Intellectually, he knew skin like hers would wrinkle earlier and be more prone to malignancy than his own. Emotionally, he bought the beach babe hype as much as the next guy.

At the footbridge across the Boise River she slowed for congestion, barely moving up the arch. The bridge spewed a group of kids like a belching cornucopia, bringing Bill to a stop. The woman stopped, too, at the apex of the arch. She leaned on the rail watching the river pass underneath, long strands of hair drifting down along her cheeks. Taking easy, nonchalant strides Bill paid close attention to his skates, waiting for that one quick, non-threatening glance he would get as he went by her. One look, then he'd speed on down river for a couple of miles before turning around and heading home. Looking up he saw her profile. Not a disappointment. A very pretty woman with pronounced cheekbones, full, sensuous lips and smooth, soft skin. She could have been a model. Bill slipped past her, still keeping that brief image in mind. Wait. He pulled his skates together and rolled slowly for a second, then turned and grabbed the rail.

"Mary?"

The woman turned and tipped her head, looking at him over her sunglasses. For a moment he didn't think she'd recognize him in cutoffs, t-shirt and Styrofoam helmet. Then she said, "Bill Clark, right?"

"Yeah, that's right."

"One of the bad guys."

His face must have fallen when she said it. She quickly added, "Oh, don't look so hurt. I didn't mean it."

"I hope not," Bill said. "I like to think I wear a white hat most of the time."

"Yeah? That one's red," she said, pointing at his fabric covered helmet.

"I meant metaphorically. Besides, this one matches my hair."

"Your hair's not that red."

"Almost."

Below them a group of about a dozen tubers called out greetings, ranging from hellos and cat calls to invitations to jump in. Mary waved. Bill nodded.

When the floaters disappeared beneath them, he said, "I watched you skate. You're really good."

"Thanks. It's probably the best part of living in Boise, getting to use the greenbelt all the time."

"How long have you been doing it?"

"Skating? A couple of years. I started when I was a ranger at Ponderosa. When I was off-duty I'd cruise the campground loops." Bill picked absently at a paint fleck on the rail. "Well, it must have been a good place to learn. You sure caught on to it."

"How long have you been skating?"

"About the same. Maybe three years. I started after we moved into the new house. It's just off the greenbelt."

"Really? That would be so cool. I live in the North End. I guess I could skate to the greenbelt." She shrugged. "Usually it's easier to toss my stuff in the back of the car and park at Vets."

Veterans Memorial was one of a string of parks scattered along the 15-mile greenbelt.

Hoping for an invitation, Bill asked, "Do you always skate alone?"

"Usually. Sometimes I'll go out to Lucky Peak and skate that part of the path with Seaman."

Bill raised an eyebrow. Did she really say semen?

"My dog. I don't like to let him run loose in the city, but he's all right out there. And he makes me feel safe."

"What kind of dog is he?"

Mary gave him an odd, fleeting look like he'd asked her in which direction the sun sets. "He's a Newfoundland," she said. "That's why I call him Seaman. They're water dogs, you know."

"No, I didn't know they were water dogs. So, Sea-Man, like a sailor, or something."

"Yeah. It's a family name, actually. My great, great—I don't know how many greats—grandfather had a Newfoundland by that name."

That struck Bill as odd. Would an Indian that many "greats" back have had a purebred dog?

"Big dog. No wonder you feel safe."

"Yeah," she said, pushing back from the railing. "Maybe I should bring him to our next meeting." She rolled slowly by and touched him lightly on the forearm. "Nice seeing you."

Bill called to her when she was halfway down the bridge. "Will there be a next meeting?"

Mary did a tight 180 and drifted backward down the slope of the bridge. "That's up to you," she said, then reversed again and started to stride.

***

Tips & Tricks from *The Private* newsletter

It's an oldie, but a goodie, and It doesn't require any tools! Find a little stick to jamb into the valve stem on a tourist's tire. Don't forget to do it to at least two tires! Remember, you're actually doing them a favor. They probably came here to get some of that famous Idaho air in the first place!

Speaking of tires a Marsing reader writes to tell us how well jacks work when you scatter them in the parking lot of a visitor center. We're not talking about tire jacks here although they are for tires! We mean the kind of jacks little girls play with. No matter how you toss them, there's always a poky side up. The Private is a little skeptical. He doesn't think jacks would hold up well, but, as usual, the Private has a simple, do-it-yourself solution. Get a section of concrete reinforcing wire. It comes in 4'x6' sections. Use your wire cutters—be sure to cut at a sharp angle—to cut out a whole bunch of crosses. Now, just bend those with pliers so that no matter how they land when you drop them on the ground, one arm is sticking up. You're welcome!

***

The cold didn't bother her. Winter held no discontent for Debbie Bennett Anderson, even though it misread its cue this year and now tripped back on stage again in early June. She counted seasons, every one, like names of favorite horses. Spring was nearly too easy to love, with its coltish exuberance. The season erupted with life, buds bursting into leaves and flowers, shoots shoving the very earth impatiently out of their way. In the natural world it was a time of birth. On the ranch, all the birthing that really mattered—the coming of the year's calf crop—was over by then. Debbie had her garden, and kept a few perennials watered and weeded, but the real signs of spring were on the desert. Someone new might not notice. An Idaho eye saw the shading across the sage shift subtly from gray to green. Not a gregarious green, lord no. Debbie had seen Seattle resplendent in leaf and vine and needle. Green everywhere! Shouting and jostling for the attention of her eyes as if she could possibly avoid it. Of course, it was beautiful. By the time she left—and it wasn't many days—she felt as if she had feasted on nothing but ice cream topped with caramel and chocolate syrup and sprinkles and marshmallows the whole time. She'd had so much of a good green thing it didn't seem good anymore. She couldn't wait to get back to the parchment soil where bunch grass grew in measured stands among the rabbit brush, barely within hailing distance of its neighbors.

Spring on the Bennett Ranch was the season for branding. Hands and friends from surrounding ranches came to help, just as she and Charlie would help them the following week. No money changed hands. It was branding. You helped each other because who else would? And who would miss it anyway? It was the biggest social event of the year, one a debutante would never see. Owyhee County, bigger than the state of New Jersey, was home to about 9,000 people. The community of ranches, and ten or twelve ranch families, around the Bennett ranch covered half a million acres. Most of that was a grazing permit on land owned by the government.

Branding brought back a handful of cousins every year. They came from Mountain Home, Murphy, Twin and even Boise to remember who they were. Debbie welcomed the help and listened to them tell the same old tired stories of how it used to be when they grew up on the ranch. Used to be was now for Debbie. A part of her felt a little resentful that her life was someone's ancient history. She didn't begrudge the cousins their memories or their enthusiasm for branding. She sometimes wished they felt the same way about bucking hay.

Who could blame them for coming back to romanticize ranch life? There was romance in it, along with the smell of horse sweat and saddle leather. Sometimes Debbie herself felt a little larger than life when she was cutting calves on Skid. She felt so much a part of the horse, felt his legs become her legs when he planted them like posts in front of a calf who thought it owned its mind, then felt her muscles and Skid's mend together, draw tight, and spring the other way before the calf knew it had even decided to move. What were those mythical things called? The horses with men growing from their front shoulders? Sometimes she felt almost like that when she rode Skid cutting, when he was more in charge than she was.

The smells of branding would never leave her if she suddenly became a sailor and cruised the oceans the rest of her life. The inevitable dust permeated the air, soaked through with cow slobber and urine and blood. The juniper smoke wound through it all, carrying the scent of itself along with that branding smell of smells, burning hair.

You couldn't convince a calf it was for its own good to be strangled and thrown on its back by a lariat, stuck with a three-inch needle, have a notch cut out of its ear, get its hair set on fire and its flesh burned by a hot iron and—if it were unlucky enough to be born male—have its testicles removed without benefit of anesthesia.

She would never say it, but Debbie had doubts too. The excitement of branding day was darkened by the violence. She had those doubts every year and every year she put them in a place deep down inside her. She imagined she had a pocket where things like that were stored. When she saw the slice of knife on skin she put it in a pocket. When the iron pulled back from the flesh leaving a raw B bar B burned into the side of a four-month-old calf, she put it in a pocket. She put it in a pocket and never took it out so she could love spring.

The seasons were defined more by the thermometer than the calendar, and when the temperature reached into the seventies it meant spring was giving way to summer, and it was time to move the cattle to the range. Some of the same cousins who loved the branding occasionally came along on the drive. They were almost an endangered species. Driving cattle meant sitting on a horse for ten hours. Those cousins who came rarely stayed for a second day, suddenly called back to town by urgent business just remembered.

Summer in Owyhee County was almost always hot, and always dry, except for the afternoon thunderstorms that blustered across the desert, dusting up jackrabbits and coyotes with lightening and wind and a spatter of rain. Debbie savored the sun, rejecting the modern mantra of avoidance the health nuts preached. Her skin was the color of her mother's saddle, the one she straddled every day. The wrinkles around her eyes and the edges of her mouth had many tributaries at 49. She could have used more cold cream and smiled less. Debbie didn't think that proposition paid. Soaking up the sun made her smile a lot.

With the cattle on allotments for the summer, ranching turned to a routine of irrigating and cutting hay, windrowing and baling it, then bringing it in to stack. For this work, the cousins were extinct. The neighbors still thrived. Handshake agreements to share equipment and swap kids got most of the work done. Charlie always ended up hiring some help for stacking. They didn't have kids to swap.

Fall, when it came, meant roundup. It was always the time of greatest anticipation. How had the cattle done? Was the feed good enough to fill them out? How many calves were lost? They called haying harvest, but the real harvest was in the fall. The real crop was cattle.

Winter, the hardest season, was also a special time. Debbie did not look forward to feeding cows in the dark, fighting frozen bales with frozen fingers, breaking ice from watering holes and sitting up all night with sick calves. She looked forward to nothing more than being snowed in. Even with the work and hardship they brought, the deep snows that buried their place every winter always brought a sense of safety. She couldn't have explained it to someone new. Someone new might have felt trapped and cut off. Debbie felt snug. Someone new might have worried about how they'd get to a hospital in an emergency and how long the food would hold out. Debbie cross-stitched, read and baked. It was her vacation.

Now vacation was over, leaving only memories and a skiff of snow on the sage. They were taking cows to summer range. Because winter forgot its exit lines, the cold slapped across her cheeks, and stung her fingers and toes. Charlie went after a runaway calf to her left, caught it, and steered it back to the herd. Stupid thing. Why would breaking for the ranch and leaving mom behind bawling like a banshee seem like the thing to do? Charlie started pushing the little knot of cows and calves that had stopped to watch the attempted escape. "Hope, hope, hope," he said, encouraging them along. Every driver had his cow talk. "Git" was especially popular. Some used a clicking sound, others said "hey there." Charlie always used "hope." When he needed to go after a breakaway, he'd nudge Red with his heels and change "hope" to "hup," to let the horse know it was time to chase down the critter.

In a movie Charlie would be cast only as a cowboy, and he would always wear a black hat. At 6' 2" he looked like a sculpture not quite finished. He had enough skin to stretch over the bones of his face, barely. On screen, people would love him, or love to hate him. In person, most would—did—avoid him. He looked a little too skinny, a little too weathered, a little too rough. This was surely a man who would soil the carpets. He'd lost the tips of two fingers taking a clumsy wrap with his lariat. A thin, two-inch scar made a higher ridge along his left cheek where fence wire whipped his face once when stretched too taut. No other scars showed, but Debbie knew where they were: a six-inch mark above his right knee where his femur had come poking through six summers ago after a fall with Red, a healed burn clear as a brand across his ribs where another running rope had caught him, and a little V-almost invisible at the base of his neck in front, where Debbie once made an airway with a pocketknife. She'd saved the bee stinger as a reminder of how a little thing could bring a big man down. Debbie watched him hope, hope, hoping the cows along. A perfect man of many scars.

Driving cows is one percent romance and ninety-nine percent dull. The rhythm of the horse rocking your hips back and forth sways you into languor. Debbie was half hypnotized by the rippling backs of the cows stretching down the road in front of her when it happened. Skid was probably in his own horse trance, or it wouldn't have bothered him like it did. Something white flew out of the sagebrush toward them, took a quick swoop up, then dramatically dived. Skid instantly forgot his years of training and trust. The horse spooked, stepped sideways, then whirled away from the attack. Debbie felt the thing hit her cheek. She batted it away just as Skid started his dance. She was two steps behind, feeling daylight slip beneath her jeans when her own years of training kicked in. Stiffening her left leg, she leaned into her right while swinging the reins almost behind her. The action pulled Skid's head around to her knee, forcing the rest of him to follow. The two made a quick, tight circle then stopped. Skid snorted once as if in warning.

Charlie loped up on Red. "You all right?"

"Yeah, I think so. He just spooked." Debbie felt something under her chin and pawed at it with her gloved hand.

"What's that?" Charlie asked.

"Just some paper. It's what scared him."

She started to crumple it up to put in her pocket. Something about it caught her eye. Probably the word Idaho. She smoothed it out on the saddle horn and held it up, protecting it against the wind with her body. Not just Idaho, but Private Idaho in big type across the top of a half-page flyer. She'd heard that name on the news. Something about a bunch of vigilantes who were against out-of-staters. Debbie skimmed the copy, then stuffed the sheet in her jacket pocket, feeling a little conflicted about the whole thing. She didn't much like newcomers, either, but wasn't so happy about someone tossing paper around to trash up the desert.

CHAPTER FOUR

Come a time

In which Jo Beth calls an unauthorized number, Blaine visits a statue, Frank reads a want ad, Griff climbs trees, and The Private sees the light.

"Oh, man," Bill moaned. He held the Outside section of the paper in one hand and his morning cup of coffee in the other. McNalley's column was all about Bruneau Dunes. It was supposed to be about Bruneau Dunes. Bill had called the outdoor editor a few days earlier with a quiet tip. He thought a little well-placed outrage in the local press about the proposed travel writers' motorized trip across the dunes might put a stop to it. McNalley wouldn't tell where the tip came from. Neither would Clark. Well, he might let it slip to Mary Lewis when the moment was right. Now the moment would never be right.

"Oh, man," he said again, as he read about McNalley's adventure at Bruneau. As Bill had suggested, the outdoor editor asked the park manager to show him where they were planning to take the travel writers. Bill assumed the manager would PR McNalley about the sensitive vegetation and wildlife. Because he was a little rushed that day, the manager took the writer to the overlook on a park four wheeler. Instead of a story about the sensitive nature of Bruneau Dunes, McNalley wrote about the all-terrain vehicle ride. He raved about it.

McNalley was so excited about riding on the dunes he planned to buy an ATV. Worse, he ended the piece with a call for the parks department to allow their use in certain areas of the park.

Bill tossed the section into the trash. He had just been trying to help. How could it have backfired so completely? He took a risk calling McNalley. Jo Beth would have canned him if she knew what he did. Scratch that. She'd probably give him a bonus now that the story turned out this way. Even so, it was more important than ever to keep his involvement a secret. Mary Lewis must never find out.

"Jesus Christ!" Bill heard the shout six cubicles away, even though Jo Beth was inside her glassed in office. "Somebody's going to pay for this! I'm going to have somebody's balls on a platter!"

Bill heard the door slam. Jo Beth's raging went on, muted now and unintelligible. He cautiously stood up to look over his divider. All over the office other heads were up, or rising up, like prairie dogs checking for coyotes. One by one, they noticed each other. Frightened, puzzled looks went back and forth. Sudden silence swooped down like the shadow of a hawk and the heads dropped.

Temper storms were often in the forecast at Commerce. Jo Beth was a meteorological wonder. Most days were sunny and pleasant but she could change inclement in a minute. When a Jo Beth front came through, wise workers brought in the lawn furniture and shut the windows. Bill diligently pretended to be busy. He knew everyone else found something just as pressing.

In a few minutes someone would sense the proper passing of time and step around a partition to ask a co-worker, "What the heck was that all about?" That would break the tension. One by one they would relax and begin the speculation. Later in the day the rumors would start. By first thing tomorrow, at the latest, the real story, more or less, would circulate.

The copier room, hallways and break room would buzz with whatever it was. Soon after that, everyone would have a...

"Clark. My office."

Bill looked up in time to see a red blur. He had not actually seen her. He could not swear it was even Jo Beth's voice. Her scent proved her presence. Bill took a deep breath of the uncontaminated air of his cubicle, and rose to follow the fragrance of oranges.

As he made the journey down the hall, others joined him from left and right, each with the look of cattle who just had a terrible epiphany. Four of them crowded into Jo Beth's office: Information Officer Rob Flowers, Promotions Director Jennifer Young, Marketing Specialist Kerry Hudson, and Bill.

"Have any of you seen this?" Jo Beth asked, holding up a copy of *Sunset* magazine.

"That the new one?" Flowers asked.

"Yes, it's the new one. It's been out a couple of days, and it explains some things." She flipped a few pages, then folded the magazine open. "See anything unusual." She held it open to the two-thirds-page Idaho ad. Under the big red word, Idaho, was a color photo of whitewater rafting on the Salmon. Bill had taken the picture himself, and was particularly proud of it. It was the first time they had used an in-house photo for an ad campaign.

"Take a close look," Jo Beth said. "Anything odd that jumps out at you?"

For a moment, silence answered. Then, Jennifer, a sweet lady who blushed at jokes that were even slightly blue, said, "Oh fuck," then said, "Oh fuck," again.

Flowers turned white. Kerry Hudson, who worked directly under Bill, made a strangled sound and reached for a chair back for support. Bill swallowed hard, and said, "What... What do you get if you dial it?"

Jo Beth gave him an oddly satisfied nod. "That's the big question, isn't it? Shall we just see, kids? Let's try a little experiment, shall we?" She punched the hands-free button on her phone. The familiar hum of a ready line came through.

"Now, first we have to dial a nine to get out, don't we?" She said it as if giving remedial instructions to an eight-year-old. "Nothing wrong with that nine, is there?" The small office suddenly began to smell like a locker room. "Then we dial the one, because we are making a long distance call, aren't we?" She stabbed the one. "Now comes the tricky part. The part we almost, but not quite got right. We'll dial a nine again, which isn't right, is it?" The four stared at her. "The number we really want isn't a nine at all, is it? Can any of you tell me the number we really wanted in that ad?"

Kerry said it, in a voice that broke with the effort, "An eight."

"What was that again? I'm not sure I heard it?"

Teeth clenched, Flowers said, "For god sakes Jo Beth, just dial the fucking number!"

"An eight," she said, ignoring him. "That's right. But again, we won't be dialing an eight this time, will we? We're dialing the number that's in our ad, just like the thousands of people who read that ad will be doing." Jo Beth punched the nine, then two zeros and the rest of the Idaho information number. The line was quiet for a heartbeat. Then they heard it ring. It picked up without a second ring, and a female voice answered. It was a recorded voice, as it should be. Rather than welcome the caller to the Idaho information line, the purring, sultry voice on the other end said, "Hi. My name's Lisa, and I'm very, very glad you called, because I've been soooo lonely."

"Oh fuck," Jennifer said, and dropped into a chair. Kerry began to cry.

Jo Beth stabbed the release button, cutting the voice off. "No reason to listen to any more of that." She clattered her fingernails on the unresponsive keypad. "No need to cost the state any more than we have to. Of course," she said, raising her voice an octave in an oh-by-the-way way, "this little boo-boo will cost the state something, won't it? I figure $150,000 to begin with for the ad campaign that's down the tubes. Then there'll probably be someone who will sue us because little Jimmy or Ashley dialed the number thinking they would get Idaho information for their school report and got a..."

Flowers interrupted. "You don't mean $150,000. We didn't spend that much in *Sunset*, did we?"

Bill had never seen Jo Beth act so sweet. The rage that shone through that confectionery overlay was just as unprecedented. "Well, Rob, the problem isn't only with *Sunset*." She smiled like someone's mother. "In fact, the problem isn't theirs at all. They printed the ad exactly the way Swope, Munson and Taft sent it to them. And guess what? So did every other magazine we bought space in."

"But that's nuts," Kerry said. "How could the ad agency make a mistake like that?" Jo Beth positively beamed. "Well, honey, they tell us they didn't make a mistake."

"They had too. We wouldn't have sent them copy with a 900 number on it," Kerry said. Her hands were shaking. "I mean, someone would have surely noticed it. Our 800 number is practically tattooed onto the back of our eyelids." She gave a light, unconvincing laugh.

"Isn't that the funniest thing?" Jo Beth said. "Everyone in this room signed off on the proof, and not a single one of us noticed."

Three quick raps on the door announced the entrance of Jo Beth's secretary, Ralph Miller. He handed her a flimsy sheet of paper and left the room like he'd spotted a grenade.

Jo Beth looked at the fax for a moment and nodded. She turned it around and held it in her fingertips at arm's length. "Recognize the initials? They're all there. And the ad is perfect, except for that one little correction someone made. That itty-bitty little 9 someone penciled in on the proof above that crossed out eight."

Flowers grabbed the fax out of her hands. "Can you tell whose writing it is?"

"It's a nine, Rob," Jo Beth said. "Just a neat little nine. I doubt if forensics could tell us."

"Well, the ad agency should have caught it anyway. They should have at least called," Flowers said. "Christ, they didn't even question that we were suddenly going to a 900 number from an 800 number?"

"Agreed," Jo Beth said. "There will be blood on some butts over this, and I intend to make sure SM&T bends over big." Her face went blank. Jo Beth seemed to focus on something way beyond the wall. Almost absently, she said, "That doesn't get us off the hook, does it?"

***

God, it was amazing how tired a man got from doing nothing all day. Blaine Stope wadded up his greasy apron and tossed it in the bin. Sometimes he said goodbye to Cyndy or whoever else was hanging around the back door on break. Today no one lurked back there sucking on a cigarette. All he had to hold his breath against was the perpetual stench of rotting food that hovered around the garbage cans.

Stope got in his 1978 F-100 short bed, a beat up old thing he had once been so proud of. Paid cash for it new. Now he could barely afford to keep gas in it. In the good days he bought a new rig every three years. He had been due in 1981, when Bunker Hill closed.

 The god damn government and its god damn regulations killed it all. Not to mention the stupid god damn parents. They were men he worked with every day and they cut their own throats, plus his in the bargain when they sued Bunker Hill over lead emissions. They claimed their kids were getting stupid because of lead in their dirt yards. It was pretty damn clear to him the kids inherited most of their stupidity.

 He took the Big Creek exit at least a couple times a week. It was out of his way, and he really couldn't afford the extra couple of miles in gas. It did not seem like a choice to him. More like a duty. Stope pulled over to the base of a rock bluff, parked the little Ford and got out. It was not a pretty place, more akin to a gravel pit than a memorial. The 1-90 traffic zipped by a hundred feet away in a constant roar and whoosh. Yet, it was a place of quiet contemplation for Blaine Stope.

 He did not have to read the sign beneath the 12-foot bronze sculpture of a miner, hardhat and lighted lamp planted firmly on his head, his drill pointing into the sky. Blaine had been there. He had hauled bodies out of the Sunshine, where the bad air from a mine fire claimed them back in '72. That was just before he went to work for Bunker Hill. Hell, the Sunshine was still going in fits and starts. He could have maybe gone back to work there a couple times. It never seemed smart tempting fate a second time.

 Stope had mourned those men plenty. It was not to remember them he paid his visits to the memorial. It was to remember him. He saw himself in that black metal man, pounding the stubborn stone with his drill, waking up ore from an eon's sleep so it could be put to some good use. He saw a man who did real work, breaking rock to turn it into car batteries, zinc casts and coatings and, before the government screwed around with it, silver dollars. It was hard work, no kidding, but it was important work. His dad and granddad had helped win the big wars by working the mines at Wardner, Wallace and Kellogg. Their sweat was part of the film on walls a mile underground, as was his own. As was the blood of the 91 miners who went down in the Sunshine in '72 and never again saw the light of day.

The crackle and crunch of gravel signaled the approach of a car. A Toyota full of tourists pulled up next to the statue. A woman in her mid-thirties made the passenger window disappear with a touch of her finger.

"Oh, come on, Jerry," she said. "It'll only take a minute." From the back seat Stope heard the protests of two children. "Mo-om," one said, stretching the word into syllables. "It's so dumb."

She threw the door open. "Come on, everybody out. We need to stretch our legs, anyway."

"You heard your mother," the man said. "Pile out, kids."

The driver got out and stretched. The kids, forgetting their objections, popped out of the rear doors like someone had squeezed the car flat. The older boy looked about ten. His brother might have been seven. They started flinging gravel toward the interstate, missing it by fifty feet with every throw.

"So what's the story?" the man asked. His wife was reading the plaque. She shrugged. "A bunch of miners died."

"Hum," he said. "Cave in?"

"Fire or something." She turned to yell at her children who crept closer to the highway with every aim. "Hey, stop throwing those rocks. You'll get hurt."

As if assigned overtime on a chain gang, the oldest slumped his shoulders, dropped a handful of pebbles and drug his heavy feet through the gravel. The younger one mimicked him, hanging his head low and groaning.

"Come see the statue," their father said.

"I don't wanna see the statue. I wanna hamburger."

"Well, you're just going to have to wait until we get to Coeur d'Alene," Mom said. "They don't sell hamburgers around here."

An automatic response almost made Stope speak. He fought it down easily, picturing the two rock-throwing angels harassing Cyndy. He walked back to his pickup, opened the door and was about to leave when he saw the oldest boy wind up for another pitch.

"Hey!" Stope yelled.

The boy flinched as he let loose the rock. It pinged off the metal miner's face, six inches beneath the glass in the helmet light.

"You made me miss!" the boy scolded. He stooped to pick up another rock.

"Hey! Stop it," Stope said. "Don't be throwing rocks at the memorial."

Both parents frowned and stared hard at Stope. He stared back. They blinked and began herding their children into the car.

"Come on, kids. Let's find a place to get a burger and fries, okay?" the father said, giving Stope one last mind your-own-business look.

"It's just a stupid statue," the boy said, as his mother shut the door.

Stope watched them drive away, as the smallest child, face pressed against the back glass showed his tongue. The head rock-thrower offered the middle fingers of both hands.

***

Tips & Tricks from *The Private* newsletter

Some visitor centers leave brochure racks unattended at night. If you run into that situation, take all the brochures you need. They're free! You probably have lots of uses for them: Insulate your house! Balance the short leg on your table! Paper the walls in your chicken coop!

We're happy to hear that several people with reader boards are giving the message to tourists. What if you don't have a reader board? You can make your own yard signs, or send for our high quality weather resistant tourist-tweakers available at cost on page 8.

***

Seven a.m. and Frank Thompson, along with hundreds of other Idahoans, was reading the morning paper. Unlike most, he was not sipping coffee. Thompson had a bowl of Cream of Wheat in front of him. His fingers rested around a half-finished glass of orange juice. Most Idahoans up at that time were getting themselves charged with a little caffeine on the leading edge of their day. Thompson was taking a break after his first two hours of work. His minority status sans coffee seemed as natural to him as the long days of a farmer.

Many of the coffee drinkers who read the same headlines found them encouraging. The news from Boise was that housing starts were up 11 percent, Micron was hiring another 300 people and planning and zoning had approved another four-lane bridge across the river. Statewide, unemployment had dropped below 4.5 percent, tourism had increased 14 percent the preceding year and Albertsons was planning a dozen new super stores.

The juice drinker shook his head. "People," he muttered.

"What about people, dear?" his wife Mildred asked.

"Ah, too darn many of them, that's all. This used to be such a wonderful place to live."

Mildred set a fresh bowl of Cream of Wheat down in anticipation of Spencer's usual late arrival. Lehi, Denton and Margaret were already there, quietly consuming the warm cereal.

"Don't you still have a wonderful life?" Mildred sounded a little bruised.

Frank smiled up at her and put an arm around her thick waist. "Of course I do. I couldn't count all my blessings, but if I did I would start right in this room." He gave her a gentle squeeze. "One." Then he pointed at his children in turn. "Two is Levi, three is J.B., four is Lehi, five is Margaret, six is Denton."

"Okay, Dad, we get it," J.B. said. He had been a little snippy since he had gone to work at the processing plant.

"Well, you may 'get it,' but it's not a good place to stop. Where was I?"

"I was six," Denton said.

"So you were. Seven would be Mary Ellen. Who am I leaving out?" Spencer came shuffling into the kitchen. "Leaving out of what?" he asked. "Eight would be Spencer. Just counting my blessings, son."

The lanky sophomore rolled his eyes.

"Now, none of that," Mildred scolded.

Spencer tossed his book bag on the floor and slumped into his chair. "Mush again?"

"It's good for you," Margaret said.

Ignoring his younger sister, whose opinion he held in approximately the same esteem as that of a centipede, Spencer said, "It ain't exactly a blessing."

"Isn't a blessing," Margaret said. "There ain't no such word as ain't."

Frank Thompson folded his newspaper and set it aside. It was his habit to pay more attention to his family than the printed word. "Good food is always a blessing. It's one of many you have, Spencer."

"Yeah, well, I think I'll pass on this one." He pushed the bowl aside and emptied his juice glass in two gulps.

"You're not going to waste it?" Mildred asked.

"Nah. Nothing ever goes to waste around here. Margut will suck it down." His sister looked like she had been slapped across the face with fish.

"Spencer Kimball Thompson, we'll have none of that," his father warned. He locked eyes with his youngest son.

After a long moment, Spencer looked away and said, "Sorry."

Boys that age always challenged. It was part of the job of growing up. Frank knew that. The challenge was harder with each boy. Spencer tested him more than the others combined. It was the lack of discipline in the schools and the influence of liberal families. It was getting worse. If little Margaret—he still thought of her as little in spite of the best evidence—if little Margaret were a boy, he thought the raising would be beyond him. Soon Levi and J.B. and Mary Ellen would marry and have children of their own. How could they possibly bring them up right in the world as it was becoming?

Denton broke the conversational ice. "Hey, Dad. Look at this ad." He pointed to a two-inch black-bordered box in the classifieds. "You're always talking about how you wish people would quit moving here. Sounds like you're not the only one who thinks that way."

The headline on the ad said, "Private Idaho."

***

Near Wallace, a man dressed in a field jacket and army green pants put a rolled-up copy of the Shoshone County Press in the plastic container next to Blaine Stope's mailbox. Sipping his morning coffee, Stope watched the guy walk down the road. More of a skip than a walk, actually. Stope saw only the back of his head. Not the regular paper boy. Not a boy at all, in fact. Something about him was so familiar.

***

Even growing up in the middle of it, his life along the Blackfoot seemed mythic, as if he had been set down in a magical place among minor gods. An abiding sense of awe permeated his early years. As the principle observer in his own life, he watched from some short distance the workings of a small ranch. Billy was ever the spectator, surrounded by people obscure enough to seem silhouettes. He was forever too little to buck hay, steer the grain truck, set a canvas dam for watering the wheat, harrow a field, or drive cattle. Johnny, six years older, was expert at all of it. His brother was a barely smaller version of the men who made life happen, working beside them on the brink of Billy's vision.

His mother made meals appear and told him every story and kept him well. She taught Billy how to play with Griff and how to care for cats and how to ride a horse. Mom was his best friend. Billy thought she loved him more than Johnny. It was the only thing he had on his older brother. Yet, he would have given that up instantly to become one of the silhouettes.

Mom said there would come a time. She said Billy would be big enough to help with the hay. He would even drive a tractor and a truck, just like Johnny. Comforting words he pretended to believe. He told himself, come a time, he would feed the cattle. Come a time, he would plow the fields. Come a time he would burn the ditch banks in the fall. Come a time he would walk next to Pop.

Waiting for that time, Billy made his own world through explorations of the one in which he lived. The Place had no boundaries as far as he knew. Fences were something to keep the cows in. He crossed them with impunity seldom knowing and never caring whether it was Clark land or the land of the neighbors he walked. Those rare times he saw someone else it was always a silhouette, usually riding a tall horse, tipping his hat to say "'Lo." The land might belong to the silhouette, or it might not. Never mind. It belonged to Billy the moment he was alone.

No, not alone. His world was populated by lesser individuals he could explain things to. Sometimes even Johnny was in that imaginary world, always a villain. After Johnny committed some awful crime Billy would track him down, regretfully bringing a brother gone wrong to justice. Griff was always there. Long before Billy Clark had heard of a boy-and-his-dog story, he lived one. He lived a thousand of them.

Griffin looked nothing like a lion, had no wings or tail, and flew only with the greatest reluctance. Mom had wanted to call the little black and white spaniel Daisy after the comic book duck. Billy had read every one of those stories a dozen times, and would never let Mom throw one away. His collection of funny books, as he called them, took up two bedroom cupboards when they were put away, which they never were. Among the Disneys there were Supermans and Hawkmans and Classic Comics. One of those featured a griffin that seemed nobler for a namesake than a talking duck.

Griff was a girl dog who had to live up to the imagination of an explorer boy. At 30 pounds, she was not well-suited to fight wolves, chase down cougars, wrestle spies to the ground or leap into burning buildings. She did it every day. She also climbed trees.

Exploring, by definition, meant that no crack in the rocks big enough to crawl into, no gully, no wild rose patch, no river bank and, most of all, no branch could go unexamined. Billy climbed. He knew every rock along the low cliffs in the upper valley. His feet found every corral pole on every corral on every ranch. No barn roof or straw bale-covered shed was a mystery to him. No boxelder went unclimbed. Griff, in the role of loyal companion, climbed with him.

When they climbed the lava rocks, Griff could hold her own. The spaniel sometimes needed a boost into the lower branches of a big tree. Once cowering there in the crook, she would follow Billy out along every bough as he commanded his spaceship crew or lived the life of the Robinsons.

After seeing a movie about the Matterhorn, with shots of climbers inching along an edgy trail and squirming through cold, tight chutes, Billy made that mountain in his mind. In everyone else's mind his mountain was the barn. To assault the summit—never mind most of the trip was horizontal—he started at the straw bale windbreak, a narrow hundred-foot-long stack that protected wintering cattle from the biting gusts that came off the river to the south. He would walk along the top of that from one end to the other, forgetting for a moment the structure was sometimes the roof of a train where he chased his bad brother while the ground shot by at exciting speeds.

At the end of the windbreak, he balanced along the top of a slat fence that kept the pigs in, ignoring the potential for a romp or ride with them. The next stop was the roof of the coop where Mom raised the little yellow chicks under a brooder lamp. Now, the chicken coop roof was a ledge along the way to the summit. Sometimes it was a stage where he belted out Elvis songs for the Really, Really Big Shoo.

Back then to the slat fence for ten feet and onto the sod roof of the bigger chicken house, where the full-grown brood spent its days making eggs. The dusty roof played the part of a desert from time to time. In this scenario it was the beginning of the mountain's snow. A short leap from the sod roof to the top of a corral corner post was a daring jump across an icy ravine. Then the tightrope walk along the poles became a dangerous trail on the face of an impossible cliff. The big square-poled gate that hinged on the barn wall was supported by a plank leading up at 30 degrees. It was the final ascent to the shake roof of the barn, and ultimately to the lofty ridged peak of the Matterhorn.

Climbing that mountain was an endless adventure in Billy's mind. What went on in the mind of Griff, one could only imagine. As the first dog to climb the Matterhorn and the second and subsequent dogs to do the same, Griff followed her master with unparalleled allegiance. The straw stack was a snap. She showed only the slightest wobble on the slat fence, which was topped with a nice length of two by fours. The chicken roofs were easy. It was not until she came to that ravine that Griff really took a test. She perched on the edge of the sod roof, all four feet scrunched together, like a reluctant gargoyle. She eyed the six-inch diameter of the post across the way, knowing it was her goal, then looked longingly behind her at the broad, inviting roof of the chicken house. Griff drooled onto the ground six feet below, smacked her lips a couple of times, then looked at Billy. Standing there on the pole, already well on his way to conquering the peak, he encouraged her with a couple of commanding words and a wave of his arm. Finally, Griff found the daring to spring. Usually she made it, landing with two or more feet on the top of the post, scrabbling to keep her balance. Sometimes she fell, without grace, to the ground. If Billy was in a forgiving mood, he would climb down the corral poles and into the ravine, pick up the dog, and give her a boost, saving her from the icy elements. A harrowing rescue became part of the game. Or, he might sigh large, click to her with his tongue and head back to the beginning of the windbreak to start the climb over. Either way the two of them would eventually balance on the corral poles, Billy holding out his arms like a diver doing a swan, and Griff walking on her claws, shaking like an earthquake with every hated step. The reward was on the 15-foot-high summit, where she and He sat looking out across the world.

***

It was not the Monster's belly. Too cold. He sat up, stiffly, testing his joints. They creaked like something very old or something very new. Coyote hugged himself against the chilly air and wondered if he had fur. It felt like he had awakened as a people, so probably not.

Light, bright as a torch, came in through a ragged horizontal crack. It hurt his eyes. He had been in the dark so long. So long. He wanted to look away, but couldn't. Instead, he began crawling in the dirt toward the opening.

CHAPTER FIVE

The history of her

In which Bill runs into Seaman, Jake carves out a living,
Someone slaps bumpers, Debbie sees a sign, Mary's ancestry
is questioned, and The Private notices a newness.

This time he knew who she was. Bill put his legs into it and
started to churn. What a lucky break. He seldom came out
this direction. For miles through town the path paralleled the
Boise River, sometimes on both sides, running through the
cottonwoods and willows, carving up the grass of the "wife"
parks: Julia Davis, Ann Morrison and Kathryn Albertson,
through Vets and Willow Lane, never far from the water.
East of town, the north side path left the river at Municipal
Park and cut through the Warm Springs Golf Course. For four
or five miles it tracked along by itself through pastures and
meadows along Highway 21 toward Lucky Peak. He seldom
found himself out on the eastern end of the path. Today, the
crowds on the greenbelt had irritated him amply. He had
decided to forgo river views for a stretch of clear pavement.
To his delight, Mary Lewis had done the same. He saw her
swaying hair a quarter mile down the path. If he needed more
proof, it came in the form of a black blur the size of a compact
car. When it first burst from the brush, he thought she was
being attacked by a bear. Deer were common along the path,
and moose trotted down from the foothills occasionally.
Not a bear, surely? Then, he remembered her dog. That
confirmation put more power in his strokes.

He caught up with her just past Eckert Road where the bike
path and highway were at their closest. Bill let his speed carry

him past her, then turned and coasted backwards on the path, facing her. A cool move only recently perfected.

"Hey, Mary. How's it going?" Her face went from puzzled, to recognition, to horror in under two seconds. Her mouth dropped as he felt the fur hit the back of his legs, solid as a davenport. The collision had him airborne and parallel to the path for a cartoon second. He might have groped at the air beneath him like Acme's best customer, betrayed again by coyote lust. When he came down it was clear time still ran. Maybe it even accelerated to give him a better body slam. Bill hit the pavement flat on his back. The pain held a heartbeat while his ears registered the squeak of Styrofoam compressing on asphalt at the back of his head. Then the pain came. His landing jolted every internal organ he owned. It scraped skin from a four-inch space between his shoulder blades and bruised his tailbone so he couldn't sit comfortably for a week. All that awaited discovery, like the surprise on your first day at boot camp. Now his body screamed for air. What wind was in him now mingled with the ozone. Struggling to get it back with lungs too startled to move, Bill saw the black cloud descend. It squatted over him like a...

"Seaman, no!" Something the size of a sock slurped across his face, getting water up his nose. He choked feebly. Suddenly the cloud was gone. In its place was a beautiful face, framed by cascading hair. He felt it drape against his cheeks. He would savor the memory of it. If he lived.

"Bill, are you okay?" She put her hands around his neck and asked again. "Bill, are you okay?" He later wondered why she thought it was a good idea to squeeze the neck of a person who was dying for lack of air. At that moment he took his first shallow breath, getting a taste of relief that came stronger with each succeeding expansion of his chest.

He put his hands on her wrists and drew her away from his neck. Not too far. She didn't object to his holding her like that for a few seconds, her face a foot above him, her hair brushing his lips. In those seconds he felt the most blessed relief. It was almost like breathing for the first time, each breath sweeter than the last. He could have remained suspended in that moment infinitely. Slowly, as if by trial and error, his other pains found pathways to his brain. He groaned.

Mary sat up and Bill let go of her hands.

"Go on, Seaman." She pushed the dog, which was desperate to be a part of the scene.

"Wow." The voice, tight and a little choked was his.

"You all right?"

"Yeah, I'm fine." He grimaced as he sat up. "I think." His tailbone shot an arrow up his spine. "I'll be a little sore is all."

Mary put her hand to her mouth and turned away. Her hair hid her face. Bill could see that she was trembling. It broke his heart.

"Mary, it's all right," he said, his pain momentarily forgotten. "It wasn't your fault."

She turned toward him again. Her eyes were moist and her shoulders were shaking. Finally, she could hold it no longer. Tears rolled down her cheeks as she let it go, laughing, then giggling, then stopping abruptly. Then laughing again.

"I'm sorry," she gasped. "I know it must hurt, but," she shook her head. "I can't help it. It was so damn funny."

She threw her arm around the dog, holding him back.

"I mean, you looked so, so," she shook her wrist looking for the word, "dashing. Then when you hit Seaman, you should have seen your face." She put her fingers to her lips and looked away. Again, she let her laugh go. "You looked like someone had pulled a rug out from under you. I mean, it was terrible, but funny at the same time. You know?"

Bill could imagine how he looked at the moment of impact. How he looked now was only a guess, but her next move gave him a clue. She put her hand out and touched him gently on the shoulder.

"Don't be embarrassed. I didn't mean to laugh."

"That's okay," he said. "I understand."

He started to get up. Mary stood, helping lift him, supporting him with her shoulder. He moved stiffly.

"God, you are sore. Are you sure there's nothing broken?"

He wasn't sure at all. Bill had never had a broken bone. Any of these pains might be the signature of fracture for all he knew. Nothing poked through his skin. That had to be a plus.

"I don't think I broke anything." He paused. "Feels like I might have bent a place or two."

"Can you walk?"

"Only if I take my skates off'

"Oh yeah," she said, looking at his feet. "Do you want to do that?"

"Would it mean bending?"

"Probably."

"Not in this lifetime."

"I can go get my car. It's parked at headquarters."

The headquarters building for the Idaho Department of Parks and Recreation was set back off the road, a few hundred feet from the river on the right, half a mile away.

"The car sounds fine," Bill said. "I think I can make it there, with a little help."

"Sure," Mary said.

She put her arm around his waist. He put his across her shoulders. They started slowly up the path. She skated. He rolled. Seaman romped.

"Nice dog," Bill said.

"Thanks. Sorry you had to meet him under such unhappy circumstances."

The circumstances were mixed in Bill's mind. He could have skipped the pain and humiliation. The feel of this woman under his arm was bliss.

"What was his name again?"

"Seaman."

"That's right. And, you named him after your great grandfather's dog?"

"Actually, he wasn't my great grandfather. He was my great, great, great, great grandfather. It's hard getting four greats—I think it's four—into a conversation."

"Wow. You've traced your roots that far back? Someone in your family must be Mormon."

She slapped his hand playfully. "No, we're not Mormon. They aren't the only ones interested in genealogy, you know."

"Sorry. I ..." He stammered, knowing he was stepping into a conversational minefield, yet not knowing how to dance out of it. "I just thought you might have been adopted by a Mormon family, or something."

"I'm not adopted. Whatever gave you that idea."

"I don't know. I didn't mean you were adopted. I didn't know. It's just that Mormons adopted a lot of ... kids, and with your last name, I thought you might have been, uh, one of them."

"You mean they adopted a lot of Indian kids."

"Kids of all kinds. Well, sure, Indian kids."

Mary pulled him along, her skin soft as ever under his arm, but Bill felt her tense.

"Look, I'm sorry. I didn't mean to get off on that subject. Race doesn't mean anything to me, really."

"Really?" She asked. "It means a lot to me."

For a moment he thought she was going to throw his arm off and skate away, leaving him in sedimentary layers of misery.

"I'm proud to be Nez Perce," she finally said. "And I'm proud of the other part of me, too."

Bill gulped, afraid to respond, yet knowing he had to. "You should be proud," he finally said, taking a neutral course.

"I would be just as proud if I was only Nez Perce, but I am not embarrassed having a white man in the family."

She looked up at him when she said it, her brown eyes so soft and warm he could barely stand it. For one irrational second he thought she meant him. He felt his face flush at the foolish notion.

"Uh, let me guess. That would be the guy with the dog."

Mary laughed. He felt a wave of relief wash over him with the sound.

"That's right, the guy with the dog, my great, great, great, great gramps."

He could see the parks building through the trees, now. Only one car was in the lot, an early Mustang convertible with its top down and tonneau cover on. The car was bone white except for three random spots of primer on the rear deck and fender.

"What was he like, your great how-many-ever granddad?"

"Well, I never met him, you know."

"Oh, yeah. I guess not," Bill said.

They cut off the path and into the parking lot, Mary guiding him toward the Mustang.

"He came to Idaho in 1805. I'm an old broad, but I'm not that old."

Yeah, Bill thought, you must be all of 25 or 26.

"Is this yours? Great car."

"Of course it's mine. What else would you expect an Indian to drive."

He laughed. "A Mustang, naturally. What year is it?"

"Sixty-six."

They stopped by the passenger door. She grinned at him and said, "I bought it new."

Bill gave her a blank look.

"I'm teasing, silly. You thought I was old enough to know Meriwether Lewis."

She opened the door for him, then chased Seaman out of the front seat when he tried to claim it. Bill stood there staring while she walked around the car.

***

Charlene loved to watch Jake work. He swept the saw up and down and back and forth, pushing it in here and there, tilting it sideways to grind out some detail, all as effortlessly as an artist using a camel-hair brush. She marveled at the critters he saw in the wood, the majestic eagles with their curved beaks jutting out in defiance and their talons wrapped around a flopping fish, the bear rising on its hind feet in a terrible attack, the snarling cougar in the stance of a predator with its tail wrapped around itself. All of them were rough-finished creatures, rugged as the woods. Jake hated using hand tools. If he couldn't bring out the detail he wanted with the chainsaw, he'd mutter about it all the while as he chipped and hammered. That's why he kept his sculptures big, though Charlene had told him so many times, as nice as possible, that the people would buy more if he'd make smaller things.

She didn't push it. Charlene felt lucky she could get him to make anything one person could carry. Jake loved his saws, the bigger the better. He loved hearing the rip as his chain bit into a standing tree. He attacked a tree like it had offended his mother, cutting one direction, then the other, until he heard the crack and made the call, "Timber!"

Charlene had seen him in the woods, running a few steps to avoid the kickback as the tree fell. A few times she had been allowed to see her man do the real work. Nowadays, she watched him all the time as he chewed out sculpture at their little shop along the Payette. She watched him with his little saw and his big artistic strokes, knowing his hands itched to be bringing down trees, one after another. She watched him hurry too fast, quickly carving out a critter, then kicking the thing across the floor because of some real or imagined mistake.

Jake's early work was better. He had some pride, then. When they first opened the shop after the mill closed, he came up with new designs, or variations on old ones all the time. Now he churned out five or six over and over, hardly varying a feather or claw. It didn't matter to tourists. They bought the sculptures as fast as he could make them. The current favorite wasn't a bird or an animal at all. It was a three-foot high woodcut of Idaho. Tourists stuffed them in trunks, or strapped them on roofs or had them shipped: Anything to get the little Idahos back home. Charlene had begun to paint towns and rivers on the sculptures, with their little spot along the Payette featured in prominent lettering, "Burrell's Saw Art." She worked on one now.

The saw sound wound down to silence. Jake wiped his forehead with the sleeve of his plaid shirt and came over to where Charlene was working under the shade of a sturdy arbor. He tipped a short log up on end and sat down to watch, elbows resting on his knees. Behind them the river roared its monotonous roar. Cars whooshed along the highway a hundred feet to the east.

Charlene was painting the Snake River across the southern half of the state, tracing its path in blue enamel.

"You should put in highways," Jake said.

"Do you think? That'd be a lot of work." She moved the river along with her brush, east to west, like the real thing. "Would people want highways?"

"That's how they get here." Jake hawked loudly and spit into the dirt. "If you had highways on it, they'd know how to find their way back."

They both laughed.

"In fact, you ought to put big red exit signs every place they can leave the state."

"Oh, Jake," Charlene scolded. "Where would we be if it weren't for tourists?"

Jake spit again. This time it was a recreational spit. "We'd be right here and they'd be on the other side of the border bothering somebody in Oregon."

The sound of crunching gravel signaled the coming of a customer. Jake stood, knees creaking as he did. He shuffled back toward his open-air shop. Charlene had made it clear he wasn't to be out front when customers were around. Fact was he scared them, the big lug. They liked it better when he was a few yards away working his chainsaw art. They loved the art. The artist made them nervous.

Two customers wandered through the forest of wooden animals, admiring the creativity. Pointing out some delightful detail to her husband, the woman clapped her hands. Jake heard her say she loved primitive art. Her husband said something about it being a little too primitive for his tastes. After a few minutes the man reached for his wallet, a little reluctantly. Jake stared at the car they had been driving. A Lexus painted like a pearl, parked right next to his battered old Ford pickup. It would take a couple of minutes for Charlene to complete the transaction, writing down the tax and item on the Visa slip. Jake stretched languidly, looking around at the stock in his shop. Quite a supply. He suddenly had the urge to go get a little more wood. He sure did hope he could get out of his parking spot without dinging that car. It looked a little tight.

***

Anyone watching the man would assume he was going about his official business, whatever that was. He wore an orange vest, so he must have been a highway department worker. The man wasn't leaning on a shovel, or looking into a hole with three or four of his compatriots, or listlessly waving traffic past a construction site. He seemed to be employed, though. He walked behind the row of cars and RVs in the rest area parking lot, skipping a few, leaning down briefly behind most of them. Around his neck hung a bag like a newspaper carrier might use. He was extracting some kind of sticker from the bag, popping the break back paper off, dropping the paper in the bag and slapping something on the back of the cars.

People discovered the stickers at various times and places. A few who were parked with their rear bumpers facing the rest rooms noticed them when they went to get into their cars. Some found the proclamations when they stopped that day for lunch or to visit Shoshone Falls or Massacre Rocks. Others didn't notice until they took the luggage out of their cars that night, or went to set up camp.

A few got all the way home, states away, before discovering the stickers.

Unless they were lucky enough to find the stickers right away, just about all of them got some unwanted attention on their trip. They noticed icy glares, kids making faces and even rude gestures from people passing them. They understood later. Until they finally discovered the stickers, they seethed at the impolite Idahoans they encountered on the highway.

Bold, black lettering on a putrid pink background, read simply TOURIST. A cartoon figure to the right of the word depicted a dumpy man in Bermuda shorts and Hawaiian shirt bedecked with cameras and luggage. The caricature was overlaid by concentric circles surrounding a bull's eye. The recipients of the unwanted tags struggled to scrape, peel and rub the stickers, only to find the adhesive notably tenacious. Most eventually opted to cover them with a less obnoxious message. One detail usually went unnoticed. Floating in the lower left-hand corner of each, no bigger than an eyelash, was a tiny black chevron, like a soldier in the army might wear.

***

Whenever Debbie felt a little blue she saddled up Skid and went for a ride. Usually, she rode up the draw behind the ranch and onto the foothills, taking the low ridge south for a couple of miles until she came out on a plateau. From up there she could look out over their ranch, a few thousand acres of neighboring ranches, and a couple million acres of BLM ground to the north. On a clear day she could see the Sawtooths 130 miles to the northeast. She could watch the weather roll in from the west; thunderheads towering 30,000 feet in the air, testing the earth by poking it with lightening fingers; broad, fluffy fronts stretching horizon to horizon like a quilt pulled up to Idaho's chin. On cloudless days when the sky was thick with color it made the whole view seem under water. She could watch the F-111s chase each other out of Mountain Home Air Force Base, quiet as flies in the distance. They changed into fire-breathing monsters that shook the ground when they got close. Debbie didn't like the jets much. They were part of living in Owyhee County. Better living with roaring jets than what lay to the northwest. From the ridge you couldn't actually see the city 80 miles away. You saw where the city was. Boise announced itself with a murky brown cloud that stayed stuck up against the foothills below Shafer Butte. Debbie looked at that cloud and wondered what it must be like to live there, breathing indecent air, fighting traffic twice a day like a salmon on a perpetual spawning run, shopping shoulder to shoulder for food wrapped in plastic and cardboard. Seeing it even from a distance made her shudder. It made her glad for the distance. That gladness almost always drove away the blues.

Some days, like this one, a different melancholy settled around her like a persistent fog. This sadness seemed so personal she felt possessive of it. She knew others suffered from grief and sickness and hunger. Those were surely dilemmas more worthy of worry than hers. Her distress was not because life treated her badly, rather because it treated her so well. She feared losing her perfect life.

On gloomy days when she loved her life so much she saw nothing but its end, the plateau would not cheer her. On days like today, she went to visit the Clara Tree.

Clara Carson Bennett was the only grandparent she ever knew. She remembered her as an old woman, in her 80s and 90s, a grandmother in every detail. She remembered gingerbread cookies that seemed, like sourdough starter, perpetually self-generating. The smell of warm cookies was the smell of Gram's house. Debbie's memories were of newspaper clippings hung on hooks beside the door, ready for Clara to back up an interesting story with proof in black and white. She remembered the electric range. Clara used a wood stove for decades, overcoming imprecise temperatures to become a master cook and an even better baker. Sometime in the 1950s, she decided she would have an electric range. If she was going to shift from one era to the next she would do it right. It would be a push-button range. The latest thing. It would have a clock and a timer to run the oven. It would have a window in the door. And it would be red.

The red range was Clara's only indulgence in 91 years of life. Debbie remembered how the family teased Gram about it. She remembered the constant quilts that came from her gnarled hands, patched together from scraps of fabric that once made dresses and aprons and shirts. She remembered sharing every Christmas Eve with Gram, and hanging handmade ornaments, adding just one new one every year.

Debbie remembered Clara Carson Bennett as a grandmother. She knew her best as a little girl.

Clara's parents, Hannah Carson and Amos Bennett, were Owyhee County pioneers. Amos sought silver on Jordan Creek, with little success, then worked in the big mines for a few years. In 1868, he was working the Golden Chariot at Silver City when miners from the competing Ida Elmore mine started a war over disputed claims. At least they started the war when Amos told the story. The Underground War, which lasted about three weeks, resulted in only three deaths. That was amazing, considering the hundreds of rounds fired inside those tunnels. As Amos told it, mine timbers nine inches thick were nearly cut in half by gunfire. The mine owners eventually worked out their differences and went about the business of getting rich. Amos Bennett put down his rifle and pick. He and Hannah homesteaded 160 acres, started supplying beef to the mines and, eventually, had four boys and a daughter named Clara.

Clara knew nothing about mining, except for her father's stories. He would sometimes drag out a little poke sack that held a couple of crusty ore samples and three smashed bullets to illustrate the tales. That was all just old-days talk to Clara. She had today to live for. She had trees to climb and calves to ride and canyons to explore. She lived the romantic life of a ranch girl, riding the Owyhee desert on half-tamed mustangs. Later, as a young woman, she wrote about it in a little book called *Owyhee Sage*. It was Debbie's bible; the history of her. She started reading it when she was seven years old, and never stopped. She could follow young Clara up the creek and through the horsetail rush, under the lava ledge that hung out over the Butterfly Pool, and into the side canyon to find the cave Clara found. Clara was her invisible friend and adventure leader. She was the laughing girl who always egged her on, begging her to explore. If you quizzed her about it, Debbie would have the right answer: Clara and Gram were the same person. Yet, they were as far apart as the years that separated the little girl from the grandmother. Farther, because Clara still lived. Gram did not.

Lately, another separation was taking place. Debbie still saw Clara running or riding across the desert as she always had. Sometimes, running there beside her was another little girl. A girl so far away in years she could barely remember what it had been like to be her.

Days like that were when Debbie felt the loss that had not yet happened. Days like that—like this—she went to her special place. A place where Clara and Gram could be one, and Debbie could be with them.

Owyhee Sage made Clara a minor celebrity in Idaho. That status followed her for fifty years, although she never wrote another book. Debbie asked her once why she didn't write something about her later life on the ranch, or even stories about her father's mining days. Clara had said, "Oh, Hon, I had only one story, and I already told it." At the time, it wasn't a satisfying answer. The older Debbie got, the more it made sense. If she wrote a story about her own life on the ranch, what could she write next? What else was worth the words?

Sometimes, when the reflection off the creek or the golden flutter of leaves or the squeaking sound of fresh dry snow made Clara's heart sing, she still wrote. She wrote poetry, not stories. She wrote only one for Debbie.

Daughter Grand

Daughter Grand, I think of you a woman.
I see you dressed in white
Standing with your special man
On life's threshold, bright.
I think of children to surround you,
All Great Grands of mine
Getting from you, love so true
As they begin their time.
I think of things I'll never see
Wishing I could stay
Instead I'll simply plant a tree
And with that planting say
Daughter Grand, always think of me.

Clara Carson Bennett, 1957

Clara died in 1971, three years before Debbie married Charlie. There would never be children surrounding Debbie. The Tree was a real live cottonwood, now 50 feet high. It grew next to the creek on the old homestead two miles from Debbie's house. On those melancholy days when she went to visit the Clara Tree, those two miles gave her a chance to think and watch for Clara in the sage. She usually saw her. Or, she would be waiting beneath the tree when Debbie got there. She would be there with Gram and Hannah and Amos, waiting to welcome Debbie back into their intertwined lives; waiting to give her the strength to love the life she had and forget her fear of losing it. That ugly thing, she could put in a pocket.

Today Clara was nowhere to be seen between the Bennett Ranch and the Homestead, now owned by Andy Bennett, one of the Boise cousins. Debbie looked for her naked footprints in the floury dust on the road. She tried to catch a glimpse of her peeking from behind a lava break, or darting between the rabbit brush. No Clara.

When Debbie and Skid topped the hill a quarter mile from the old house, she saw the sign. The sign itself was, by now, just a small annoyance on the landscape. It hung there, a little crooked, from a corner post next to the county road, where it had been hanging for six years. The paint had begun to fade, though you could still read the agent's name. There were half a dozen depressions in the sign that looked like someone with an iron thumb had tested its tenderness. Debbie straightened in her saddle, hearing the familiar creak of leather.

There was something new. A smaller sign, with neat red lettering was bolted on top of the first. It was the worst four-letter word Debbie Bennett Anderson had ever read.

***

"It seems like I would have heard something about it, that's all."

He had his eye on Seaman in the back seat. The dog was determined to show his affection by licking the wound on Bill's back. Paying strict attention to sitting up straight kept the scrape from rubbing on the back of the Mustang's bucket seat, or sticking to the vinyl. That exposed it to the dog. He had to be vigilant.

"How would you have heard about it, history books?" Mary asked. She let the engine wind out until the pipes began to get throaty then shifted aggressively to third.

"Well, sure. Or their journals."

She shook her head. "Right. And who wrote the journals?"

Bill shrugged. Bill winced. "They did, Lewis and Clark. Or was it just Lewis?"

"Okay," she said finding fourth. "And how would you describe those two?"

"Uh, explorers. Heros."

"Yeah, and..?"

"I don't know what you're looking for?"

"Let me give you a clue. They were men."

"I'm a man, so what?"

"So, don't you think their story might have been told differently if Sacajawea had written it?"

"Granted, her viewpoint would be different. Not that much different, though. The facts would still be the same."

Mary rolled her eyes. "Don't bet on it. What I'm getting at is everything we know about the Lewis and Clark Expedition has been told to us by white males. A woman would have had a different point of view. An Indian would have had a different point of view. An Indian woman might have told a story you wouldn't even recognize."

Bill grabbed a handful of hair on Seaman's neck, kneading the dog in a friendly way with his thumb and holding him at arm's length. "You're right, of course. I still think there would have been some mention of Meriwether Lewis fathering a child by an Indian woman."

"Have you read their journals?" Mary asked, not waiting for an answer. "They are full of references to the men sleeping with Indian women. But no, Lewis didn't say anything about sleeping with my great grandmother. My dad mentioned it. So did his father and his father all the way back."

Mary backed off the accelerator as she came around the bend where a side road led up to Warm Springs Mesa. The pipes rumbled pleasantly and echoed off the road cut. "And like a fool, I mentioned it," she said. "I don't know why. I never do that. It just leads to complications."

"Hey, don't get me wrong. It's not that I don't believe you. I'm just surprised, that's all." He wasn't handling this well. Now that he thought about it, he hadn't handled anything well since about the time he caught up with her on the path. "Actually, I think it's kind of neat." He laughed.

"What's funny?"

"Oh, I was just thinking. My family came here in 1863. I rarely find someone who has me beat, but you sure do. I mean, Meriwether Lewis discovered Idaho. You can't be much more native than that."

Mary didn't say anything for a moment. She seemed to be thinking hard as she clicked her fingernails on top of the windshield frame. "I'm not sure what to do with you, Clark." Her tone was resigned. "You seem harmless enough by yourself, but I'm afraid you might reproduce."

"Huh?"

The road straightened out in front of them. She shifted down and made the Mustang leap. "Forget it," she said.

For the next few minutes the conversation was a dialogue of directions. Bill concentrated on removing his skates. If Mary drove in deference to his injuries, it was not apparent. She obviously enjoyed working the gears of the convertible, matching them precisely to the speed and the road, treating each corner as a challenge. When she swung up into Bill's driveway the Mustang bounced on its springs, giving his tailbone a jolt it did not need.

"Nice house," she said.

"Thanks. Would you like to come in?"

"I don't think so," she said, making no movement to turn off her car. Her refusal disappointed him, but he needed a hot shower more than company right now.

Bill heard the familiar squeak of his garage door as it began to disappear. A pair of shapely legs, feet dressed in running shoes, began a slow, vertical exposure behind it. He thought of a novelty pen he'd seen once where the woman was dressed in a bathing suit when you held it right side up then— whoops!—her suit went away when you turned it over. These legs stayed unclothed longer than he expected. Finally a pair of short shorts, a bare mid-riff, a loose blouse tied in front and enough other visual clues came into view to positively identify Pauline Clark.

Adding a puzzled look to her wardrobe, Pauline came out to greet them.

"Bill? I thought you were skating."

Before he could answer, Seaman made a short lunge toward Pauline. The dog gave her a woof so powerful his lips shook. She drew up her arms and stepped back.

"Seaman!" Mary scolded. "Stop that!" Turning to Pauline she said, "Sorry, he's not good around strangers."

The Newfoundland dropped his ears and nuzzled his nose under Mary's arm. "Go away," she said.

Finding no solace there, the dog tried the same tactic with Bill, who pushed him back gently.

"Pauline, this is Mary Lewis," Bill said. "Mary, my wife, Pauline."

"Hi," Pauline said, smiling thinly. "Big dog."

"Yeah, he is. Sorry about that. It's nice to meet you."

Pauline looked suspiciously at the animal. It probably outweighed her by forty pounds.

"I thought you were skating," she repeated.

"I was," Bill said. "Took a spill. Mary was nice enough to bring me home."

"My god, Bill, that scrape!"

He rolled his shoulders experimentally. "It probably looks worse than it is. Doesn't hurt too bad."

"No, I meant on the back of that skate."

He looked into his lap. Just above the heel his shiny, metal flake purple Rollerblade looked like the plastic had been left on a hotplate.

"I just got you those for Christmas." Pauline folded her arms and glared at the dog. Then she asked, "Are you okay?"

"I'm fine, a little shook up, that's all."

"Hey, great car." Nick Hawthorne crossed the street.

"You thinking of buying that and classing up your image, Bill?" Just what he needed. A chance to be humiliated in front of the golden boy.

"Not a chance," Mary said. "It's not for sale."

"Yeah, I'll bet not. This beauty would bring $15,000 in California."

"Mary, this is my neighbor, Nick," Bill said.

"Hi, Nick."

"Pleased to meet you. Mustang Mary, is it?"

"Nope. Just Mary. Mary Lewis."

Seaman made a move toward the other side of the car, but Bill had his fingers in the dog's collar.

Nick ran his fingertips along the fender ridge.

"Looks like you've got it all smoothed out, ready to paint."

"Yeah, a friend of mine in McCall took out the dings for me this past winter, just before I moved here."

"You're new to Boise?" Pauline asked, brightening. "Have you found a house, yet?"

At the sound of Pauline's voice, Seaman turned and curled his lip. Again, Bill kept him calm.

"I'm renting in the North End. It's a little small, but I love the neighborhood."

Pauline reached in the front pocket of her shorts, pulled out a thin, gold case, and extracted a business card. She started to reach across Bill to hand it to Mary. Seaman gave a warning rumble.

"Pass that to her, will you?" she said to her husband.

Mary took the card.

"She'll make you a deal, Mustang," Nick said, nodding toward his house. "Pauline set me up with that one a few months back."

Mary glanced at the card and slipped it under a clip on her visor.

"I'll keep it in mind, but my name's not Mustang."

Nick crossed his arms and leaned on the driver's door. "Not even your middle name?"

God, Bill thought, where did this guy learn his pickup routine. He eased the door open and started to slowly make his exit.

"So what is it?"

"What's what?" Mary said.

"Your name."

"Mary."

"Yeah, I've got that memorized," Hawthorne said. "What's your middle name."

Mary tilted her chin and said, "Who wants to know?"

Nick extended his hand. "Nicholas Randolph Hawthorne."

She put her hand in his and said, ''We've been through this. I'm Mary Lewis, remember?"

Quietly, Bill said, "Pauline, can you give me a hand here?"

Seaman, now unencumbered did not know what to do with his freedom. The dog looked from the driver's side to the passenger side where Bill was exiting, then quickly looked back again. He sat up straight on the middle of the seat and suspiciously guarded both sides.

"But there isn't any symmetry," Nick was saying. "All I know about you is you drive a great car and your name is Mary." Nick started counting off on his fingers, "You know where I live, who sold me my house, who my neighbors are and my first, last and middle names. I think that calls for a little reciprocity."

"Nice try, but you left out some things." Mary started her own finger count. "You know I rent my house, it's in the North End, that I have a 160 pound Newfoundland, and that I know Bill Clark."

Pauline, who was helping Bill out of the car said, "I thought you two just met."

"Oh, no. Mary works out at State Parks. We've known each other a couple of weeks."

"Yeah," Mary said. "He's trying to ruin one of my parks for a movie."

Nick said, "Hey, I'll protect your park, Mustang. With me around you'll have nothing to worry about.

"Mary laughed, "I think I'd have a lot to worry about. And it's not Mustang."

"Okay, okay. I'll stop calling you Mustang, but I still don't know what I should call you."

"How about Mary?"

"Maybe." Nick frowned and scratched his chin. "I'd like to know what my options are."

"Maybe you don't have any options," she said.

"There are always options."

"Yeah, well, my middle name isn't one of them, okay?"

"Ah ha! So you do have a middle name."

Mary sighed heavily. "Yes, I have a middle name. It's stupid, for a person."

"Uh, you've thrown me there," Nick said.

Pauline took Bill's Rollerblades, licked her finger and wiped at the scrape with it, to no effect. Bill took a couple of experimental steps.

"My mother named me Idaho, all right? And if you call me that, I'll slap you."

"Idaho? I think that's a pretty name," Nick said. "What does it mean?"

"It doesn't mean anything. It's just the name of the state."

"Well, it has to mean something. It's a Native American name, isn't it?"

"No," Mary said. "Well, yes, but only kind of. It's my name and I'm Native American, but it's not an Indian word. Some politician made it up and thought it sounded Indian."

Bill straightened nearly to his full height and shuffled his body around so he wouldn't have to turn his neck. "You sure?" he asked. "They taught us in fourth grade that it meant 'Behold the sun coming over the mountain,' or something like that."

"Yeah, right," Mary said. "Did you ever think about that? How often have you needed a word that meant 'behold the sun coming over the mountain'?"

Bill shrugged. "Well, it was something like that."

"Guess what? The history books got it wrong." Sarcastically, she added, "Hard to believe, isn't it?"

Mary put the transmission into reverse and started to roll back down the driveway. Nick, leaning again on her door, matched the car's pace while continuing to lean, talking faster as the car rolled.

Nick's words faded into the background of Bill's pain. Pauline helped her husband shuffle up the driveway and onto the front step. Bill rotated his bruised body to avoid the screen door. He had always had good peripheral vision—hardly had to turn his head at all at a four-way stop. Using that gift now he was able to watch Mary hanging onto Seaman's collar while Nick Hawthorne climbed into the passenger seat of her Mustang.

***

He stood and stretched, put his hands on his waist, then arched, throwing his shoulders back. He looked out over the sage and lava rock. In the distance a black river cut across the desert like a snake. On its back colors moved, squares and squares hooked to squares and not squares at all, but all moving. Fast. He grinned. Something new, he thought, then dropped to all fours and trotted into the brush.

Chapter Six

Blading with the beast

In which Mary has a Private moment, Blaine shares a secret, Nick gets papered, Frank learns the value of property, Bill makes a memory, and John makes a move.

She was thinking about Nick. Not obsessing, mind you, just thinking. Her mind drifted from subject to subject as she drifted from side to side on the path with each subtle shift of her weight. It was early on a Saturday. Six o'clock early. Mary liked to beat the heat by gliding out before most people were awake.

Last night had been good. She and Nick had gone to the Brick Oven, then to a movie, and finally ended up at her place. It was their second date. They did not sleep together. That was a major triumph, in her estimation. Gawd that man had angles! He kept poking at every defense she had, constantly testing for some weakness.

Fighting him off nearly wore her out.

No, she had to stop thinking in terms like that. It wasn't a fight, or a battle, or even a contest. She would not "lose" anything when she finally consented to sleep with him, which she would. Nevertheless, she wanted to make sure Nick knew he had won something when it finally happened.

She skated through the Warm Springs Golf Course, enjoying the smell of freshly mown grass. There were a few duffers queuing up for carts at this early hour. One waved at her.

Mary waved back, limply. She felt no kinship with golfers. You did not golf alone.

She enjoyed being alone, coasting along without worrying about who would win. Nick would win, of course. Only when she was sure she would win, too. When he understood she was not something to be conquered, he could conquer her at will. When he realized it was a partnership, no matter how short the duration, the two of them could be more than their sum. It would mean giving up a lot of control. Maybe he couldn't do that. Most men could not. Most men took what they wanted and ended up with nothing.

Nick would not be the one. Part of her knew that. He was too full of himself to have room for someone who had a self of her own. He would end up with some woman empty enough to hold his ego's overflow. Mary sighed. Maybe they could have a little fun together in the meantime.

Coyote! She caught it in a glance toward the river. It sat and watched her for a second, then started to run. She expected that. She expected it to go off a little distance, and turn to watch her again, if it stopped running at all. What she did not expect was for the animal to run toward her. It came at her like a greyhound with its nose in fur, streaking through the tall, dry grass. Her heart went on hold for a beat. Then, six feet from the path, the coyote turned and slowed. It matched her pace, loping along easily, acting for all the world like Seaman. She had left the Newfoundland home with a sore rib, a memento of his recent run-in with Bill Clark.

The coyote matched her strides in an easy trot, as Seaman sometimes did. Instead of stopping every few feet, sniffing, then catching up, the animal seemed content to parallel her. Mary slowed. The coyote slowed. She stretched out her strides. The coyote broke into a run to keep up.

He must be someone's pet, she thought. There was a guy who lived along the river not far from there who raised exotic animals—emus, water buffalo, alpacas. Maybe he kept a coyote, too. Mary grinned. Whatever the explanation, she enjoyed the company. She found herself paying more attention to the animal than the path. Every time she glanced over at him the coyote was looking straight ahead. When Mary looked back at the path, she had the odd feeling the coyote stole a glance at her. He was right there, six or eight feet away, yet she felt like she never got a good look at him. What if she stopped? Maybe he would stop and she could stare to her heart's content. Or maybe he would keep on running and that would be the last of him. She didn't want that.

The decision was soon made for her. Where the path crossed Eckert Road, bicyclists and bladers were supposed to stop. She usually blasted on across, unless there was traffic. This morning there was. She would have to stop. Mary straightened up and coasted toward the red sign. To her horror, the coyote failed to match her movement. He kept running and running.

"Wait! Stop!" She yelled. The animal did not indicate he heard a sound. A car came rolling up toward the stop on Highway 21, a couple of car lengths beyond the bike path. It wasn't going fast, but it was obvious the driver did not see the coyote. The reverse seemed just as true. The coyote ran through the grass, onto the shoulder and across the road without faltering. Mary saw the car's bumper go right over the top of him. She closed her eyes and stopped. She heard the car stop at the sign, and quickly turn onto the highway as if nothing had happened. The heartless son of a bitch.

Afraid of the mangled mess she would see, and already feeling guilty because she had been a part of it, Mary opened her eyes. The coyote sat across the road, looking at her, unharmed. Relief surged through her, then was quickly followed by something else. Recognition. Full face and close up she knew this beast, though she had never seen him before. She knew the driver had not seen him; knew a hundred bladers or bikers, had they been on the path, would not see him.

As if that moment of recognition was all he wanted, Coyote turned his tail to her and disappeared.

***

Being out of work had its advantages. Oh, sure, he had a regular job at the Prospector, so technically he was employed. Blaine Stope didn't consider it work, and it only took 24 hours out of his week. He spent another eight as a volunteer on the mine tour. That was nothing like the 60-hour weeks he put in back in the old days. Even after all those months—months that had without notice turned into years—he still felt like he was on temporary leave. He'd grab that time card in a second if someone held it out, ready to put in the hours again. Until someone did, he knew how to fill his spare time.

Some guys just sat around the house and got in their wives' way. That wasn't Blaine's style. Nor did he spend every morning reading the promises and lies in the classifieds, and every afternoon down at Job Service, like some. He even knew men who spent weeks working on their resumes, changing the words over and over to find a better way to say "I dug rock all my life." He knew what would happen to those men. Blaine wasn't going to let it happen to him. He'd taken the burger-flipping job at the Prospector because his brother-in-law owned the joint. He was helping the kid out, actually. It put him in a position to be ready when they called miners back to work. Blaine would be at the head of that line, without any two-week notice necessary. Hell, he'd leave the grill between flips if he got the word. Those other guys, they were stuck, the way he figured it. If they had some other kind of job, say working in a parts store or driving truck for a logging company, they wouldn't be miners anymore. Not really. They'd be used to calling themselves a counter man or truck driver. They'd be used to working in the sunshine and wearing a clean shirt every day. They'd hesitate when the call came for miners, and the real miners—men who had never given up—would beat them out.

Meanwhile, there was fishing. His daddy had taught him to fish. He'd shown Blaine where to look for the lunkers, in the shadow of a rock or under the edge of a cutbank. He taught the boy to keep his tip up when walking with a rod so as not to jam it into the ground and ruin a perfectly good pole. He'd shown him where to find worms no matter how dry it was, and how to catch grasshoppers with a stick and a Ball jar. It wasn't fancy fishing, like the Yuppies were all starting to do, beating the water's back like they were whipping an ornery mule. Why that was supposed to be fun, he could never figure. Blaine used a little K-Mart rod and a Zebco reel that had run him something under twenty bucks. Give him a bamboo pole and a bobber and he'd be just as happy.

Blaine had a special place he liked to fish, not more than three miles from his house. He drove the F-100 to within a couple hundred yards of the pool, and parked it in the brush where nobody would see it. Then he wandered through the trees for a few minutes never quite the same way twice, so as not to make a trail. Eventually, he would reach the hole, approaching it sometimes from the east, sometimes from the west, and sometimes from the north. He treated the spot like a mining claim. He'd never even brought Sally here. Blaine owned it by virtue of his being the only one who knew it existed.

The creek meandered through the pines and brush, then over a series of short rock steps before falling over a two foot ledge and into a pool not much bigger than a hot tub. The water seemed to pause there to rest a few minutes before easing over another little ledge and down through the woods toward town. The fishing wasn't really that hot. Blaine sometimes went for days without a single bite. He liked the way the place looked and the way it felt. It felt like him. A big, smooth rock poked into the little pool on the west, providing a Blaine-sized laying spot. He could drop his worm in the water, stretch back across the warm face of the stone and feel more at home than he did at home. Blaine lay there for hours sometimes, the pole propped between his legs, one hand curved casually around the cork handle, his Cat hat pulled down over his eyes. The sunshine warmed his bones better than on some Hawaiian beach. The trickle and tumble of water talked to him in soothing tones, always a friendly voice.

"Right here. Hey, this is great!"

Blaine tensed.

"Perfect!" the female voice said. Blaine did his best to become a part of the rock. "Oh, oh," the voice said, excited. "Shhh! Look at that. It's perfect! What a great shot. Shhh! Don't wake him up."

Blaine opened his left eye a slit. The sun filtered blue through the mesh of his cap. Beneath the bill he could see a piece of what was going on. Across the creek a small blond woman was standing thigh-high in weeds gesturing excitedly toward him like she had discovered a rare bird that might fly at any minute. Two men, one with a video camera and the other holding a microphone, were taking direction from her. Maybe if he just stayed quiet, ignored them, they would eventually go away. He closed his eye and pretended to sleep. Maybe he looked relaxed. He did not feel relaxed. Blaine kept the position like death had taken him. Not a muscle moved. He barely breathed.

The intruders talked in whispers that would have wakened the dead, occasionally snapping a twig or kicking a stone into the water to punctuate their intended silence. Blaine blew a burst of air through pursed lips, bouncing the bill of his cap. Would they ever go away?

Something in the intensity and rhythm of their whispering signaled a change. Blaine cracked open an eye again. Now the woman was standing with her back to him, while the man with the microphone held it toward her at chest level. The cameraman pointed his unit at her face.

"Okay," she said. "Do you need a white balance?" She held up a clipboard she was carrying and the cameraman focused on it, apparently making some adjustments to his equipment as he did.

"Got it. We're rolling."

The man with the mic said, "So what is it you're trying to accomplish with this study?"

The woman's answer came across smooth as pudding. Yet, she sounded like she was used to giving orders. "Well, everyone knows about Redfish Lake, the floating golf green at Coeur d'Alene, McCall's Winter Festival and Sun Valley. Everyone wants to go to those places. Unfortunately, because they are so well known, those destinations tend to get a little crowded. But there are hundreds of other places in Idaho not as well-known and every bit as beautiful. Places like this." She nodded over her shoulder to where Bill played possum. "We're trying to identify the best lesser-known places, so we can develop materials that would attract people to them."

The reporter—Blaine assumed now he was a reporter asked, "What kind of material will you be developing?"

"Just what you'd expect. We'll be doing brochures, maps and guides. We'll take pictures of spots like this and use them in magazine advertising and TV commercials. It will continue our theme from some years ago that Idaho is the Undiscovered America."

"And why is that important?" the reporter asked.

"It's important because those popular places—the Redfish Lakes and Sun Valleys—are getting overcrowded. Letting people know about Idaho's other beautiful areas will take some of the pressure off. But, the big reason is economic development. Smaller communities like Wallace and Kellogg really need the dollars tourists can bring in. We need to share the wealth with the smaller communities in Idaho, by sharing some of their secrets."

Blaine felt the heat of the sun. There was an internal heat churning up inside him that threatened to match it. They were going to tell people about his fishing hole?

"Okay," the reporter said. "That was pretty good. How did it look to you?"

The cameraman peeked over his eyepiece and said, "Not bad. I've got some good cutaways of the fisherman. I'd like to shift a little and get a little different angle of him over Jo Beth's shoulder. Can we run through the questions one more time?"

"Sure," the woman said.

"No problem," said the reporter.

The two of them shifted and shuffled as the cameraman directed. Blaine felt like a bug skewered by a pin. He felt trapped. Worse, he felt like a pawn in a game he could only lose. Tourists. These people wanted more damn tourists! More tourists to flip more hamburgers for. More assholes who would show their dicks to his sweet Sally.

"Ready?" the reporter asked.

"Rolling," said the cameraman.

Then Blaine smiled. Sometimes you had to fight fire with fire. While the blond rattled on about tourism, he unbuttoned his

501s and did a different kind of fishing. Too damn bad about that second take.

***

When he saw the red flyer stuck under his windshield wiper Nick stopped whistling. He did not like people touching his car. There was rarely a problem in the well patrolled Micron parking lot. He yanked the paper from the wiper's grip and glared at it. Whatever business or charity had set such a bad tone for his long lunch with Mary would pay for it. He planned to turn the offending announcement over to the guard at the entrance kiosk. Security would put a stop to the pamphleteering, especially after they got a piece of his mind because it happened in the first place.

Nick expected to see a discount offer for pizza or a car wash special. The flyer read: "Welcome to Idaho. Now get out!"

His fingernails cut through the paper as he stood there looking quickly from side to side. No one suspicious in sight. A few other early lunchers getting into their cars. Just getting in. Not stopping to pull flyers off their windshields first. There was not another flash of red in the lot.

***

Frank Thompson let out a long, breathy whistle, then shook his head.

"What is it, dearie?" Mildred asked.

He reread the paragraph to make sure he was right. There was nothing more embarrassing than to get worked up over something then find out you had put a comma where there was not one. Yes sir, he was right.

"Listen to this," he gave the paper a snap and began to read. "Average Boise home now costs $150,000."

"No. That can't be right."

"It surely is, Mom," he said. "Look at it right here."

Mildred put down her spatula and wiped her hands on her apron. She leaned over his shoulder and looked where he pointed.

"My word, it does say that, doesn't it?"

"As sure as I'm living," Frank said. "And listen to the rest of it." He ran his finger down the column, moving his lips quietly for a couple of lines until he found the part he wanted to share. "It says, 'Last month's 23 percent increase was the most dramatic in a string of astonishing gains that began last January.' 'Astonishing,' it says. Well, I guess so. Who could afford such prices?"

"Californians." J.B. said the word like it was a hairball he found in his Cream of Wheat.

"Likely true," Frank said. "That's who buys the big houses around here. They sell their home for half a million in California, then come here and pay for one twice as big with pocket change."

"Fa-ther," Margaret said.

"What? What did I do now?"

"You exaggerate so much. Its right next to lying, you know."

Frank saw Mildred was on the verge of saying something sharp to the girl. He stopped her with a glance.

"Well, I don't mean it that way. You're right, though. I should be more careful."

The dear girl wanted everything to be so perfect. She could not understand why others had such a hard time living up to her expectations. There were rules, after all. It was as simple as that.

"It was just an expression. Sort of a lazy way of making a point."

Margaret frowned. "What point?"

"That houses shouldn't be that blamed expensive."

He saw her eyes widen at the suggestion of a profanity twice removed. Before she could rebuke him for the slip, he quickly said, "It is awfully irritating to hear of a house on a tiny little lot selling for three times what your Uncle Eldro got for his share of the home place. Think about it. He got less than $50,000 for 160 acres, with a frame house on it."

Margaret narrowed her eyes, looking for some crack in his statement. "I thought Uncle Eldro always lived in town."

"No, of course not. He farmed the Higley place—what's now the Higley place—for several years before you were born."

"Well, when did he sell it?"

Frank straightened and looked thoughtfully at Mildred. "When was it, Mom? Late sixties?"

"Nineteen sixty-five." Her tone was gentle, yet authoritative. She liked to say she didn't know a lot, but she knew what she knew.

"Sixty-five?" Margaret said. "That was more than 30 years ago."

"So it was, yes," Frank agreed.

"Well, what would it sell for today?"

"Billions and billions," J.B. said, doing his best Carl Sagan.

Margaret gave him a look that would fry eggs.

"Sue me, Sis."

"I expect he's closer to right than you might think, sweet one," Frank said. "It's right up against town near about. Lots sell for what ridiculous price? Ten thousand? I've heard as much as $30,000 for an acre, even right here in Bingham County."

Margaret dropped her jaw, exposing a complicated cage of braces. "That'd be $5 million!"

"Would it?" Frank was not as fast with math as his daughter. Five million? She must have a coma wrong somewhere. That could not be.

"Sure. Thirty thousand times 100 acres would be three million, then the next 50 acres would be a million and half, then the remaining ten acres—you did say 160, didn't you?"

Frank nodded dumbly. "The last ten would be $300,000. That adds up to four million eight hundred thousand." She blushed. "Okay, it wouldn't quite be five million. Sorry."

Frank Thompson sat and stared at her. "Dad, does that mean people are getting rich when they sell their land?"

J.B. answered for his father, who seemed to be somewhere else. "Of course it does, dodo head."

Could it be possible that land prices had gone up 100 times when he was not looking? Well, yes, he knew that, actually. Eldro had sold the farm to the Higleys for about $300 an acre, throwing in the little ramshackle house. He knew that. He had never really thought about it before.

"Dad, why don't we sell some land and get rich, too?" As soon as she said it, Margaret knew it was a terrible mistake.

She had ventured out beyond a well-known family sign that said "No Skating."

Everyone got quiet.

In a tiny voice, Margaret said, "Just asking."

To say that Frank Thompson rarely raised his voice would understate the case. He never, ever showed anger that way. Like his father and his grandfather, Frank gained more by showing his broken heart. He shook his head so slowly and so little, a stranger would not have seen it. No Thompson child would miss the movement.

"Now, little one," he said, his voice so low it hummed, "you know the answer to that one."

Margaret nodded, hoping the acknowledgment alone would be enough. But he waited, expectantly. She knew the answer as surely as she knew the day of the week, Monday. Monday night was Family Home Evening, a time set aside in their religion for the togetherness of kin. Some with lesser faith let the tradition slide from time to time, making excuses for their lapse. The Thompson family had never forgotten a Monday in her memory. Her father extended the doctrine of family unity beyond his wife and children to include the land his grandfather had homesteaded.

After a moment, her lower lip quivered lightly, and Margaret dropped her eyes. "Because family and home are one and the same," she said, "and you do not sell your family."

***

As a child, Billy tried three or four times to build a model world. He did fine with the models—1/25th scale cars from AMT and Revell. The world was a tougher task. He laid out a complicated network of train tracks on a plywood board, painted on roads for his cars, and placed Lincoln log houses and plastic trees. He could always imagine the world he wanted. He could never quite build it. No matter how much detail he put in, using pieces from his brother's old farm sets and miniature cowboys and army guys, it still looked like toys on the basement floor. He needed mountains in his world, and rivers and lakes.

Billy bought books on model railroading. Trains were not a special fascination. People who were fascinated by them knew how to build little worlds for those trains. He spent hours bending chicken wire into the framework of mountains. He planned tunnels and ravines where tracks could dart out of the dark and fly across the sky to plunge again from view into the bowels of the next mountain. He made a "hell of a mess," to quote his father.

It took experimentation to get the right mix of flour and water for papier-mâché' to put the flesh of earth on the bones of buttes. Billy was too impatient. He wanted the world to take shape in well short of seven days. The mountains he plastered with strip after strip from the Daily Bulletin, never seemed to dry. The paint he sprayed to mimic grass always smudged, or peeled, or flaked. In the end, he got disgusted with his efforts and played Godzilla with his feet.

Something happened in the intervening years between childhood and 44 that made world-building possible. Bill Clark had not worked chicken wire and soggy paper in 30 years. When he began The Place project, he was suddenly a master. Maybe it was because as a child he tried to create something that never was. Now he tried to recreate it.

His memory was near-perfect. He recalled every rut in the lane on the way to the mailbox at the top of the hill. He knew the folds of the gullies, the dust of the cow paths, the lean of the fences. And for the rare times when he questioned his memory he had the picture.

Bill knew every detail of the warm summer day the plane had flown over. Mom was hanging laundry to flap in the wind in the back yard. The sheets and shirts hung on lines between the log garage and the boxelder tree where he had his rope swing. Billy played on the grass with a toy tractor Pop had brought home from the implement dealer's.

Seeing airplanes fly over was not unusual. This was the 1950s, after all. Modern days. Seeing one flying so low was something. It wagged its wings. He and Mom waved. The thrill of the low-flying plane might have faded if it had not made three passes. The incident might only have been a mental shrug when recalled later, if it were not for the pictures that came in the fall.

He remembered walking up the lane, up the hill to the county road to get the mail, looking for lizard tracks in the dust. With the usual letters and daily copy of the Bulletin, was a round cardboard tube. When Mom opened the tube, they were amazed to see an aerial photo of the house, the barn, the corrals—all the things that made up the heart of The Place. They had never seen any of it from the air, but they recognized it instantly. Someone had stamped PROOF across the photo in big red letters. That ruined it, which was the idea. They wanted you to buy a perfect picture, or maybe two or three.

Billy wanted one more than anything. More than the slot car set in the Montgomery Wards catalog he was already bugging Mom about. When Pop and Johnny came back from moving cows, they looked at the picture too. Mom and Billy told the story about the day the airplane came over. How they waved and it waved back. Look. You could even see Mom's laundry hanging on the line. You could not see him and Mom. The shadow of the house was too dark.

Billy was afraid Pop would think it was foolishness, buying a picture of something you saw every day. In fact, he said almost exactly that. They were among the few words Bill could really remember him saying. To his surprise, it took little persuasion to convince Pop to order the pictures. One for him and Mom. One each for the boys.

From the air The Place was flawless. The fences looked straight and tight. The barn and chicken coop looked freshly painted, although neither ever saw a drop. Even the "boneyard" where they kept rusting, outmoded equipment for spare parts looked neat.

The big joke about the picture was on Johnny. Another reason Billy and Bill liked it. Beyond the fenced yard, across the driveway from the little log house was a grassy area where Pop had planted half a dozen apple trees and a row of lilacs. For reasons long lost they always called it the "park." A dirt driveway encircled the park. Trees followed it around on three sides: A row of boxelders along the ditch to the east; legions of pines and ash serving as a windbreak on the south and west.

That spring, ahead of that airplane summer, Johnny had the job of fertilizing the park. Since the park was only the size of a big lawn, Johnny spread the fertilizer from a sack, scattering it by hand. His goal was to get rid of the fertilizer as quickly as possible and get onto something more pleasurable. Johnny threw the granules haphazardly by the handful. He flung them in sweeping arcs and spun around watching centrifugal force rip them from his fingers. In a few minutes, the job was done and forgotten. The results lasted a lifetime. The photo captured the momentary capriciousness forever. From above you could follow Johnny's path back and forth across the park, tracking every wobble and weave, every circle and spin where he had scattered the fertilizer and the grass responded by putting on a dark green coat. The black and white photo of the park looked like a tangle of pasta, or worm tracks in mud, or the meanderings of memory.

Bill always smiled when he looked at that part of the picture. It was his favorite memory of John.

Today, as he sat on his work stool in the basement looking at the photo, the barn was his focus. The diorama of The Place, a perfect miniature of the fish pond, the cottonwood-lined lane, the log house and outbuildings, took shape before him in HO scale. There were details of the backside of the barn that were not yet right. The front and roof were perfect. Both ends were just logs, with only a small, high window to the granary on the south side breaking up the design. They presented no problem. The back puzzled him. He knew there was a door. For the life of him he could not recall just what it looked like. He had hoped the photo might jog his memory. The angle was wrong. There was no getting around it. If he wanted the model to be right—and he wanted nothing more—he would have to go look at the original. That was something he had not done in thirty years.

***

That evening the phone rang a little after nine. Pauline, who was just home from showing a house, picked it up, automatically assuming it was for her. Bucking all odds, it was not.

"It's for you," she called, putting her hand over the mouthpiece. "It's your bro."

Bill muted the TV and reached for the telephone on the end table. Bro. Pauline always called him that, implying a closeness not altogether there. Not that he and John were estranged, really. There had been a constant coolness in their relationship for as long as Bill could remember.

"Hey, John," he said to the phone. Pauline listened for the connection and hung up.

"Hey yourself. What's happening in Boise?"

Bill hated questions like that. He always felt compelled to give an intelligent, informative answer, when the real answer was, "Not much, how's Idaho Falls?"

"Oh, business is booming. Micron just announced another expansion. Should mean 1,500 jobs. Pauline sells houses like they were French fries. We've got a little problem at work remembering what our phone number is. You know, the usual."

John laughed. "I heard about your number problem."

"Yeah, who hasn't? The networks are so tickled they can hardly stand it."

"I saw them talking about it on the CBS morning show. They were having all kinds of fun at your expense." John paused. "It's not really at your expense, is it?"

"What do you mean?"

"It wasn't your fault, was it? I mean, is anyone going to lose their job?"

"So far the jobs are safe. They don't know how it happened, so it's hard to pin it on anyone. It could have been anyone of a hundred people, I suppose. Actually, someone might end up getting a medal. The calls to our 800 number have tripled."

"No shit?"

"Really. With all the publicity, everyone in the country knows our number by heart."

"That's great."

"Yeah, I suppose."

There was silence on the line for a few seconds, or what passed for silence. In that void Bill always imagined he could hear other conversations drifting in and out, sometimes setting up rhythms and harmonies, almost like music. It sounded that way now, like a familiar song he could not quite make out.

Bill asked, "How are Jenny and the kids?"

"They're fine. Well, actually, they're going to be fine, but they aren't feeling great right now."

"Sorry to hear that. They got some kind of bug?"

"No, they're not sick. Just unhappy. We're moving."

"Moving, really? Where?"

"Rock Springs."

"Wyoming?"

"That's the one. And I don't want to hear about it being where they'd give Earth an enema. It's not that bad."

"But Rock Springs ... That's not even in Idaho."

"Mom always said you were the genius of the family."

"Man, what do you want to move out of Idaho for?"

There it was again. The almost song filling in the silence.

John said, "I don't want to move. There's a job over there that pays nearly enough to live on."

"A job? Hell, there's all kinds of jobs in Idaho. You could move over here, if you're set on moving somewhere."

"There are all kinds of jobs I'm not qualified for, that's what kind of jobs there are. You've got to remember I don't have a degree."

How could he forget? Bill had gone to college on the GI bill following two years in easy stateside duty after being drafted into the Army during Vietnam. John missed the draft because he was too old, which no one could be sorry about. He missed the education benefits, too, and seldom passed up a chance to remind Bill of his good fortune.

"There are plenty of jobs that don't require a degree."

"Tell me about it. I've been looking for two years. There's nothing out there I could get that pays what I'm making now, let alone more. Everyone's moving in from California with a resume an inch thick. Employers can hire the cream of the crop from out of state. That sorta puts us local boys in a bad position."

Bill sighed heavily. He had heard about that. Occasionally he had lunch with a friend from the Idaho Personnel Commission. He talked a lot about the number of applications they got for state jobs. The numbers were up two and three times from just a few years earlier. Highly qualified people—mostly from California—were moving to Idaho and taking lower wages to get away from big city problems. They could afford it. The houses they'd paid maybe seventy or eighty thousand for a few years back were selling for half a million. It was nuts.

"So, will you work in a dental lab over there?"

"You kiddin'? That's another problem. Everybody's teeth are lasting better nowadays. I'm getting out of dentures." John Clark laughed unconvincingly. "Getting into mud."

"You're what?"

"I'm getting into mud. I'll be working for a trucking company over there that specializes in hauling mud for oil wells."

"What the hell do they use mud for?"

"Lubricates the drilling. Actually, mud is only one thing they haul. They branched out into a lot of other areas when the oil business went bad a few years ago."

"So what makes you qualified to haul mud? You'll need a commercial license, won't you?"

"Yeah, I'll get one. I'm qualified because the owner of the company is an old high school buddy. Remember Ron Wrigley?"

Bill remembered him, vaguely. The conversation flailed along for a few more minutes, then finally died with their goodbyes.

John moving away. How could that be? His brother had been a constant in his life since his earliest memories. Not that every memory was terrific. Johnny had considered younger brother Billy a pest, and frequently tried to eradicate him. Though no more ignored, scorned or slighted than any other little brother, constantly being left out of everything had its effect on Billy. Jokingly, he talked about those days when "Johnny wouldn't let me play any reindeer games." It was funny now. It hurt then.

They never really were close. But Bill needed his brother, like he needed wilderness. He rarely visited the wilderness. He needed to know it was there as a possibility. Johnny was an essential possibility, too. Bill could not say why. Maybe it was because they were never close. Maybe it was the possibility of reconciliation that beckoned. Maybe it was that John was a part of their little family, his place in Bill's life a birthright.

Maybe it was because he was here first.

The here was Idaho. Beyond the borders of the Gem State, the world barely existed for Bill. Intellectually, he knew it was there. Californians came from somewhere. The land beyond the borders really didn't matter. Everyone believed tenaciously in something. For some, it was religion. Others had race, ethnicity or tradition. Still, others clung to family. There was a part of each in Bill Clark's beliefs and the sum of it went by the name of Idaho. Idaho was not just a place on a map. It was a place in his heart.

Now, John was leaving. Driven out by forces that seemed neither fair nor fathomable. Idaho would be less without John. What would John be, without Idaho? Bill Clark felt hollow. The brothers had more than a mother in common. Though they had never talked about it, he knew they felt the same way. Without Idaho, John would be nothing.

CHAPTER SEVEN

Get out of the state you're in

In which a catchy tune infects Jo Beth, Mary discovers the nature of Nick, Jake has lunch, Debbie uses tools, Pauline ponders plots, and The Private gets a goose.

Morning staff meetings at the Division of Travel and Tourism were often an opportunity to catch up on a little rest. Jo Beth usually rattled on about meetings she had attended and letters she had received in an effort to keep the staff up to speed. Most of it could be safely ignored.

Some days even the furniture could not ignore her.

Jo Beth walked into the conference room five minutes late and slapped her Franklin Planner on the table like a beaver protecting its territory.

"What is this 'Private Idaho' crap? Does anybody know?"

Her staff gave her blank stares to prove they were paying attention.

"Didn't you even read it?" she asked, unfolding a Statesman and giving it a flip onto the table. "It's called a newspaper. You really should pick one up sometime."

Everyone shifted uncomfortably.

"Front page of the local section," said Jo Beth, still standing. "You've read it, surely, Rob, haven't you?"

Information Officer Rob Flowers stiffened in his chair. "Uh, actually I was running a little late this morning. Didn't have time to read the whole paper. Local section did you say? I haven't gotten to that yet."

"What does an information officer start with, the comics?" Jo Beth launched an eye rocket at Flowers, then looked up. "Since none of you seem to know what the hell's going on, let me summarize. The Statesman has discovered there is a 'conspiracy'—that's their word—to discourage people from visiting Idaho." She let her words hang like laundry on a line.

After a moment, Kerry Hudson asked, "Are they talking about the porno number?"

Jo Beth looked like someone had elctro-shocked her pond. Her eyes stared through Hudson like the woman was Thermopane. Then she blinked.

"No. No, this isn't related to that fiasco. At least I don't think it is. The Statesman is trying to sell papers with this 'Private Idaho' thing. Somebody—they say a bunch of somebodies—is going around putting bumper stickers on tourists' cars, and sticking flyers under their windows that basically encourage them to get the hell out of the state."

Flowers gave a low whistle. "That's not good. It's not exactly new, though."

"Of course not," she said. "We've had that kind of crap cropping up every once in a while for years. The difference this time, according to the Statesman, is it's organized. The group is called 'Private Idaho,' like the song."

Kerry Hudson asked, "What song?"

"Welcome to the world, Kerry," Jo Beth said. "'My Own Private Idaho'."

"U-2," added Jennifer Young, the promotions director.

"Me too?" Kerry looked puzzled.

"The rock group, U-2."

"B-52s, Jennifer, not U-2," Flowers corrected.

"Not U-2?"

"Stop it! I don't care who sang the song," Jo Beth said. "I won't be able to get it out of my brain all day." She shook her head like a bug was bothering her. "The paper says they have a newsletter. They even have a logo, if you can call it that. It's a private's chevron or hash mark whatever you call those things on their shoulders."

"So, who are these people?" Bill asked.

The state travel director shrugged. "The newsletters come out of Boise. It's published and distributed by The Searchlight."

The groans were near harmony. The Searchlight was a small right-wing monthly that had few friends in a state government it deemed largely unnecessary. Max Madsen was the editor and most of the staff.

"Madsen claims someone else pays him to do it. He isn't saying who. Says he doesn't know who."

"Oh, right," Flowers said. "He hasn't got a clue."

"I don't believe him, either, but that's what he says. Supposedly he gets the copy electronically, then someone calls and asks how much it will be to print and mail it. Madsen tells them, and he gets a money order within a couple of days. The Searchlight handles the marketing for it, too."

"Does he have any idea who the person is?" Bill asked.

"Oh, Clark, for Christ sakes, it's Madsen himself," said Flowers.

"Yeah, probably. I was just curious."

Kerry, who had been skimming the article looked up.

"He swears it isn't him. Says he supports it, though."

"It doesn't matter who it is, "Jo Beth said. "What matters is it's happening. If out-of-state media start to pick up on this, it'll be bad news for tourism."

"Yeah, well, count on it." Flowers put his finger on the paper. "It's a copyrighted story. That means the Statesman thinks it's big enough they want credit for it. You can bet AP has picked it up. Every other daily in the state will have it tomorrow. So will the Spokane papers. I wouldn't be surprised if Seattle and Portland pick it up right away, too."

"Can we keep it out of the Times?" Jo Beth asked.

Flowers shook his head. "No way. If they decide it's interesting they'll have a reporter up from LA by the weekend."

Jo Beth mouthed an expletive.

"We've got to go proactive on this," Flowers said. His right leg was bouncing up and down like a telegrapher's key finger. "We need to get the word out this is just a bunch of harmless spoilsports. A minority. Hell, not even a minority. Just a handful of people too selfish to share the state." He snapped his fingers. "Hey, maybe we can even turn it into a positive. We use the angle that they're trying to keep America's best secret hidden. Keep it for themselves."

Jo Beth nodded enthusiastically. "I like it. We don't take it seriously at all. We treat the group like a bunch of local characters—colorful characters. They're harmless old curmudgeons sitting on the front porch of a general store somewhere, stuck in the '40s."

"Are you sure that's who this group really is?" Bill asked.

"Doesn't matter," Flowers said. Now both legs were twitching. "We define them. We can talk to the media every day. They have a newsletter that comes out-how often?"

"Once a month," Clark said.

"Big deal, then. They've got nothing if they don't have a spokesperson." Flowers rubbed his hands together. "We'll bury them."

Flowers' confidence brightened the looks on everyone's face, except Kerry Hudson's. She looked like she'd just given two pints too much to the Red Cross.

Jo Beth asked, "What's the matter, Kerry, still trying to place that pesky song?"

"Huh? No. It just struck me. Max Madsen's daughter, Michelle. I went to Boise State with her."

"Fascinating," said Jo Beth, looking around the table. "Anybody got anything else for the good of the order?"

"Wait. That's not it!" Kerry said. "I don't know her real well or anything, but I do know where she works."

The state travel director gave her a weary look.

"She works at Swope, Munson and Taft. She's the receptionist for our ad agency."

* * *

"Hey, it's cold!"

"Oh, it's not cold, you big baby," Mary said.

Nick was sticking his toe in the water and feigning agony.

"You won't even notice after a while. Before you know it, your butt will go numb."

"Uh-oh, can't do it. Haven't I told you it's a rule of mine to avoid sports where my butt goes numb?"

"Nice try." She tossed her tube into the Boise River and expertly threw herself into it backward. "It's not a sport, so your rule doesn't apply."

Nick gingerly sat down in his tube and pushed himself off. "If it's not a sport, what is it?"

"It's fun, that's all." Mary stroked the water with her hands until she caught the gentle current. "Better hurry or you'll never catch up."

Responding to the challenge, Nick began churning the water. In a minute he caught her, then passed her and kept on churning. "You're never going to win that way," he called.

"Neither are you," she said, under her breath. Louder, she said, "It's not a race. You wouldn't want to do that for two hours, would you?"

He stopped paddling. "Two hours?"

"Yeah. I guess it would be less if you were paddling all the time, but who'd want to."

She pulled a beer out of the six-pack she'd lashed to the side of the tube, popped it open, and said, "Kick back, relax. That's what tubing the Boise's about."

Nick pulled off a beer of his own and let himself drift. He took a generous swig and let his head drop back against the tube. Mary sipped her beer and watched him behind the privacy of her sunglasses. She had to admit he was a good catch. Hell, he was a great catch, by most standards. He kept himself trim and fit—a little more muscle than she normally liked. She could live with it. He had a strong handsome face and a thick thatch of blond hair. He was bright. Very bright, even by engineering standards, which were the only standards he accepted. That bothered her a bit. Like most engineers, he was a linear thinker. He could not imagine a problem that did not have a solution, given enough time, money and resources. Which was what made him so certain about her. She could see it in his eyes. There was no question in his mind. She would eventually be his. He was so damn cock-sure of himself. The problem was, he was right. Today was the day.

"It is pretty," he said, drifting a little closer. "Not as pretty as you, but pretty just the same."

She smiled at him, then mischievously flipped water his direction. A few drops landed on his chest and spotted across his shades.

"Hey! Is that any way to treat someone who just gave you a compliment?"

"What compliment? I thought you were stating the obvious."

Mary splashed him again.

"All right, Miss Conceit, you asked for it!"

He cupped his hands together and tossed a pint of water in her face. Mary shrieked, and splashed him back.

"It's *Ms.* Conceit, to you, beach bum."

They splashed and pushed and laughed until both tubes finally went over, dumping the pair of them into the river. When they came up for air, they stood waist-deep, facing each other. Either could have escalated the battle with heavy splashing or dunking. They chose instead to kiss. Mary ran her fingers across his chest, dragging her nails through his curly blond hair. She broke the kiss first and started to speak. He quickly re-engaged. After a moment she reluctantly slid her mouth to the side far enough to say, "The tubes, Nick. We'll lose the tubes."

He released her and dove after the inner tubes like a lifeguard on a rescue mission. It took him a dozen strong strokes to catch up with his, then a few quick kicks to snare hers as well. While he did it, Mary found the two beer cans they had lost in the scuffle. His had sunk; hers had floated. She emptied the water/beer from both, crushed them, and waded to where Nick stood holding the tubes like runaway mounts recaptured. The cans went into the net sack tied to her tube.

They floated along making small talk. Mary found it hard to concentrate remembering the kiss. She had to concentrate. There was a spot not far ahead where the river parted around a small island. It was obvious to any floater the best route was to the left. She planned a side trip to the right. She knew a spot along the back on the north side of the river where they could pull their tubes out of sight. Near there was an even more private spot in the grass. It would take some care picking their way back in without getting scratched up. Nick would probably complain. She thought she could convince him to follow her. A loosened bikini top ought to be incentive enough. Or—and this was a wicked thought to savor—a bikini bottom suddenly missing.

There were other floaters around them. Half a dozen tubes were in sight. Two rafts full of people throwing buckets of water on each other were coming around the bend behind them. Those people might wonder what was up when she and Nick took the channel to the right. Or, they might know what was up. She didn't care. This was the time. The place was just around the bend. His house, or even hers, would be wrong. He would have the upper hand in either situation, she thought. Outdoors... Well, there was something equalizing about making love beneath the cottonwoods.

"A guy could get a great tan doing this," Nick said.

He was kicked back again, working on another beer. The California sun worshiper was already almost as dark as Mary, who needed no extra help to be fashionably brown.

Mary did things to his body in her mind, practicing plays for the main event, only minutes away. Then she saw him do it.

Nick drained his beer, then casually let it fill with river water and slip from his fingers. Mary caught a flash of light from the can as it drifted deeper. She quietly slipped over the side of her tube and plucked it from the bottom of the shallow river. She got back in her tube, crushed the can vigorously and put it in her net bag. In a moment, when the island came up, it slid by on their right.

***

About noon every day Jake Burrell climbed the steep hill across the road from his shop to eat a quiet lunch. Jake's shop would be a studio for a man with more pretension. He didn't figure he had an artistic bone in his body. What he did to tree stumps was like whittling. It was something to keep him busy between jobs. The between had stretched out longer than the jobs in recent years.

Halfway up the hill he turned to look through the trees at his shop. Three cars in the lot right now. Lunch time was always busy. He could never figure why. He himself was more inclined to eat lunch at noon than buy a knickknack. Jake continued climbing, with occasional stops to catch his breath. He reached a place at the top edge of a clearing. Here a rock outcropping provided a sitting spot beneath a yellow-barked ponderosa pine. He appreciated the backrest the tree offered. The ponderosa must have been 150 feet high; maybe 300 years old. Not another one nearby of its same generation. He often thought about how it would feel to bring that momma down. Jake wondered why someone had not cut it years ago.

Maybe other loggers had enjoyed lunches beneath its boughs and decided to spare it.

From the outcropping, leaning back against the bark of the tree, he watched toy cars come and go below. In her red bandana, he made out Charlene, flitting back and forth, answering questions and taking money. She rarely came up to his spot with him, though he often asked. Charlene always said it was too important waiting on customers. Jake thought shutting down the shop once in a while would not hurt a bit. He had to hand it to her. His income from the carvings would be about zero if he tried to sell them himself. Even when he tried to be nice, he made customers nervous. If they were nervous, they would say some stupid thing that would rile him. Next he knew, they were hightailing it down the road with their wallets still bulging.

Jake pulled a worn, folded newsletter from his shirt pocket and spread it open. For two weeks he had gone over it and over it looking for ideas. Every paragraph was a good one. He had sent for the bumper stickers and installed his share of those. Charlene caught him and made him stop. The woman did not have a sense of humor when it came to customers. Sometimes she would not speak to him for days after one of his little parking-lot "accidents." He had to admit her silence slowed him down. Some.

The newsletter had a lot of things you could do with potatoes. He liked the idea of shoving a potato in a tourist's exhaust pipe. What a treat to watch one of those faggy little creeps in their alligator shirts cranking and cranking and cranking. They would probably open the hood and stare at their engines for a while, as if they'd know the difference between a manifold and a mannequin. Eventually, they would run down their batteries. Satisfying as the look on their pasty faces would be, that was why he always rejected the idea. They would surely whine until he let them use the phone.

Then they would sit around for 20 minutes asking asinine questions until the tow truck came.

The tow truck. Jake stopped in mid-bite. Gary Peterson down river in Gardena had an old tow truck. Hell, he probably had a battery charger too. Ol' Gar was no genius when it came to mechanicing. He could probably fix a pipe potato, though, if someone were to tip him off.

Jake slapped his knee. By hell, he thought, it might just be worth the aggravation. He slipped *The Private* back in his pocket and gave it a friendly pat.

***

Tips & Trick from *The Private* Newsletter

Want to divert some of those thousands of dollars the state spends on advertising to tourists? Call the state travel information line and order up a pile of brochures. Have them sent to someone you know who has a garbage can. Or, make up some clever addresses of your own! It doesn't cost you a thing because the number's toll free!

Too much trouble to leave addresses with the automated state system? No problem! You can help by simply putting the number into your speed dial. Then, while you're baking cookies or watching TV, dial it up and leave the phone off the hook. It'll hang up eventually and signal you that it's time to dial again.

Don't get frustrated if the line is busy. It just means you have a lot of friends out there!

***

Debbie held a two-inch staple between her lips. She tasted the tang of rust. Mixed among the new galvanized steel staples in the bucket were some old-timers, saved because they came out as straight as they went in. They tainted all their neighbors. She did not mind the taste. It reminded her of second chances.

Charlie ran the wire through the stretcher while she fed it to him with her leather gloved hands. He clamped the device down and began to ratchet the lever back and forth. A wire stretcher was about as ungainly a piece of machinery as was ever made. Theirs looked like an orange praying mantis with stomach cramps. Whoever invented the blamed things seemed to have put as much thought into how they might best cause injury as how they might stretch wire. You could hardly pick one up without tearing off a piece of flesh, or banging a knuckle. Depending on where you grabbed one, it would scissor to pinch you as you picked it up, or unscissor and flop down to make a mark on your shin. You'd probably drop it on your foot a time or two during the season, just to remind yourself they were heavier than they looked. Whether they were 50 years old or brand new, they were a special trial every time you used one. That was Debbie's opinion. Charlie worked a stretcher like he'd pulled a thorn out of one years ago and the whole tool species was forever grateful. Fine with her. She'd as soon eat staples anyway.

Charlie handled tools like they were surgical instruments, with an easy confidence that came from years of practice. Practice did not always make perfect. Debbie had years of practice too. She was still a danger to anyone who happened by whenever she picked up a tool. Usually, it was because she was trying to use the wrong tool.

How many times had Charlie told her that? "Debbie," he would say, not even waiting for the blood and/or cursing to stop, "that wouldn'ta happened if you'd used the right tool."

Sometimes it would make her so mad she would about show him another handy use for whatever tool it was started the discussion in the first place. The problem was, she never had the right tool with her. Seemed like she always had a close cousin that might save her walking a hundred feet. If she needed wire cutters, well she had a pair of pliers that would worry through wire if you twisted it enough. If she needed a

Phillips screwdriver, she had a flat blade that might turn the screw if you pushed on it with both hands the same time you twisted. If she needed a hammer, you could bet the closest thing she had was a pipe wrench the size of a calf's leg. She would use that wrong tool every time, rather than put everything down and go all the way back to get the right one. That was true whether "all the way back" was a mile or 50 feet.

Debbie smiled thinking about that particular personality flaw. When she smiled, it was a special joke on herself. She could feel the little dead spot on her lower lip, where one day about ten years back she used the wrong tool. She was putting a new light in the chicken coop. The plastic coating on the old wire was a brittle hazard. She decided to correct it before they lost the coop to an electrical fire. Charlie, of course, had an affinity for tools and always had a passel of them tagging along with him. Debbie liked to carry the bare minimum. In practical application that meant one tool less than she needed. She had been getting along real well with a pair of wire cutters, a knife, a screwdriver and a hammer right up until it came time to strip insulation off the wire. It was heavy copper wire, 14 gauge, maybe even 12. The wire strippers were back in the shop, a round trip of about five minutes.

Strippers had never been her favorite tool. They lacked versatility. Sure, you could strip wire with them, if you needed to, but what else were they good for? They looked like pliers, but they would not turn a bolt worth a darn. They were too light to hammer with, and too short to be much use for prying.

Rather than make a five-minute trip back to the shop, Debbie cut the insulation in a radius with her knife and grabbed the plastic in her teeth. She stood on one end of the wire, pulling it taut with her teeth and her wire cutters. Holding the cutters with both hands, pulling as hard as she could in the direction of her face, the folly suddenly dawned on her. In the time it took the thought to register, the insulation pulled off. The sudden release sent the tip of the wire cutters right through her lower lip.

Balanced equally with her wrong-tool flaw, was the ability—nearly the need—to laugh at herself. Charlie came along just then to see how she was doing. He found her sitting on a straw bale, a tiny tube of plastic insulation clenched in her teeth, blood streaming down her chin, her head rolled back, laughing like a fool.

The first thing he said was, "Are you okay, Hon?" When she nodded and continued to laugh, he was not sure what to say or do next. Since it was on his mind, he pulled a pair of wire strippers from his back pocket and said, "I thought you might need these."

Debbie nearly swallowed the insulation. She curled up in ball and fell over on the straw bale laughing. And crying. And bleeding.

The little dead spot on her lip beneath the tiny V-shaped scar was tied up in her mind with laughing and using the wrong tool. She remembered those things, and forgot the pain.

Debbie ran through that memory while Charlie cranked the wire stretcher. Charlie, meantime, concentrated completely on the job at hand. Neither of them noticed the wagon rolling up the road alongside the fence.

It was a covered wagon, like the Oregon Trail pioneers once used, pulled by a fine pair of matched mules. Instead of barrels of sugar and flour and dishes and water, the bed of the wagon held tourists. Seven of them sat along each sideboard on padded benches. Fourteen pair of hands went up the minute Charlie and Debbie looked up. Fourteen cameras clicked, freezing them forever in frames of fencing.

"Good afternoon, neighbors," the driver said, tipping a crisp straw hat. The brim of the white hat was wide enough to hide under. Its crown was nearly a foot high and banded by a snakeskin with a red feather stuck in one side in case you had somehow missed seeing the rest of it. "Just go about your business. Don't mind us a bit."

As if struck dumb Debbie and Charlie both nodded.

It might have been anybody talking beneath the shadow of that brim. The Andersons assumed it was Bill "Bruneau" Baker, new owner of the old Bennett homestead. They suspected the nickname was recently acquired. Bruneau was a local name shared by a canyon, a river, hot springs, sand dunes and a town. It was unlikely to come as standard equipment with someone who just moved in from Pasadena.

"That wire was the cause of many a fight in the old days between the cattlemen and the sheep ranchers," the man was saying. "There's more than one grave up on Boot Hill that got there because of a battle over barbed wire."

Boot Hill? What Boot Hill? Debbie wondered.

"It was men like this who settled the West," Bruneau said, holding his hand out as if introducing a local celebrity. "Tough as nails. Made it possible for the rest of us to bring women and children into the wilds."

Debbie felt her teeth come down hard on the staple. Men? Was Baker blind? Did he really think... She looked down at what she wore. It was pretty much the same thing she wore every day: Levis, cowboy boots, a wide leather belt with a silver dollar buckle—minus the dollar so it wouldn't get all scratched—a chambray shirt, leather gloves, and a sweat-stained felt hat to shade her face. But she did not look like a man. Even though she did not wear make-up—hadn't bought a tube of lipstick since she and Charlie were married—any fool could see she was a woman.

The wagon was moving again, mules kicking up dust, weary travelers rocking with the pitch and sway. Debbie's eyes darted to the staple bucket. A good, fiberglass handled hammer rested in there, head down. For a moment, she thought to pick it up and fling it through the air in the direction of the wagon. She did not. Partly because she would get a one sentence lecture from Charlie on using the proper tool.

As the team topped the little ridge a hundred feet to the south, she heard Baker say, "Yep, it's a way of life that's all but gone, folks. All but gone."

***

Mary Lewis was on TV. Bill did not know how he picked her out in the crowd. Hers was one of many heads of long dark hair in a three-second clip of placard-waving protesters. About 50 of them stood like militant choir members in a half circle behind the reproduction of the Liberty Bell on the statehouse steps. Their protest had nothing to do with the statehouse, or even state government. The granite steps in front of the Idaho capitol were simply the preferred site for political demonstrations of every stripe.

He saw her again—confirmed the sighting, really—in an even shorter close-up that showed her in profile for an eye blink. She was shouting or chanting something. The reporter's voice-over drowned out whatever the precise message was.

Bill tapped the rocker on the kitchen TV's remote and saw the readout climb to 12. "...traditional tribal fishing area and," the Channel Seven reporter looked dramatically over his shoulder, "even more important for these protesters, the alleged burial site of their ancestors. At the statehouse, I'm Gary Call reporting."

"'Alleged' burial grounds," Pauline said. "Either it is or it isn't. Assholes."

"I'm sorry," Bill turned the volume down. "What did you say?"

"The 'burial grounds.' There's not a shred of evidence anybody's buried out there. It's not like the Indians put up markers."

Bill gave her a vacant look.

"At Eagle Rock." Pauline gave a ponderous sigh. "I thought you were listening. They're trying to stop the project now by claiming there are Indian burial grounds out there."

"Really?"

"Yeah, really." She tossed a multiple listing book she had been thumbing through onto the counter. "First, it was the wetlands, then the damn Oregon Trail remnants, then the eagles, and now this. We haven't even asked for annexation yet, and look at all the grief we're getting."

Briefly, Bill considered saying something about the water rights they had yet to secure, the potential drainfield problems and the diesel plume the developer had so far kept a secret. Briefly. Pauline was not in a mood to be toyed with.

"I think we should find out once and for all. We take a backhoe out there and dig. If we don't find bones, fine, it wasn't a burial ground." She tipped her lips into a crooked grin. "If we do, well, oops. We might as well move them since they're dug up anyway."

Now that he thought about it, Bill could not remember the last time Pauline was in a mood to be toyed with.

"Where do they think the burial ground is?" he asked.

Pauline shrugged. "Up along the cliffs on the southeast I think. Burial isn't the right word, anyway. They used to put their dead in a ravine, then start a rock slide to cover them up. Some ceremony, huh?"

"I guess they didn't have shovels."

"Besides, who really cares, anyway? I mean, I couldn't care less about where my grandparents are buried."

"Santa Monica," Bill offered.

"Yeah, but so what? They're dead, for Christ sakes."

"Still, you wouldn't want somebody building a house over their graves."

"Why not? I wouldn't want to live in it myself, maybe, but who am I to stop someone else from living there?"

Bill was absently sketching something on their shopping list pad, to one side of the scribbled word yogurt. "You know," he said, "maybe you should look into it. You probably own those lots your grandparents are buried in. Maybe it's a real estate possibility."

For one scary moment he saw the spurious suggestion find its mark. She dismissed the jibe almost, but not quite, instantly. He reflexively grinned at her when she stuck her tongue out at him, then went back to his doodling. He drew a straight black line across the roof of the barn, then went over it again, and again.

***

Thirteen of them came flying northeast toward the Snake River. Canada geese, wedged out in traveling formation. You could have heard them honk as they cleared the rushes on the Oregon side. You could have heard their wings creak as they pumped through the air. No one was there to hear. No one was there to see.

The first indication something was wrong came from the back of the formation. Three geese fell away and banked sharply 180 degrees. The remaining ten began to break up. Their wings tipped in peculiar ways. Their feet swung forward as if landing were imminent. Yet they were a hundred feet over the river. Over the exact center of the river their flight stopped.

The geese struggled and cried, then fell. They dropped like stones. Splash. If you had been there you would have heard ten splashes in all. You would have heard frantic honking as the three lucky ones formed a minimal V and flew like demons toward the setting sun. You would have heard it if you were there. No one was.

He watched the bodies drift down river, then absently kicked a rock into the water with one Doc Martin. He laughed at the dead birds, then remembered who he was. He shifted and jumped into the river to grab a goose neck in his canines.

***

CHAPTER EIGHT

You use what you've got

In which Bill and Mary do lunch, Blaine makes a fashion statement, Frank gets an offer, and Pauline wants to trim a tree.

Twenty-five or thirty restaurants dotted downtown Boise within blocks of the Capitol Mall. The LBJ building named after Senator Len B. Jordan, not the president, featured a lunch concession in its basement. With all those choices within walking distance, Bill Clark usually chose to walk down to the first floor of the Hall of Mirrors and out the door to where a hot dog vendor set up her cart for a couple of hours each day. The dogs were good, as dogs went. Usually he ordered a chorizo.

To his surprise, he spotted an unmistakable head of hair at the end of the lunch line. For a moment he thought about walking on by. Their last meeting had been such a disaster. The sun shimmering off her hair was too much to resist.

Bill slipped in behind her, put his face close enough to catch the scent of her... shampoo? Perfume? Self? then said, "Hi, stranger."

Mary turned around.

"Clark. What are you up to?" She seemed pleased to see him.

"Oh, just eating in my favorite restaurant. What brings you into town?"

"Testing," she said, wearily. "I'm reviewing applications at the Personnel Commission."

"Yeah? What for?"

"I'm an information specialist. That makes me a 'subject matter expert'." She said the last with fake importance. "I get to check the applications to see if people are minimally qualified. If they are, they get to take the test for information specialist. If they're not," she said brightly, "I flunk them and their lives are ruined."

"Wow. I didn't know you wielded so much power."

"Yeah, right. Mostly they call on me to do reviews because I'm too stupid to say no. It's getting to be a real job too. They used to get maybe 25 or 30 applications. Now, they get over a hundred, and most of those are overqualified. Everybody wants to move here from California."

"Yeah, I'd heard that," Bill said, remembering John's complaint about the competition for jobs. "Seems like everyone I know is from California."

"Except me," she said. "I've never even been out of the state."

They got to the front of the line, where Bill announced he was buying for both of them.

"No, you don't have to do that," Mary said.

"I insist. You saved my life, remember?"

"Oh, that's right. You owe me big because I didn't let my dog finish you off when he had the chance."

"That's it," Bill said.

They chatted for a minute while waiting for their chorizos, then found an empty picnic table. Bill saw heads turn to watch Mary. Mostly men. He saw a couple of women watching her, too, in a clinical way. He did not know the scale they used, but he was certain Mary got the highest marks. She was dressed in a burgundy double breasted suit with a cream pleated-placket blouse. Her earrings were burgundy, with silver inlays of eagles or osprey, the only clue of her heritage. A meager one at that. She wore a cloisonné pin depicting her agency's emblem, itself prominently featuring an osprey. Bill noticed a thin gold and silver bracelet on her right wrist. She wore no rings.

"So, I saw you with Nick a couple of times," Bill said.

"Spying on me, are you?"

Bill reddened. "No, no. I just happened to see you. He's my neighbor you know."

"I know." She touched him lightly on the sleeve. "I was teasing. You won't be seeing me much around Nick's anymore."

Bill felt clumsy when conversations turned to personal matters. He had a knack for saying exactly the wrong thing. What was he supposed to do next? Ask what happened? Change the subject? Take a mammoth bite of chorizo?

Mary saved him the decision by saying, "We had a little disagreement, that's all. Besides, he's not really my type."

Bill saw the opening. He was ready to ask what her type was, when she quickly changed the subject.

"Hey, what do you think about this Private Idaho thing?" she asked.

"Oh, not much." Bill idly stirred ice with his straw.

"Really? I'd think it would be the big buzz around Commerce."

"Yeah, people are talking about it. I personally don't think it's anything to worry about."

"You don't think it could hurt tourism?" she asked.

Bill shrugged. "Maybe. A little. Tourism can take it."

"That's an understatement." As soon as she said it, Mary looked like she regretted it. "I'm sorry. I didn't mean to be negative about your work. Sometimes I get a little tired of tourists. That's all."

"Hey, who doesn't?" Bill said. "Tourism is great. It brings in lots of money to the economy, creates jobs—yours and mine included. I still get tired of the extra traffic and the crowds."

"Wait a minute. You think mine is a tourism job?"

"Sure. You produce brochures to attract people to your parks, don't you?"

"But we don't promote out of state. The parks were created for Idahoans."

"That may be why they were created, but who uses them? Out-of-staters mostly, right?"

"A lot of Idahoans use the parks," she said. "But, yeah, about 60 percent of our campers are from out of state."

"My point exactly. They're tourists. In fact, so are the Idahoans. If they travel more than fifty miles to play, by the definition we use at Commerce, they're tourists."

"But that's not why I became a ranger. It's not why I took this job, either. We're providing a place for people to recreate, but our number-one job is protection of the resource."

Mary looked uncomfortable.

Bill softened his tone. "And you do a good job. Like I said, I get a little tired of tourists too. Sometimes I'd like to close off the borders."

That seemed to relax her.

"Maybe you should join."

"Join what?"

"Private Idaho. I hear they're looking for a few good men."

"Uh, that might be a little difficult, given what I do for a living."

"Yeah, I know. That's why I haven't been active."

Did that mean she would be active if it wasn't for her job? Bill remembered the six o'clock news from the night before.

"Say, I saw you on TV last night."

"Yeah? The Eagle Rock protest?"

"Yeah, I think so."

"Was I beautiful?"

"Well," he stammered, "of course."

Mary laughed. "I have a talent for embarrassing you, don't I?"

"I guess I'm easily embarrassed," Bill said. "You're really against that project?"

"Who isn't? It's a terrible project. It's going to obliterate Oregon Trail ruts, scare off the bald eagles, maybe even destroy Native American graves."

"Uh huh. I've heard all that." Bill began swirling ice with his straw. "It's my wife's project."

"Your wife!?"

"Yeah, Pauline. You met her."

"I remember. She's in real estate, isn't she?"

"Guilty as charged," Bill said. "She's working with the guy who's developing Eagle Rock. Kreigh Sparks."

Mary shook her head. "Well, what does she think about all the problems? What do you think about it?"

"She thinks the problems will go away if they throw enough money and influence at them." Bill shrugged. "I'm not so sure. To tell the truth, I'm not a big supporter."

"Have you talked with her about it? I mean, do you guys fight?" She touched her fingertips to her lips. "I'm sorry, I didn't mean to get personal."

"That's all right. No, we don't really fight about it. I guess we don't even talk about it much."

Mary began digging in her purse. She pulled out a green brochure and handed it to him. "Put this under her pillow."

"What is it?"

"It's a brochure we developed about the eagles. Our agency manages the wildlife area where they roost. It's got a lot of good information in it."

"I'm sure it does." Bill opened the brochure and glanced through it. "If it's not a multiple listing book, Pauline isn't likely to read it."

For a moment Mary put her hand on his. "Maybe you could read it for her. Maybe you could talk. Maybe ..." She stopped. "I shouldn't be taking advantage of you like this. I'm sorry." She reached for the brochure. Bill pulled it back.

"I'll look it over," he said. "Maybe I'll get a chance to talk to her tonight." He looked at his watch. "Will you be testing again tomorrow?"

Mary nodded.

"Good. Let's meet again for lunch and I can tell you how it went."

"It's a date," she said. "Tomorrow I'm buying."

As he waved goodbye, Bill resolved to approach Pauline about the eagles. He wanted to do something for Mary. He still felt bad about the ATV article that had gone wrong. He thought maybe he had already corrected that mistake. If he could only tell Mary a little more. Someday, when they knew each other better, he might be able to open up to her. Lately he itched to talk with someone. Someone who would understand.

***

Break time and Blaine Stope sat out back enjoying a few minutes to himself. He always took the picnic table closest to the back door. The smell from the garbage that made his stomach edgy kept company away. He'd have sipped his Coke inside the Dumpster if it meant a few moments of peace and privacy. A warm breeze stirred up the leftovers and sent the scent his way. Ugh. Times like this he thought about taking up smoking again to cover the reek.

As the wind backed off, he caught a trace of laughter. Blaine turned toward the source and saw three young girls sitting three tables away. They instantly turned from his glance, going into a half-huddle across the table.

Nice looking girls, he thought. What, 16, 17? Hard to tell nowadays when teenagers looked 30. Two of them wore oversized shirts tied at the waist. The third had on a blue halter top. All wore short shorts. Blaine took it all in. For a moment he thought about them in a very basic way. Then he stopped himself. All his life he had enjoyed looking at women. Lately he couldn't look long before he remembered how other men looked at Sally, and what that led to. He got angry at those men. Then at himself. The same damn thing was inside him, if he'd let it out. Hell, hadn't he flashed that newswoman or whatever she was? That wasn't a sexual thing. That was a statement. Still, he was not proud of it after the fact. Especially when he thought of those motel men.

As if an offstage prompter had whispered it, the three girls slowly turned their heads toward him. Their eyes met his in unison. In unison they turned quickly away and back to the huddle. Blaine heard their girlish laughter. Were they flirting with him? He felt a little rush at the thought. One of them stole a glance at him again, whispered something to her friends and started another chorus of laughter. What the fuck was so funny? Automatically, he checked his fly. Hell, even if it were open his apron covered it up.

The wind carried the sound of them closer in fits and bursts. He made out only two words: troglodyte and hairnet. He felt the heat rush up into his cheeks. Son of a bitch! He'd forgotten to take off his fucking hairnet! The miserable state inspector made the cooks wear hairnets, which was bad enough back behind the grill where people could hardly see you. It was terrible if you forgot about it when you got off shift. Crap, he'd stopped at a bar one night on his way home and almost wore the thing inside. He didn't know what made him glance in the rearview mirror. He never would have lived that one down.

Now these damn girls were making fun of him. His hand went for his head before he could stop it. Instead of pulling the thing off, Blaine scratched his scalp as if he had planned it all along. It took guts to do what he did next. Damn near more guts than it took to go into a mineshaft looking for bodies. He pulled his legs out from under the picnic table and swung them over the bench. Then he slowly stood, and ambled toward the girls. All laughter stopped.

Blaine Stope, who weighed 273 pounds, put his beefy palms on the end of their table and leaned forward. The table creaked. "Anything else I can get you ladies?" he asked, pleasant as could be.

They stared at him like panicked rabbits, not moving a muscle. Finally, one of them stammered, "No, no. We were just finishing."

"Yeah," said another. "In fact, we're through, aren't we Ronnee?"

"Done. Yeah, we're done."

Blaine grinned at them and said, "Now don't rush off on my account,"

Like leaves caught by an October gust, they scattered. They were up from the table so fast it began to totter under Blaine's weight. In ten seconds they were inside a Honda with Washington plates, forgetting all about their half-eaten burgers. As he watched them go, he savored the look of pristine fear in their eyes. To his surprise, he found he liked that look.

***

Tips & Tricks from *The Private* newsletter

Whenever you enter a museum, souvenir shop, or other tourist trap, remember to turn the sign so it reads "closed." If the place doesn't have a sign like that, do them a favor and install one for them. They're cheap!

Bumpers aren't the only good place for anti-tourist stickers. Every stall in every rest area in Idaho should have one at eye-level. While you're at it, slap 'em on self-serve gas pumps!

***

Two years ago, when she was in seventh grade, Margaret decided she was going to become a doctor. Though Levi, at that age, wanted to be an astronaut, a firefighter, a stock broker and a mechanic all within a period of six months, Margaret's decision meant something.

"She gets it from you," Mildred said at the time.

"From me? I never thought a minute about being a doctor."

"Not that. Her stubbornness." She smiled at him. "Have you ever thought a minute about being stubborn?"

Frank admitted he had. Margaret took the stubbornness he passed on to her and piled some more on top for good measure. That was all right. Stubbornness could be looked on as dedication. She would need a lot of dedication to get through college and medical school.

A lot of money, too. That thought kept Frank's stomach churning many a night, including this one, when he sat going over records.

Margaret was one of seven. Some of them were already in college. Each would be called for a mission, in their turn. All of it took money, a commodity that got scarcer each season. Even when the crops were good, money did not always follow. Last year's spud crop was a record for the Thompsons. For everyone else, too, unfortunately. There were so many potatoes on the market the price fell to $4 a hundred weight. Frank had contracted half his crop at $6.25 the spring before. If it were not for those contract spuds, he might have lost the farm. As it was, he had to borrow more heavily than he liked to get this year's crop planted.

Well, the hay was bringing a good price. He wished he had more than the 40 acres in the school section and the 20 acres on the homestead. Of course, if he did, the price would probably fall through the floor.

"Fa-ther!" Margaret yelled. "Tel-e-phone!"

"All right, all right. I'm coming." He got up from his work table and went to the kitchen phone.

Margaret dropped the receiver with a clunk when she heard him say, "Hello?"

"Mister Thompson?" Not Frank, not Brother Thompson. Not a good sign. It was probably someone wanting to sell him a new long distance plan or three rooms of carpet cleaning for a special price. You used to never get calls like that.

"Speaking."

"Mr. Thompson, how are you tonight?"

"Fine, thank you. Yourself?"

"I'm just great, thanks. Say, Mr. Thompson, this is Barry Hardinger, from Smith Realty. I understand you own twenty acres over in the Meadowview subdivision, is that right?"

A Realtor. He had this conversation a few times over the last couple of years, never with the same one twice.

"I own a hayfield, not a subdivision."

"Right, right. Of course. It's right up against the subdivision isn't it?" The man laughed. "They've about got you surrounded out there, in fact."

"It is not for sale."

"Oh, wait. You're getting ahead of me. I haven't even asked, yet." He laughed again, a television laugh.

Frank frowned.

"I will admit I was going to get around to asking in a minute."

"Well, I saved you the trouble. Goodnight."

"Wait, wait! Please don't go yet, Mr. Thompson. Please just give me a minute more of your time. Then if your answer is still no, I'll say goodbye and not bother you again."

Frank felt his neck getting warm below his ears. He was too polite to simply hang up on the man.

"That okay, Mr. Thompson?"

"Say your peace."

"Good. Thanks. I work with a developer who is interested in putting some homes on that site, and one right across the highway."

Frank chuckled. "The Whitmill place? You won't have much luck with Orrin Whitmill. His family has owned that ground longer than we have ours."

"That may be true, Mr. Thompson, but he was willing to sell it."

Frank did not think he heard right. "You said ..."

"He sold it. We've already signed the papers and he has a check in his hands as we speak."

Jacob Whitmill, Orrin's great-grandfather homesteaded that land the season before his own great-grandfather came to Idaho Territory in 1875. The families had history together. Why, his Aunt Alma had been a Whitmill.

"Mr. Thompson?"

"I'm sorry. What were you saying?"

"Just that we know you and Mr. Whitmill go back a long ways, so it won't be a secret for long how much we paid him for his 160 acres. We want to be fair with you anyway, so we're willing to go the same price, $10,000."

"Ten ... Orrin took $10,000 for his father's farm?"

"Yes, he did. Oh, wait. No, I don't mean for the whole thing, Mr. Thompson." The man laughed again. "That's per acre, of course. What do you think about that?"

Frank dropped into a kitchen chair.

"Well, where's he going to live?"

That 160 was the Whitmill home place. They did not have another acre anywhere, as far as he knew.

The laugh again, like off some game show. "I guess he can live pretty much where he wants. He's a millionaire now," Hardinger said.

Slowly, Frank hung up the phone. He could hear the man's laugh until the receiver dropped into the cradle. Later he would feel bad about his rudeness. Now he just felt numb.

***

The weather report was half over on Channel Seven when Pauline rustled into the room undressing as she went. "Sorry," she said. "It ran late."

Bill grunted. "They always run late." From their king-sized waterbed he watched through the open door of their bathroom as she took out her contacts.

"Anything on the news about it? They had cameras there."

"Yeah, they had a report. I saw the back of your head."

"My best feature," she said. He glanced at that very feature now, as she took out her earrings in front of the mirror. Her reflection said, "What was the coverage like?"

"A lot of people saying you were destroying eagle habitat, a couple of Indians talking about their heritage, the Historical

Society upset about the Oregon Trail, some mountain bikers worried about the Ridge to Rivers plan. Oh, and Kreigh Sparks mentioned how wonderful the development would be for the economy."

Pauline stepped out of the bathroom and pulled her blouse over her head in that impossible crossed arms way women do. "What was the tone of the piece?"

"Geez, I don't know. Neutral, I guess."

"Yeah, I'll bet. The media's trying to fry us on this one."

Bill pulled his pillow from behind his head, gave it a couple of good whaps with his fist, and stuffed it up against the headboard again. "Media are," he muttered.

"What?"

"Nothing, nothing."

"They are so short sighted," Pauline said. "That development means jobs for construction workers, architects... "

"Real estate agents," Bill offered.

She wrinkled her nose and pointed her tongue at him. "It's a sound, environmentally sensitive project. I'm proud to be a part of it."

"The eagle people don't agree."

"Oh, screw the eagle people. They don't know what they're talking about." She kicked her shoes off into the corner and began working on her panty hose.

"They claim the slightest disturbance will scare the eagles off. They say people walking quietly will flush them and they won't come back. Ever. What a bunch of horseshit! You see eagles all the time—bald eagles—right next to the Connector in the middle of town. Like the traffic doesn't bother them but someone out for a Sunday stroll will?"

She tossed her nylons into the wicker hamper at the foot of the bed and slammed the lid. Naked now, her body drew his attention more than her words. She slept in late, so he never saw her in the mornings. Many nights she didn't come to bed until after 11, which meant Bill was already asleep. The sight of her like this wasn't rare, but it was unusual enough for him to notice with all his nerves. For a moment he lost track of the conversation.

"I'm sorry, you said what?"

She frowned at him. "I said," she said, "you can't stop progress. That area's going to be developed whether those people like it or not. They may as well let Kreigh do it with some sensitivity than have someone come in and rape the land."

Bill couldn't remember a single sensitive thing Kreigh Sparks had ever done. He let it pass.

"Actually, you can."

"Huh?"

"Stop progress," he said. "They stopped Hulls Gulch and Castle Rock."

Pauline began buttoning her nightshirt savagely. "They didn't win either of those completely. I've sold houses in both developments."

"Yes, you have. And, as I remember, you sold them partly on the attraction of the open land and wildlife."

"Sure, you use what you've got." She hit the button on the remote control, swung into bed and turned out the light. In the darkness, she said, "I'd do the same thing at Eagle Rock. I'd sell the eagles."

Bill turned his pillow from its upright position and beat it down for the night. "You can't sell them if they're not there."

"Oh, hell, they'll be there. Where are they going to go, out onto the desert?"

Let it pass, he thought, let it pass. He should forget about eagles, forget about Mary Lewis, and concentrate on the bird in hand. He should.

"I don't know where they'd go, but there's good evidence they would go."

"Yeah?" she asked. "What makes you a sudden expert?"

"I'm not trying to be an expert. I did talk with someone recently who knows something about it."

Pauline put a fist into her pillow, then shook the feathers soft.

"Who's the expert? Some enviro-wacko?"

"No, an information specialist for state parks." He did not see a reason to remind Pauline she had met Mary. "They manage that whole Barber Pool area where the eagles roost."

"Right, and they built their new headquarters closer to the river than any of our trophy houses will be. What's good for the goose should be good for the gander."

"The river isn't the issue. Their building is way out of the setback, anyway. It's the roost tree that's the issue. There's apparently only one tree along that whole stretch where the eagles like to roost at night. Without that tree they'd move up the river, maybe way above Lucky Peak, or maybe down river clear the other side of town."

"Really?"

"That's what they say. They've done some studies on it."

"Just the one tree?"

"Ey-up."

Pauline snuggled down into the covers. She was quiet for a moment. Bill began to get hopeful. He was awake, she was awake. Something could happen. Spooning with her, he slid his hand into her nightshirt and cupped her breast.

"You know what?" she said.

"No," he whispered in her ear, "What?"

She rolled over quickly. "If something were to happen to that stupid tree... "

Pauline sat up, leaving Bill's hand to slide down her chest and into the inhospitable night air.

"They talked about that at the meeting, but it didn't sink in until you brought it up. They're claiming you can't put anything within 1,500 feet of the damn tree. That cuts the heart right out of the project. The first-class homes would be right on the ridge overlooking the tree, and down even closer near the river. Without those houses, the project wouldn't be worth it."

She was quiet for a minute, then said, "But without that tree, there wouldn't be a problem."

"Pauline, wait a minute. You're not really talking about cutting down the tree."

"Oh, of course not." The moonlight coming through their bedroom window shown on Pauline's face. She grinned. "I could hire someone to do it."

"Pauline!"

"What? It's just one tree. There are hundreds of them up and down the river. The eagles would just move a little ways."

"Maybe, maybe not. What if they're right and the eagles go clear out of the area? What would you call the project then, Stump Rock?"

She sighed and turned her back to him, scooching down into a tight fetal ball. After a moment had passed she said, "Goodnight, Bill."

Still sitting propped up against the headboard, he said,

"'Night."

***

His sleep had been a long one. Or maybe he had been dead. It was all the same to Coyote. He liked waking up, or being alive. He liked the new things. He liked the metal tepees that rode the frozen black rivers. He liked extra eyes. He liked food that killed itself and waited to be eaten. He liked the dams.

The people—not Nu Mee Poom, but people—had built dams to catch the salmon. He had tried that once himself so he could have salmon all winter. It would have worked, because everything he did worked, except that he got lonely. The people had all gone to hunt buffalo while he worked on his dam. It was too lonely, so he stopped.

It was not lonely now! There were more people than Rabbit had family. They wanted to trick each other so some of them would go away. Coyote liked that, and he liked his new name. He especially liked helping.

CHAPTER NINE

A meantime thing

In which Debbie visits the City of Trees, Bill and Mary plot to go underground, Jake spots an owl, Bill takes a plunge and Coyote learns new trick ways.

"Well, honey, it's been darn near a year."

Charlie Anderson sat behind the wheel of the Bronco, headed west on 1-84 on the eastern outskirts of Boise. Those outskirts were a lot further out than Debbie remembered. For a good minute her mouth hung open as houses drifted by on either side.

"This is unreal," she said. "This was nothing but cheatgrass last time we were here." She shook her head in disbelief. "A year, you say?"

"Pert near," Charlie said. "We did some Christmas shopping last November."

"November? That's only, what? Eight, nine months. Charlie, they don't even build houses in the winter. These things have gone up in the last four or five months. And there are already people living in them."

Charlie nodded. "Mild winter. Probably got an early start."

She tore herself away from looking at the houses. It was like witnessing a bad traffic accident. You did not want to see it, yet you did not want to not. Debbie stared at Charlie's face as if there might be pictographs left there by an earlier culture, something that might have meaning if she could just puzzle it out.

"Doesn't it bother you?"

Charlie shrugged. "I'm just buying supplies. I don't have to live here."

She slumped against the door, letting her head feel the vibration of the window for a moment.

"What about the people who do have to live here?"

Traffic in front of them began to pile up going into the city like leaves crowding a culvert in an irrigation ditch. Absently, Charlie's tongue explored the end of his toothpick.

"I'm thinking they live here because they like it."

"Like it? How could they possibly like it? Those houses are crowded up together so close they may as well share the same wall."

Charlie smiled. "Some do. They call those apartments, and-what is it?-condo-hom-iums."

"That's not living. It's just not living." Debbie folded her arms and hugged herself tightly. "It's not Idaho."

"Well, I guess they think it is. They've got their microwaves and computers and video games. They've got their swimming pools and hot tubs. Maybe those are all fine things. We don't know."

She sat there watching the traffic build, watching the houses get closer and closer together, until they began to turn into apartments and "condohomiums," watching the big buildings downtown creep nearer, watching the haze thicken over the valley.

As they passed the city limits sign, Debbie said, "If that doesn't take the cake. 'City of Trees.' I didn't see a single tree in any of those new yards."

"I suppose they'll plant 'em eventually," Charlie said.

Debbie gave a short, derisive grunt.

***

She nearly bumped into him when she came striding out the door from the Personnel Commission.

"Whoa. Is the forest on fire, lady?"

"Oh, hi Clark. Sorry. I thought I was going to be late. If I don't discipline myself, I lose track of time."

"You're just right," he said. "Ready for a chorizo?"

She wrinkled her nose. "Not two days in a row. Let's go to Dolly's."

Dolly's was the food concession in the LBJ building.

"Have you ever eaten there?" Bill asked, raising one eyebrow.

"No, why? What's wrong with it?"

"Oh, nothing's wrong with it, I guess. The food's a step up from a vending machine. Maybe a baby step."

Mary looked through the glass doors at the hot dog cart.

"I really don't want another dog, and I don't think we have time to walk anyplace else. Do you mind if we try it? If it's awful, you can say 'I told you so.'"

"Sure. Let's take the tunnel. It's quicker."

They descended from the ground floor to the basement of the Hall of Mirrors, then pushed through the double doors to the tunnel. Their footsteps echoed off the concrete. If gravity suddenly took a holiday the ceiling, floor and walls would be virtually indistinguishable from one another, except for the occasional mural. Some years back a high school art teacher had convinced building services to let her students paint 12 or 15 murals on the bare walls. The amateur art was a welcome relief from the unbroken gray corridors. Adding color to the tunnel apparently frightened some bureaucrat. They never allowed another mural on the remaining three or four hundred spaces. Now the art was as familiar and invisible as the bare walls had been.

"This floor is like glass," Mary said. "Wouldn't it be great if we could..."

"Skate on it?" Bill interrupted. "I think of that every time I'm down here."

"Well, you know what they say about great minds. Think of the speed you'd get."

"I know. And not a ripple or a crack."

"Or a tree root," Mary said.

"Yeah, and no gravel to stop you dead." Bill stopped walking. Mary took another couple of steps, stopped and turned. "Hey," he said. "I bet we could do it."

"Really? Wouldn't they have a tizzy about liability?"

"Only if they knew about it. I know a couple of the guards. I bet if I played my cards right I..."

Bill suddenly realized there were half a dozen other state workers walking nearby. He gently grabbed Mary's arm and pulled her closer.

"I think I could get us in late at night," he said, quietly. "Maybe on a weekend when there wouldn't be anyone around."

Mary grinned. "That would be so cool. I had no idea you're such an adventurer, Clark."

"Hey, I'm practically Indiana Jones."

"More like Idaho Jones, don't you think?"

Bill loved to see her smile like that.

"I thought you were 'Idaho.'"

"It's big a state," Mary said. "I think there's room enough for two of us."

***

Jake Burrell thought up his carvings using images from the woods. Critters, mostly. He had done so many eagles and ospreys, carving another one like to about made him sick. He kept on carving them. They were his best sellers. Jake lined up five or six three-foot logs stood on end atop his workbench. Then, he went at each one in turn, first with what he called his shaping saw, swinging it up and down in broad strokes, bringing out the rough form of the bird and defining its stand. Henry Ford would have been proud of the way he turned them out. At this point, the carvings stood at a crossroads. With a little wrist twist here or an extra blade bite there, they could turn into the Statue of Liberty, a space shuttle or a giraffe. They could, if Jake were in a whimsical mood. About ninety-nine percent of the time they just turned into eagles standing on rocks.

Some tourist once asked him how he knew what animal was hidden inside the tree. It was the dumbest damn question he ever heard. You needed some eagles, you made eagles. If squirrels were selling, you made fucking squirrels. Kee-rist.

That answer, which was the $64,000 answer, as far as Jake was concerned, did not satisfy the idiot tourist. The tourist set about explaining art to him. He said a sculptor with a calling could look at a stone, or a tree, or a lump of clay, and see the art inside it. Then, all the artist did was remove the excess and free the figure. The guy gave a little sniff when he was done with the lecture. That was what set Jake off, he was pretty sure. It was like the son of a bitch lived way up in the clouds where the gods played poker, and being down here in the regular air was a little distressing. Well, Jake had to set him straight. He couldn't remember exactly what he said. The gist of it was that Jake's artistic eye could see right deep inside the pile of shit standing in front of him, and the figure waiting to get out was a prick about the size of a toothpick.

That was the day Charlene made that rule about his not talking to customers.

Jake switched saws for the finer work, using his little Stihl to bring out the beak and the wings, one eagle at a time, three, four, five, then moved back to the first eagle and started cutting in the feathers. He kind of liked that part. The next part he always hurried through. He used a tile knife to scratch in the deeper lines, and an odd assortment of implements that stood in for carving tools to fuss out what details he bothered with.

Charlene tried to get him to use real store-bought carving tools. She said it would be an investment in the business. She even gave him a good set of tools made special for working wood. He made her take them back. What Charlene did not understand was this carving thing wasn't what he did, it was what he was doing. He was a logger, for Christ's sake. If he bought tools he didn't already have, it would be like giving up. Right now he didn't have a dime invested. As long as that was true, it meant this was just a meantime thing.

The eagles all looked about the same nowadays. When he first started, they were better. That was when he could take his time. Now, he could hardly keep up with sales. That didn't leave much time to get creative.

He did get creative once in a while. Just so he wouldn't get bored out of his rabbit-assed mind, he came up with a new thing now and again. Like the owl. It was kind of a goofy looking owl. That's the way he wanted it. Right in the middle of its forehead he'd had Charlene paint a spot that looked like a bullet hole.

"What do you want to go ruining it for, Jake?" she asked, even as she swirled her brush around.

"Ruinin' it? Why, hell, that's what makes it art. That little dab of paint is a statement, don't you see? It's a spotted owl! Get it? A spotted frigging owl!"

Charlene frowned. "Yeah, yeah, I get it." She blew on the spot to dry it off. "It won't sell, though, I'll tell you that right now."

"Won't sell? Why the hell won't it sell?"

"Because loggers don't take vacations, that's why."

She seemed so sure of herself it simply stunned him. He planned on turning these out by the hundreds. All the while he carved that silly owl he imagined cars pulling into the lot and guys getting out to point and laugh at those spots. They'd laugh, then they'd just have to have one. They'd want to meet the guy who came up with that great idea. There'd be a lot of back slapping and joke telling. He'd be a hero, is what he thought. And Charlene thought he wouldn't sell one. As soon as she said it, he saw the truth. Guys like he imagined never pulled into the lot in the first place. They didn't take vacations, that was a fact. Even if they were local guys, which now that he thought about it was exactly who he'd pictured, they wouldn't have the scratch to buy a wooden bird, no matter how much they liked it. They couldn't hardly afford corn flakes.

The owl sat out front, getting pretty much ignored, for about a week. Jake got tired of looking at it, and took it down to Curly's. Curly gave him a couple of beers for it. They had some laughs over the owl. About everybody who came into the bar liked it a lot. He never made another.

***

The back of the Bronco might still hold an envelope, if the letter was not more than two pages thick. Charlie and Debbie went to Boise only one or two times a year, so they made the trips count. They never got out of Costco without spending a thousand dollars. There was the Farm Store to visit and now the outlet mall, where Charlie bought his work shirts and Debbie shopped for underwear.

"With all this stuff, I feel like one of those survivalists you read about," Debbie said. "I half expect to see an atomic mushroom in my mirror."

"Isn't the Cold War over?" Charlie asked.

"I guess. There are still people who live up in the woods by themselves, afraid something's going to get them."

Charlie smiled. "Or out in the desert?"

She gave him a tired look. "Oh, I know what you're saying. We've always lived there. We haven't changed." She gestured at the windshield. "This is what's changed."

Trips to Boise depressed her more every time. They were headed home, so Debbie smiled a little. Increasing stands of sagebrush on either side of the road marked their progress. They passed the Micron campus, then the last of the new housing developments.

Debbie saw something. She pointed to their left. "Charlie, look. Those weren't there when we came in this morning."

"What? I don't see nothin'."

"The flags. Right, there."

"Those are just stakes."

"Yes, with ribbons tied to them. You know what that means?"

"Well, sure. They're laying out another development. Didn't you get your limit of bein' riled up about that this morning?"

"But they weren't there this morning. They've put those up while we were shopping!"

A sign had gone up, too. It was a six by eight billboard placed there by Sparks Development, proudly announcing the new Eagle Rock project, a planned community that would include parks, shopping, a recreation center and bike paths. Lots starting at $40,000.

Debbie kept her eye on the sign until it disappeared behind the groceries in back, then stared at a case of Green Giant nibblets, not seeing it.

"If you're gonna let it bother you, I'm not gonna bring you into town no more."

"But, they weren't there this morning. It's growing so fast it's like a cancer. It scares me."

"You're not even scared of rattlesnakes, and a little thing like survey stakes gets to you?"

"It's not the stakes. It's what the stakes mean. You can't even turn your back before there's another development going up. They're getting closer all the time."

"To us?" Charlie arched a single eyebrow. It was an expression Debbie had tried to match many times, but found impossible. "We're 70 miles away. They could pound stakes 24 hours a day and not get to our neck of the woods before we die."

"They leapfrog, too, you know. They can pound stakes wherever they want." Charlie opened his mouth, but Debbie cut him off. "And don't give me that slop about how they can't build close 'cause it's BLM ground. I don't trust the bureaucrats as far as I can pitch 'em."

Charlie stroked his chin with his left hand. "You know you're right. We've been gone all day. They could be on the edge of the ranch right now. There'll probably be a K-Mart next to the creek before morning."

Debbie slapped his arm with the back of her hand. "Stop making fun of me."

Charlie rubbed his bicep dramatically, although a mayfly would have survived the blow.

"If bringing you into town leads to husband beating, I'm sure as heck not gonna do it anymore. We don't even need to come at all. Bill Baker said he'd pick up things for us whenever we wanted. He's into town two, three times a week."

She turned and looked at him. "That's because he's never quit living in town. He sleeps in a house on the desert, but his mind's still in town. Always will be."

Charlie took his hat off and slid it upside down into the wire holder mounted on the headliner of the Bronco. He smoothed his hair back. "You still upset about him thinkin' you were a man?"

Debbie reddened. "No! That's got nothing to do with it. He just doesn't belong out there with his city ways and his city people, that's all."

"Well, maybe not. He's a nice enough fellow, though, if you get to know him. I don't mind him at all. Maybe you should try to be a little more neighborly."

"What do you want me to do, bake him a cake?" She said it like he had asked her to give up her virginity.

"Well, that's not a bad idea. Anyway, it wouldn't hurt to pay him a visit." When she said nothing to that, he added, "Would it?"

***

For years, Bill had sketched scenes of The Place from memory. He was a fair artist, and might have improved if he bothered with training. Classes required you to draw cubes and pyramids and boxes so you could better understand shading and perspective. Then you moved on to bowls of fruit. Bill had no interest in drawing fruit. He wanted to draw barns and boxelder trees.

Pauline gave him some perfunctory encouragement at first. She liked a couple of his sketches, and even suggested they hang them in his den. He could not remember the last time she had commented on one. When he started work on the diorama, she practically ridiculed him for it.

"'Aren't you at least going to put in some tracks for a train?" she had asked, after several weeks' work was starting to bring it into shape.

"There weren't any tracks out there."

"So what? How can you have fun with it if nothing moves?"

"It's not for fun. It's like a picture, a snapshot. It's not supposed to move."

Pauline had considered that for a moment.

"You know, that's not a bad idea. We could use something like that to show what Eagle Rock will look like when it's done." She began to talk faster. "We could show where the canyon was, and the river. You could build little trophy houses for the view lots, and people could really get an idea of what they'd be seeing. You could put in little trees and shrubs, and paint in the roads. We could color code by phases, and ... "

"No."

"What do you mean, no? We'd pay you for it. Hell, I bet Kreigh would pay you a bundle for a model like that. We could invite him over to see this one first."

"No."

Bill moved in front of the diorama, putting both hands on it behind him.

"Sparks is not going to see this. No way. And I'm not interested in building one for him, either. Get someone else to build it, if you want. It's a good idea, but I'm not doing it."

They never really talked about it after that, except for the time he caught her using the diorama as a place to put frozen hamburger while she rooted through the chest freezer for bagels. Freezer runs became his chore. Increasingly, she avoided the basement altogether. Bill found himself spending more and more time there, sometimes working on the diorama, more often just sitting and looking at it.

He and Pauline had shared 14 years together. They had mutual friends and mutual funds. Their religious views, which lacked much conviction in any direction, were compatible. Politically, they got along by talking only about what they agreed on. They were sharing their seventh house, their third set of living room furniture, their fourth bed. They did not share The Place. Until the diorama, it had not occurred to him they should. Until he met Mary Lewis, he had not thought anyone could.

Tonight he could not get Mary off his mind. He was thinking about showing her the diorama of The Place. He knew she would understand it. They had spent most of their lunch together talking about their travels in Idaho. They had so many experiences in common, it was a miracle they had not run into each other before. Mary loved Idaho in a way he imagined was uniquely his. She had history here and a sense of place at once remarkable and familiar. He felt an affinity for her, an attraction that went beyond her native beauty, easy charm, athletic grace and intelligence. Any fool could recognize those traits. Which meant they were conspicuous to the fool he was becoming. In spite of what he considered his inherent good sense, Bill knew he was falling.

***

Fun. The old tricks were fun. Sure, he got killed sometimes. What mattered about that? Magpie would come to peck his eyebrow fat and wake him up. Sometimes Magpie would tell Coyote what he already knew about how to take revenge for being killed.

The new tricks were even more fun. Coyote could be The Private inside a people's head. That way he did not have to pull off his own legs or pluck out his own eyes like in the old trick days. He had new trick ways.

CHAPTER TEN

A special fear of spiders

In which traffic takes its toll, Sally gets a surprise, Frank's racing days are about over, the writers get a bite, and Bill kills a hobo.

Bill sat at the light waiting to turn left onto State Street. His mind went down another road. He went to sleep last night thinking of Mary. This morning, while showering, he realized his mind had taken up the thread of thought where it left off the night before. Mary was on his mind still on the drive into work. He hardly even noticed the traffic.

Behind him someone honked. Bill let off the brake and surged forward.

Lunch today would be a solitary affair. Mary was finished reviewing applications. She would be back at her desk five or six miles out of town. Even so, Bill would not lunch alone. He had a date with a security guard. Though it would be a little soon, he thought he could risk asking Mary to lunch tomorrow. He didn't want to become a pest, but it would be all right if he had a good excuse. Making plans for an underground skate was excuse enough.

Bill wheeled into the parking garage and began looking for a place in the shade.

Mary waved, but Clark didn't see her. She was waiting to cross State when she saw the red Explorer go by and recognized him behind the wheel. Personalized plate, she noticed. 4IDAHO. Vanity plates, she usually called them. That one seemed okay. Really a good choice, in fact.

She heard the squeal of tires and had long enough to grimace before she felt the impact. The sound of the door slamming behind her Mustang convertible was almost as loud as the collision. The bump had jostled her mirror askew, giving her a view of her trunk. Pieces of taillight lay scattered across both sides of it like big red confetti.

"Hey!" a voice said from behind her. "The god damn light turned green, sister. I thought you were going to go! Jesus, what color do they use on the reservation?"

Twenty. She would count to twenty this time.

***

Blaine beat Sally home from work by about a minute. He had popped a beer and was sitting at the kitchen table when she came through the front door. He watched her dump her purse on the couch and kick off her shoes. Even dressed in that uniform he thought she looked like a cover girl. Sally was almost 50, but she could still fit in her high school prom dress, he was sure of it. Better than him, he thought. He couldn't fit in his pants from last year.

"Hi sweety," she said, giving him a wide smile. "How was work?" She kissed him quickly on the forehead.

"Sucked," he said. "Just like usual."

She offered him her back and said, "Unzip, me?"

"Pleasure's mine."

She stepped out of her uniform as she made her way down the hall. Her disappearing like that shedding clothes as she went was the sexiest thing he had seen all day. It gave him an idea. He got up and followed her into their bedroom.

"How was your day?" he asked from the doorway.

"Okay," she said, putting her dress on a hanger. She looked up at him then quickly looked away. "About the same."

Something in the way she said it bothered him.

"Work was okay?"

"Sure. It was fine."

"Yeah? How fine?"

"Oh, Blaine, it was all right. I just had another... You know."

"No, I don't know. You wouldn't be talking about a weenie wagger, would you?"

Sally's only answer was a blush. He saw it start on her bare shoulders and rise along her neck to her cheeks.

"Son of a bitch!" He spit the words out one at a time. "Did you call the police?"

She shook her head.

"I told you to call the police. Didn't I tell you that?"

"Hon, it wouldn't do any good. He'd just say I walked in on him."

Stope could feel the blood rise in his own face. Calm down, damn it, he told himself. She's all right. "So what happened this time?"

"Oh, sweets, you don't want to hear about it."

"What happened?"

Sally sat down on the bed, wearing only her bra and panties. A moment ago Blaine wanted to see her right there. He had wanted to be there next to her making her laugh. Now he wanted to kill someone.

"Well, I knocked, just like I always do, and said 'housekeeping.' Then I listened and didn't hear any answer, so I opened the door and backed in. I grabbed some sheets and turned around to make the bed, except the bed wasn't exactly ready to be made. There was this guy in it."

Blaine frowned. "Sleeping?"

"Pretending was more like it. He was laying there naked without even a sheet over him. Skinny bald guy, with a big red mustache. Had his eyes closed, but no way was he sleeping." She gave Blaine a pouty look. "Do I have to spell it out? If he was asleep, he wasn't all asleep, if you know what I mean."

Stope moaned. "Son of a bitch!" he said, and pounded his fist on the doorframe. "So, if you didn't call the police, like I told you, what did you do?"

"I excused myself and left the room."

"Excused yourself? The bastard was flashin' you and you excused yourself?"

"Well, yeah. What am I supposed to do? He was a customer. We're not supposed to make trouble with the customers. We're supposed to pretend it was a mistake and leave. That's what they tell us to do."

"It's not what I told you to do."

"Sweety, I know it's not, but if I'd called the police the guy would have just denied it, said I walked in on him. He would have made it look like my fault and I might have lost my job."

"Oh, your damn job!" He was pacing now, first to the dresser, then to the nightstand and back. "Your damn job isn't worth it if you're not safe."

"I'm safe, Blaine," she said, softly.

Ignoring her he went on. "You don't make enough money to have to put up with that kind of shit."

When Bunker Hill was running, she stayed home raising the kids. They got along fine on what he made. In fact, better by a long shot than they were doing now.

Sally folded her arms across her breasts and bowed her head. She looked so tiny, like a little lost wild thing. He stopped pacing. God how he hated her going through this. Once or twice a month some asshole would leave her a dirty note or walk out of the bathroom with his pants unzipped or let a towel drop or... She was crying.

He sat down beside her on the bed. "Oh, baby, it's all right. I didn't mean to be yelling at you." He put his arm around her shoulder and rocked with her. She rested her head against his chest. "It's all right. Someday they'll start up Bunker again and you won't have to work. Or maybe I can get on at Sunshine." Those words were so well worn they came out of his mouth easy as breathing. That did not stop them from tasting bitter.

***

Tips and Tricks from *The Private* newsletter

A reader in Coeur d'Alene writes that he enjoys sharing his catch with tourists. If he pulls in a sucker or whitefish, he doesn't waste it. He tries to find an open car with out-of-state plates so he can slip it under the seat! If he can't find a door open or a window down, he jambs his gift on top of the car's catalytic converter. That fries a fish in no time!

Boise's Booster Bureaucrats at the Tourism Office want everyone to think every dime spent in a restaurant, motel or gas station comes from a tourist! Prove them wrong by writing "Idaho Native Dollars" on your check in the lower left-hand corner.

***

Frank felt the road hum through the rubber cleats of the tractor's big back tires. The red metal seat of the little Ford sprang gently up and down in a lazy rhythm that might have matched the slow, even beating of his heart. He had the tractor in fifth gear, and the hand-levered accelerator set to its highest notch. In a field, the speed would clearly be dangerous. He could quickly lose control of the red-trimmed gray crawler and find himself in a ditch. On the highway, 17 miles per hour would not get him a speeding ticket in any jurisdiction he knew.

The old faded-red FarmAll baler trailed behind him faithfully like a duckling following its mother, swinging back and forth with the ripples in the road. Frank had tied a battered slow-moving-vehicle sign onto the chute of the baler, using baling wire. Hanging that triangular symbol still caused him to mutter. The law that said you had to have one was older than his oldest child. That didn't make it right. To him, it was one of many "new" rules the bureaucrats in Boise came up with just to irritate him. Oh, he knew they were trying to be helpful. No one wanted people running into the back of balers and plows. He couldn't remember when that had ever happened. If people wouldn't drive like every road was the home stretch at Indy, well, they wouldn't have a problem, would they?

It must be about 85 today, he figured. Hot enough to make the pervasive southeastern Idaho breeze feel refreshing. Days like this made him understand why people bought convertibles. He had even remarked a time or two that this tractor was his convertible. It was low slung, as tractors go, and nobody could argue it was not open to the air. Cruising along at close to 20, feeling the heat drift up off the pavement, smelling the new-mown hay from the fields on either side, well, that was some kind of living, wasn't it?

The little Ford saw less and less farming as the years went by. It had long since been replaced by larger tractors as the main implements of work on the Thompson farm. Those big

International Harvesters and John Deeres were a sight more comfortable. All of them had cabs with air conditioning, radios, heaters, and stereos. They even had CBs so he could keep in touch with the house. Some of his neighbors had cellular phones in their tractors. Frank's father probably would have thought it was all foolishness. Not Frank. Though a little embarrassed by the luxury, he was not ready to go back to the days when combine drivers were covered an inch thick in chaff and boys pulling a potato harvester wore three pairs of gloves. He wasn't near ready to give up the little Ford, either.

The smell of the air on a perfect day was part of that. So was nostalgia. The main reason would not get on a list of guesses one hundred guesses long. Frank Thompson had a secret life inside his head. The Ford was an essential part of it.

Whenever he plowed, or windrowed or baled; whenever he pulled a disk for hours or planted seed or spread fertilizer, Frank really ran a race. He was a race car driver of international fame, always coming from behind against incredible odds to take the checkered flag. Sometimes the race was a Grand Prix in Monaco or Long Beach. Other times he drove an Indy car taking tight rights lap after lap. During rough land work, like plowing, he liked to race Baja in a nimble little coupe covered with numbers and stickers and lights. Frank raced often, no matter what he operated. The best ride was the little Ford. He felt more like he actually drove that tractor. Steering was the only possibility with the others. In a true race, he knew the newer tractors would leave the little Ford behind. In his head it still had the heart of a champion.

Frank would have undergone excruciating torture before letting his secret spill. His family would surely begin to wonder if he was capable of other acts of insanity. He could easily imagine standing in a winner's circle drinking champagne from a trophy cup. He could not begin to think about the humiliation he would suffer if anyone knew he could imagine it.

Two short sharp beeps brought him back to the day. An old Plymouth full of teenagers rumbled right behind the baler. Oncoming traffic on the two-lane road made it impossible for them to get around just then, even at his postal pace. Frank glanced back and saw them gesturing for him to get off the road. He was already off the road with one set of tires. What did they want? They couldn't expect him to pull into the borrow pit and bind up his hitch. They honked again. For a moment, Frank wished for one of the new tractors. One with a cab. He felt exposed sitting atop this one. He knew every one of them was staring at him and talking about him. He did not know what teenagers said at times like that. He knew it was not nice.

Finally, the oncoming traffic slacked long enough for the car to get around. When it made the run, he wasn't certain it would complete it. At least one cylinder worked only intermittently, making the car chug, lurch and backfire as it pulled alongside him. Eyes straight ahead, he did not intend to even glance their way. Experience told him they would be flashing rude gestures his direction, or worse, exposed buttocks.

"Fuckerrr!" one of them yelled over the booming sound of some irritating song on their radio.

It was too much. He had to twist his neck slightly, enough to see if he recognized any faces. For a chilling moment he thought he did. One of the kids looked like Levi, his own son. He would have given Levi a tongue lashing he would remember into the next life, except the boy put his face closer to the rear glass to better give Frank the finger. It was not Levi after all, praise the Lord. He had seen the teenagers before. They were locals. The Plymouth finally got up enough speed to jerk back in front of him, swaying on what once were shocks. The rear end of the car was jacked up like a perturbed stinkbug. It belched blue smoke.

Frank the racer wanted to go after them and blow their doors off. Frank the father wanted to sit them down for a timely scolding. Frank the farmer wanted the highway to be as deserted as it once was.

It was five miles between the main farm and the little 20-acre hay patch. Only three of those miles were blacktop. He could remember summers in years past when he saw not a single car on his way to the field. For heaven's sake, he could remember when the road was all gravel.

Progress. That word had begun to taste bad. Not that he was reactionary. Mormons were future thinkers. Brigham Young knew a little about progress when he laid out Salt Lake City with streets wide enough for four lanes of traffic—what, 50 or 60 years before cars? Mormons built most of the canals that really tamed Utah and Idaho. Their vision a hundred years ago still brought water to his farm today. Mormons knew about progress. Frank knew about progress. Sometimes he wished it did not come so quickly or bring so many people with it.

This was a farm-to-market road. It existed so he and others like him could transport crops from where they were grown to where they were sold or processed or shipped. Yet, all along the road, in fields that once grew potatoes and alfalfa hay, houses now grew. What a crop it was. Frank could still recognize some of the old places. The "Cook place"—though the Cooks had not lived there in 25 years—was on his left now. He could still see the old Higley house up the road a bit. It once had been considered huge, sheltering a family of ten. Now it cowered between two three story monsters that looked like they had slave quarters in the rear. And they were not the biggest. Every house that went up competed with the last one built in a contest to use every stick of wood in the lumber yard. Why did they need them so blamed big? They were twice the size of his house. Near as he could tell none of the families had more than two or three kids. Where did they get the money? Payments on those things were over a thousand dollars a month, he had heard. Why, that was unthinkable. And where did the men find ...

A car honked behind him. Frank felt the hair on the back of his neck bristle. He was not going to turn around. Was not. The car honked again. And again. Why didn't they just go by? The road was clear. Again it honked. For the first time in years, he fought the urge to give them the sign those teenagers had given him. He fought it and won. Instead, he vigorously waved them around. When they didn't go by right away, he made the same motion again, with even more enthusiasm. This time he heard the car speed up.

To Frank's surprise, it was not another jalopy loaded with grade B children. It was a clean, conservative sedan. Foreign car of some sort. A nice looking family—father, mother and two girls—sat inside. Both little girls waved at him as they went by. Letting the trace of a smile come across his hard-set face, he waved back. The driver waited until he had gone by a respectful distance then signaled and eased back into the lane in front of the tractor. The car drove at moderate speed until it was about a quarter mile in front of him, then pulled over and stopped.

Frank saw the emergency blinkers go on as the doors opened. The whole family got out and walked around to the back of the car. Strange. He continued to chug up the road, no longer counting the houses arisen since the third cutting of hay last year. What could be the matter with the family?

About a minute later, Frank pulled up behind the car, eased the throttle back and turned the tractor off.

"Do you folks need some help?"

"No thanks," the dad said. "We're fine. Just want to take your picture, if you don't mind."

The man might have offered to paint the tractor purple, as much sense as it made. It was so unexpected it took Frank a few seconds to comprehend. Then, still not so sure he heard right, he said, "I'm sorry, come again?"

"Your picture. We just want to take your picture." The man gave him a big grin and reached for his wallet. "We'd be glad to pay you for your trouble."

Frank held up one hand. "No, no. You don't have to do that. But, I don't understand why you would want to take my picture."

The mom said, "We're on vacation," she gestured toward their license plate like one of those women on TV who show off prizes on a quiz show. California.

Lamely, Frank said, "Nice to meet you."

"It's all right then?" Dad asked.

Frank shrugged. "I guess it's all right. I just don't..."

"Super duper. You don't have to do a thing." He was already making his camera click.

One of the little girls tugged on her mother's slacks. She whispered something when the women bent down. Frank only heard her say, "Ask him, Mom."

And she did: "Sir, would it be all right if we got a couple of shots with the girls on the tractor with you?"

It was a strict rule no Thompson child ever road on a tractor they were not driving. That one had gone into effect the summer Aunt Melba's little boy fell off and was crushed when Uncle Carl could not stop. Of course, this tractor was not moving. It was not even running. Frank nodded.

The little girls galloped over and scrambled up onto the machine like they had been doing it all their lives. One plopped right onto Frank's lap. The other stood on the axle and leaned against him with her hands on the metal seat. They struck that pose for the clicking camera before Frank had time to react, then jumped down and ran back to the car.

The dad put out his hand. Frank automatically took it.

"Thanks a lot. Are you sure you don't want any money."

Frank shook his head.

"By the way, what does this do?

Frank frowned. "The tractor?"

"No, gosh no. I know what a tractor is. The thing you're pulling."

As if he had to double check Frank twisted around in his seat.

"Why, that's a baler."

"A baler, huh? What does it do?"

"It bales. Hay."

The man looked perplexed, then suddenly brightened. "Like, to feed horses?"

"Well, sure. Horses and cows. Livestock of all kinds."

"Do you have horses to ride?"

"My kids have a couple. I don't ride much anymore myself."

"No, I mean, do you have horses we could ride. For pay, of course."

Frank hesitated. "Uh, no, we don't do that. You'll have to find a dude ranch someplace, I guess."

The man looked disappointed. "Well, thanks for the pictures anyway." He turned toward his car, then stopped. "By the way, I meant to ask you. Are you Amish?"

Slowly, Frank shook his head. "No. I'm Mormon."

The man gave the air a little punch, as if his team had scored a point. "Yes!" Then he turned and walked away.

Frank watched the car until it disappeared. He watched a string of cars disappear. He sat there for ten minutes thinking about what had happened. Eighty-five degrees. He still felt chilly.

***

Landing the World Travel Writers Association annual convention for Boise was probably the biggest prize of her career. Jo Beth Crowder and other tourism industry honchos would host them for five days, showing them Bruneau Dunes State Park, McCall and Cascade, Redfish Lake, Sun Valley and Idaho City. They would have optional excursions that took them into the Snake River Birds of Prey Area, to the ghost town of Silver City, through the museums and old penitentiary in Boise, into Hells Canyon by jetboat, and on a tour of Canyon County farms, where 80 crops ranging from pussy willows to onion seed grew. The resulting stories that came out of those familiarization, or fam, tours would generate tens of thousands of dollars worth of positive publicity for Idaho over the next 18 months. What a pleasant change that would be, after the 900 number fiasco.

They were starting off the convention tonight with an evening under the stars at Ste. Chapelle Winery, where they would be treated to music performed by Boise jazz great Gene Harris and a performance by the Oinkari Basque Dancers. The catered meal started with lamb cooked Basque style, smoked trout from one of the Magic Valley trout farms, an Idaho wild-rice dish featuring sugar snap peas—developed in Idaho—and, of course, Idaho bakers. Dessert was a potato again, faux this time. The ice cream, shaped like spuds, then rolled in a dusting of powdered chocolate, looked like mini-bakers. The wine and champagne flowed freely, courtesy of the host site.

Governor Jim Mathews welcomed the gathering. He was in rare form, giving a mild roast to half a dozen well-known names, including Jo Beth herself. He razzed her about the 900 number. She had fed him that one herself, hoping that bringing it up in a light-hearted way would put the right spin on it for this important crowd. The Guv's zingers brought roars of laughter from the writers who, after a one-hour hosted social and a well-lubricated dinner, were primed to be entertained. Most people were starting their desserts when the Guv sat back down.

Jo Beth sat at the head table with Governor and Mrs. Mathews, Boise Mayor Helen Hunter and her stockbroker husband Ralph, two writers—one of whom was the president of the association, and a photographer whose specialty was travel.

WTWA President Terry Wheeler took one last bite of ice cream, dabbed at his lips with a red linen napkin, and said, "Governor, I hope you're going to give this lady a raise for putting on such a fine welcome banquet for us."

Mathews lifted his glass of champagne before answering. "She did do a nice job, didn't she? I think she deserves a toast." He lifted his flute, and said, "To Jo Beth Crowder, the finest travel director the State of Idaho has ever had."

The group lifted their glasses, murmured an enthusiastic assent, and drank. Jo Beth smiled appreciatively. A few days ago, when the 900 number problem came to light, she wondered if she would even be sitting here.

The governor put down his glass, and said, "Of course a raise is another matter entirely. That will depend on you folks in the press. You write up some real nice stories about Idaho, and I'll take care of little Jo Beth."

Mathews' wife, Judith, said, "You just be careful how you go about doing that."

The group laughed politely.

"Looks like your future is secure," Wheeler said to Jo Beth. "As long as this Private Idaho thing doesn't get out of hand."

The smile froze on Jo Beth's face. Governor Mathews, said, "Now, Terry, you gentlemen aren't even supposed to know about that."

Oh, nice job Guv, thought Jo Beth, tell writers there's something they aren't supposed to know about. This group rarely covered actual news, but she knew many of them had been reporters once. Best if she could downplay this fast.

"The Governor is just teasing," Jo Beth said, giving him a quick, pleading glance. "I'll tell you everything you want to know about Private Idaho. It should take about twenty seconds. It doesn't amount to much."

"Okay," Wheeler said. "We've got twenty seconds. What are they all about?"

"First, we're not even certain it's 'they.' I think it's mostly one sour little person who happens to own a printing press." Jo Beth looked longingly at her potato dessert. She had taken one polite bite. Chalk one up for keeping her figure. "He has a few subscribers, I guess. There are always people who get their jollies from trashing tourists in every state." She saw heads nodding. Good. "It's the same old thing. Oregonians were telling people a few years ago to come visit, but not to come to live. Seattle has its Lesser Seattle Society. We've got some natives who let off a little steam by putting bumper stickers on their cars."

"And on other people's cars, I hear," Wheeler said.

"Yes, there's been a little of that. And a little graffiti, too." This last was a calculated risk. No news story had yet carried anything about the graffiti. It was a meaningless detail she hoped might appease the innate curiosity of an ex-reporter.

"'Get out of Idaho,' that kind of thing?" Wheeler asked.

"Yeah. Mostly, 'Welcome to Idaho, now go home.'"

She decided there was no point bringing up the symbol. Jo Beth would like to avoid seeing sidebars, with art, about Private Idaho in otherwise positive travel pieces. To her relief the questions stopped. In a few seconds someone started talking about the next day's activities.

That minor bump behind her, Jo Beth's naughty side tried to convince her to have some more ice cream as a little reward to herself for handling it so well. Her eyes drifted toward the dessert. She pulled them quickly back. No. She would not even look at it. If she let the damn thing melt, she could have another glass of champagne.

Oh-oh. Rob Flowers was on the move. He had been sitting four tables away. Flowers was in charge of riding herd on the caterer. He finished his dinner early so he could do the last minute running around that came with that job. He was running right now. Jo Beth was afraid that meant there was some catering disaster. No. It was all right. Flowers was just on his way to the bathroom. Why he was making a spectacle of himself by running, she did not know. Then, she noticed three or four other people making their way toward the rest rooms rather quickly.

"Jo Beth," Terry Wheeler said. "Aren't you going to eat your dessert?"

"What? Oh, no. Trying to keep my girlish figure."

"Would you mind if I helped you? It's really great ice cream."

Six or seven others got up and made their way across the grass. Jo Beth saw one woman upset a full glass of wine and leave the table without a word of apology.

"Uh, go right ahead, Terry."

Wheeler pulled the dessert plate in front of him. Jo Beth glanced that direction and bid the ice cream a regretful goodbye, then she jerked back and stared. A tiny green squiggle of frosting decorated the faux potato. At other banquets, green sprinkles had stood in for chives. She assumed that was what this was supposed to be. It did not look much like chives, now that she thought about it. In fact, it looked a little out of place. Sitting in front of her own plate, the squiggle on the ice cream potato had resembled an artist's representation of a bird in flight, a quick V to depict a sea gull, perhaps. When Wheeler pulled it in front of his plate, he turned it part-way around. Jo Beth saw another possible interpretation of the squiggle.

"Oh god."

Governor Mathews asked, "Are you feeling well, Jo Beth? You look a little pale." Then, the governor put one hand on his tummy. "Oh. Oh my. I'm starting to feel a little off myself. If you'll excuse me..."

Mathews got up and bumped into a woman from the next table, who held one hand over her mouth. They both began to trot in the direction of the rest rooms.

All across the sweeping lawn where the banquet was taking place, travel writers were jumping to their feet and heading toward the rest rooms. They would find a knot of people already gathered in front of each one.

"What's going on?" Wheeler asked

Her honor the mayor suddenly turned and retched on the grass. As if that were the cue everyone were waiting for, the sounds of retching began to drown out the band.

To one side of the banquet, sitting on the grass beneath a tall black cottonwood, unnoticed by the revelers, was someone in an army field jacket, eyes closed, nodding his head in rhythm with the music. He had not heard this one before. Or the one before that.

***

Bill wasn't feeling well. At least, that's what he told Jo Beth when he called to beg off hosting duties at the WTWA banquet. The banquet was one of the biggest plums of the year. No one would malinger to miss it.

Jo Beth would think he was crazy if she knew what he ate in lieu of the banquet. First, he thawed a couple of wieners in the microwave. Then, with a dull knife, he cut them into ragged, bite-sized knobs. Next, he opened a can of pork and beans, flipping the little bonus chunk of fat into the disposal. He mixed the ingredients together in a Corning bowl, sprinkled a little freeze dried onion over the glop and nuked it for four minutes. The onions were a move toward sophistication he made some years earlier when bachelor beans and weenies began to seem a little dull.

Pauline, who was an excellent cook if he remembered right, was selling something to someone somewhere.

After dinner and a few minutes conversation with CNN, Bill retired to his study. Pauline called it that. Bill heard a note of sarcasm in her voice when she said it. He had a real study, a room with leather furniture and books and an antique writing desk. The one he used was in the basement where the floor was concrete and the uncovered walls showed the Western white pine bones of the house.

Bill had entered his password and clicked into PageMaker when he saw it out of the corner of his eye. He kicked himself back from the desk and felt the rumble of chair castors on the cement beneath him. Bill squinted at the creature, then took a deep breath and pushed a shudder back beneath his skin. His brain had tricked him. Bill saw the tiny shadow first, cast on the wall behind his makeshift desk. Its blackness conjured a reality that was not there. Or was it?

He had a special fear of spiders. Not cat faces, or wolf spiders, or yellow garden spiders. Not even daddy longlegs which weren't really spiders anyway. He did not fear the tiny spiders of fall that cast their webs to the wind and drifted on air in search of greener pastures, or whatever spiders searched for. He had no fear of the dozens of species of spiders that called an average lawn their home. Even tarantulas would not give him sweats. He feared only one spider. The spider of shadows. The black widow.

Bill remembered that first time on the ranch when Johnny found one in an old burn barrel. His brother teased the spider with a screwdriver, trying to get it to attack the tip. Billy stayed well away. It frightened him instantly, for no reason he could name. To his relief, Johnny did not thrust the spider in his face or threaten to put it down his back.

This was no June bug. Big brother eventually crushed the spider with a board. He did so carefully, choosing a long board and holding it at arm's length. Johnny, the invincible, respected the spider's power. Billy saw that and absorbed the healthy fear, doubling it for good measure.

There was something primal in his fear, Bill thought. A dread hard-wired by heritage. The look of them fit some slot in his mind perfectly. They were "shinyblack" as he told his mother that first time. The widow looked mean and hard, as if armor-plated; as if its only business were death. He knew he could crush it in his hand, if he dared. The thought made his shudder surface, then sink. Its legs were... skittery. That bold red hourglass on its belly was a caution sign. Or a tattoo.

Added together, those features equaled phobia. Over the years Bill worked to overcome it. The older he got, the less the thought of black widows bothered him. On brave, sunny days he even caught and killed one or two. Yet, he knew if he were in the crawl space beneath his house, and felt his hand go through the tough, tangled web of a widow, his heart would simply stop.

Bill pondered this when he saw tonight's spider and the spider's shadow. This one shared none of the traits that made him dread its black cousin. It was brown and slightly fuzzy. It looked soft and gangly with its over-sized legs. Its body was long and thin, not a shiny metallic little pod that looked like it should have a stinger. The spider's only distressing feature was its size. It was about twice as big as a black widow.

For years, Bill had made it a practice to catch these common spiders—often at Pauline's vehement insistence—by trapping them with a tissue. He would make a grab for them, usually catching a couple of legs. With the spider writhing between his fingers, he would toss it outside, often with the admonition, "go play." Pauline, who was always glad to be rid of the spider, nevertheless chided him every time for not killing it. He paid her no mind. Bill did not take killing lightly.

Recently he learned the brown spiders had a name. An article in the paper, accompanied by a six-inch blow-up, gave their history. Once, they were called the aggressive house spider. An Idaho venomologist thought their common name gave them a bad rap, so he came up with another: the hobo spider. Black widows had been in Idaho forever, as far as Bill knew. The hobo was a newcomer. European in origin, it came to the Pacific Northwest in the 1930s along with other immigrants, spreading by hitching rides on the underside of boxcars. Hobos.

Bill stared at the spider for ten minutes. Maybe it stared back. It did not seem concerned. Perhaps he had picked it up by its back legs more than once already, tossing it outdoors. Maybe it returned now, merely a persistent visitor encouraged by his hospitality. Now Bill had a dilemma. Live and let live was his credo, even with black widows if they stayed out of sight. He had begun to feel differently about this particular breed of arachnid. The visitor he had assumed benign was dangerous. According to the article, they were as poisonous as black widows. People had died from their bites.

Slowly, keeping an eye on the big spider, he picked up a copy of Idaho Wildlife, rolled it up and prepared to strike. In that moment when someone chooses to kill the most insignificant creature, they justify the act on some level, though they are not always conscious of it. Bill, for whom killing did not come easily, was very conscious of his justification as the magazine came down two, three, four times. The spider, like cheatgrass and starlings, was simply not a native.

CHAPTER ELEVEN

Semi-sanctioned vandalism

In which Mary comes to the Eagle's Perch, Jake does spuds, Pauline wants a room with a view, and The Private eyes some fun.

It had been years since Bill had lunched at the Eagle's Perch. He remembered it as a place where farmers and hunters and construction workers could stop for a hamburger piled with onions, fries on the side and a Lucky Lager. He remembered Formica tables and red plastic tumblers for water; squeeze bottles for mustard and ketchup, with most of the menu on the wall. Tall booths catered to illicit meetings of the heart. Located five or six miles out of town on the road to Lucky Peak Reservoir, the little restaurant was secluded enough to assure privacy from prying eyes.

He and Mary were meeting there because of its proximity to the new Parks headquarters, only a mile away. Mary suggested the site because she could skate to the Eagle's Perch on her lunch hour. Bill offered to pick her up, but she declined, saying she enjoyed the skating. He counted on that. This meeting would lead to another where they would skate together.

The Eagle's Perch differed little from his memory. The management had acknowledged the popularity of the greenbelt path that ran behind and below the restaurant by adding open air dining. It was a cheap deck with umbrella tables and plastic chairs, but the view was great. He sat there a few minutes waiting for Mary, watching the raptors circle above the tree-lined Boise River a quarter mile away. They looked like dark little chevrons floating in the air. This time of year the bald eagles were somewhere far to the north in Canada or Alaska. The birds he saw were probably golden eagles. Maybe just hawks. The thermals from the river canyon made drifting in the midday sky easy for them. He could see cliffs turn into bluffs that stair stepped up from the river and onto the sagebrush covered flats above. If you knew where to look, you could spot the thin scar of the Oregon Trail as it traced along the edge of the highest plateau. There were other scars as well. Bill saw a set of recent tracks cutting diagonally down the gentle slope. He could barely make out a few flashes of red ribbon on survey stakes. It was the temporary road leading down to the Eagle Rock view lots.

Both scars had a story to tell. The story behind the Oregon Trail ruts was epic. He thought they should be preserved. Those sentimental feelings about the scar of the old trail caused spirited debate with Pauline.

"How is it different from the motorcycle trails on the Boise Front the environmentalists are always in a tizzy about?" she had asked.

"Those trails are ugly. They cause erosion. They are nothing more than semi-sanctioned vandalism," he had replied. "The Oregon Trail is a part of our heritage."

He remembered how smug she looked when she said, "And how do you know someone a hundred years from now won't want to preserve motorcycle ruts as a memorial to twentieth century recreation?"

How could he answer? He was pretty sure that wouldn't happen. But who knew what they might value in the future? Archaeologists got much of their best information from ancient dumps. Should we protect dumps, then? What would environmentalists have thought of the Oregon Trail when it was new? It wasn't a finite road, like people thought. The pioneers didn't hit an on-ramp in Missouri, point their wagons in the direction of the Willamette Valley, and set the cruise control. Their oxen and mules and horses had to find food. The trail often wandered, split into fibers, then rejoined like an undone rope mending itself. In some places, if you had stood in the middle of the "trail" you would not have seen a blade of grass for miles in any direction. The stock grazed it to dust.

The Oregon Trail remnants would be saved in the Eagle Rock development. Kreigh Sparks eventually conceded that. Pauline instantly turned it into a selling point. Just as the eagles were a selling point. If eagles quit coming because of the development, well it was still an evocative name.

He heard the clatter and rumble of a skater arriving on the deck. Bill turned to see Mary Lewis rolling toward him from the greenbelt entrance.

"Hi," she said, coasting to his table. She plopped without grace into one of the plastic chairs.

"Hi yourself."

Mary checked her wrist. "Nine minutes five seconds," she announced. "Not bad. Let's see, call it ten minutes to get back, 20 minutes for a shower... Okay. Almost an hour for lunch. Fifty minutes, anyway." She began to unbuckle her skates. "I'm in the wellness program at work," she explained. "We get an extra half hour three times a week to exercise. I'm cheating a little today."

"Cheating?"

"Yeah. I'm only exercising for twenty minutes. I should be going at least thirty. I'll have to make it up next week." Mary slipped off her socks and stuffed them into her skates. "Hope you don't mind looking at my feet while you're eating. I promise they're clean."

Bill did not mind at all. He noted that her feet were attached to a pair of bare legs that went all the way...

"You guys ready to order?"

"Hi Christy. I'll just have a lunch salad and a Coke. Low cal ranch on the side."

Bill ordered the same, foregoing the cheeseburger and fries he would have preferred.

Mary cocked her head. "You look pretty chipper today, considering."

Bill smoothed his tie, absently, and said, "You heard, huh?"

"Yeah, it was on the radio on the way to work this morning. Sounded pretty bad."

"I guess it was. I didn't go. I wasn't feeling well last night."

"Before?"

"Yeah, before. I guess it was unanimous. Must be a curse on the division."

"You've had your share of troubles, lately, that's for sure." Mary laughed. "You know, I was a little miffed when I didn't get an invitation to the banquet. Sounds like I lucked out after all. Do they know what caused it?"

"Some kind of food poisoning, I guess. The state epidemiologist is looking into it."

"Yuk. It sounded awful." Mary wrinkled her nose. "Maybe we should talk about something else."

They talked about the weather for a moment. When the conversation lulled, Bill said, "I've done it, by the way."

"Good for you," said Mary. "What have you done?"

"We're going skating in the tunnel. If you're up for it."

"Really? You got permission?"

"Well, not permission, exactly. I got the guard on duty to look the other way, though."

"Fantastic! What night?" Bill hesitated. This was where it could fall apart. A woman as beautiful as Mary was probably booked up solid every weekend.

"Saturday. Hawkins—he's the guard—didn't want to do it on a week night. Too many late workers."

"Tomorrow night?"

"Yeah." Bill swallowed. "Can you make it?"

"Sure, I guess I can. What about your wife?"

"Here's your drinks," said the waitress, setting the tumblers down in front of them.

"Uh, thanks," said Bill. The woman disappeared back into the restaurant. "I'm sorry, what did you ask?"

"Your wife. Pauline, is it? Is she coming?"

For a moment the question threw him. He tried to picture he and Pauline on Rollerblades zooming down the tunnel. In his mind he got her on the blades. That's as far as the image would go. He could not make her move. When was the last time they had done anything like that together? Their mountain bikes hung like dusty carcasses from hooks in the garage. They had matching racquet ball racquets. They had cross-country skis. When had they last used any of those toys? When had they had fun together?

"Oh, Pauline doesn't skate," he said. He almost added that she would be out of town all weekend at some Realtor's shindig. Unnecessary information, he thought.

"Too bad," she said. "She doesn't know what she's missing."

Mary put her feet up on an empty chair and took a sip of Coke. She faced Bill. He could not tell exactly where she was looking because her sunglasses hid her eyes. He hoped her gaze was on him. She was smiling. Then her smile faded and turned into a frown.

"What's wrong?" he asked.

Mary dropped her feet to the floor, leaned forward and tilted her sunglasses to peek over the frames. She looked past him. He turned and followed her stare. They looked out across the black cottonwoods that announced the presence of the Boise River.

"Clark, it's gone." It was almost a whisper. "The roost tree is gone."

***

She had more cookies than she really needed, anyway. It wasn't like she went out of her way to make him something special. She decided Charlie had a point. Maybe she needed to act more neighborly.

There was another reason she wanted to pay a visit to Bill Baker. Since he bought the old homestead, Debbie had not gone to the Clara Tree. She missed those quiet, cathartic visits terribly. Baker would probably not mind her coming to sit beneath that special tree from time to time. She respected property rights enough that she would ask permission.

And it was his property. Debbie's teeth clenched tight when she thought of that. Money made it so. History and tradition and family meant nothing. Only money counted. She was angry with Andy Bennett for selling the homestead. It would have fit her plans just right if he had simply kept the place, visiting it two or three times a year to make sure the roof wasn't leaking. Ah, but that was selfish. She could not blame

Andy. He had offered the place to her and Charlie enough times. Seemed like they never had the money. At least, that was their excuse. Truth was, they never believed the homestead would sell. It was way too small to do anything with. Except put in a dude ranch, as it turned out.

Cinching her saddle Debbie yanked a little too hard on the latigo. Skid grunted.

"Sorry ol' cuss," she said. "Didn't mean to take it out on you."

She tied the plastic bag of chocolate chip cookies to the front of her saddle by the rope string, and swung up.

She set Skid to an easy lope. The quicker she got this over with the better. This Welcome Wagon role was not one she played often.

The day was bright and clear, except for one big thunderhead coming up out of the southwest. Those towering clouds rolled through about every afternoon when the weather was hot. Debbie wasn't worried about getting wet. They brought more bluster, thunder and spit than rain. There was always a danger of lightning setting the cheatgrass on fire, so she would keep an eye on it.

She watched the approaching storm more than the road. A woman could afford to do that when her "cruise control" was named Skid. When she did turn her full attention to where she was, they were nearly to the entrance of the homestead. A big log arched across the gate between two huge posts nowadays, with the words Bruneau Guest Ranch burned into its side.

Some elemental portion of her brain registered it first. A primal part that preceded thought. Debbie reined Skid in hard and slid from the saddle before he could stop. She ducked under and in front of the horse. At the same instant Skid planted his front hooves in the dust like posts to avoid stepping on her, and skidded his back legs like a roping champ. She did not notice the horse's heroic effort to stop. Debbie staggered through the weeds in the borrow pit and came up next to the barbed wire fence of the homestead. She grabbed the top wire—a wire originally strung by her granddad fifty years before, with the help of Grandmother Clara. Her bare hands turned white from her grip on the strand. She did not notice. Nor did she notice the trickle of blood oozing between the clenched fingers of her right hand. She noticed only the matte black satellite dish mounted securely on a concrete pad where once the Clara Tree had stood.

***

Putting spuds in pipes was fun at first. While customers oohed and clucked over his statues, Jake would sneak behind their Accuras and BMWs and jam a number one baker in their exhaust. After they had paid $59.95 for a hunk of pine that would cost them a nickel as a piece of firewood, they climbed into their cars and tried to start them. No way, Jose. Crank, crank, crank, all the while with Jake barely able to keep from laughing out loud back in his shop. Finally the "man" would open his hood—probably for the first time ever, Jake figured. He would stand there looking into the engine compartment like he could really tell the difference between an alternator and a refrigerator. Pretty soon he would start touching things, pushing on sparkplug wires, wiggling hoses. One guy checked his brake fluid level. Jake liked to about split a gut over that.

Sooner or later Mr. Tourist would come ask him for help. Acting real concerned, Jake would lean in and do the same sort of meaningless poking, only with more enthusiasm. He pulled plug wires right off, disconnected vacuum lines and always removed the air cleaner. That seemed to assure them he really knew something about cars. Try as he might, he could never figure out the problem. Eventually, he mentioned as how there was a mechanic—a fine mechanic—up the road a piece who could fix any problem. If the tourist seemed reluctant, Jake pointed out the towing was covered by insurance anyway, likely as not. It sure would be a shame to ruin a vacation over something ol' Gary could fix in a few minutes.

Ol' Gary, who normally could not tell how many cylinders a car had without using a paper and pencil, was a genius at fixing potato pipes. He crawled under the cars, and climbed in and out of the engine compartments, trying this and that cure, asking Mr. Tourist to "try it" six or eight times. Finally he stumbled on some wire that worked loose somewhere, or found a blown fuse. Of course, what he really found was a Russet spud he could secretly remove and save for dinner while Mr. Tourist pondered the complexities of valve cover bearings.

Towing a car from Jake's to Gary's cost between $75 and $150 on a sliding scale that roughly matched the value of the car. A similar scale existed for work performed. The total bill was always over $200. It was hardly worth the trouble for less than $100 apiece.

For a while, when that state travel lady, Jo Beth Crowder, came on TV to say how good tourism was for Idaho's economy, she had two believers in the audience named Jake and Gary.

The scam turned into more trouble than it was worth for Jake. First, these were the same tourists he had his little accidents with. He hated cutting back on that. For a while, he consoled himself with another little trick he discovered. If he wore a big brass belt buckle, like the one that said Idaho across the rack of this big-ass elk, he could cause a couple hundred dollars worth of damage just by "helping" when he leaned across a fender to jiggle things under the hood. The first time he noticed a pair of three inch gouges in the paint on the driver's side fender of a Mercedes he almost apologized to the guy.

Fun as that was, he still had to talk to tourists when he would rather be throwing rocks at them. Being nice to them galled him.

The real trouble with the enterprise was Charlene. That woman should have been a detective. Nothing got by her for very long. He and Gary were careful not to do more than a couple cars a day so as not to make anyone suspicious. Even so, Charlene caught on by the third day. It took her most of a week to figure out exactly how they were doing it. She knew they were doing it almost from the beginning. She gave Jake a lecture like he hadn't gotten since he went to Catholic school, a portion of which went:

"I cannot believe a relative of mine—even though you ain't blood—I cannot believe you would do something so slimy and underhanded and rattlesnake-low to people who stop here to spend their money on your carvings."

"Ah, Hon, they can afford it. It's not like I'm taking the money from orphans or something." Jake figured logic might work.

"I don't care if they can afford it. Of course they can afford it, but you wouldn't steal their wallets, would you?"

"No, of course not."

"Well, what's the difference? You're stealing their blamed money just the same. You may as well find out where they live and break into their homes while they're away."

"Oh, now you're exaggerating. It's not like that at all."

"It's just the same."

"It is not the same." For some reason the woman could not see the fine lines here. Jake brightened. "A big part of it isn't even their money. Insurance pays for the towing." Let her argue that one.

Charlene rolled her eyes. "So it's better to steal from an insurance company, you're saying?"

"It ain't stealing. But, yeah, it's better to get it from a company. A company's not people."

"Not people? Who do you think owns the company, monkeys?"

He knew there was a good answer to that. He could not think of it right then, so he jumped another way. "We're making a lot of money off this, you know. Gary and I can pull in three or four hundred a day. That's each. Hell, that's better than we can make selling this shit," he said, waving at the rows and rows of wooden figures. "Think of what we can do with that money."

"Oh no you don't," Charlene said, backing away from him.

"What? No I don't what?"

"Don't you go saying 'we' when you're talking about that money. At least not if you're including me in that we. I don't want to have nothing to do with it. It's bad money as far as I'm concerned."

"Bad money? It spends just fine."

"Yeah? You planning to spend it on hookers quite a lot, then, are you?"

Jake frowned. "Well, of course not. Is that what you're worried about? Hon, I don't want no one else but you, you know that."

"No, I don't know a damn thing about you anymore, Jake Burrell. Except that you're being downright mean to those folks, and if there's one thing I hate it's meanness."

He was looking so hurt by the argument Charlene almost backed off. Did back off, a little. "Oh, I know you aren't planning on sleeping around, Jake. That's not what I meant. I hope you've got some real friendly carvings back there in the shop, though, 'cause you'll be sleeping with them for the foreseeable future."

Charlene got colder and colder over the next few days. Finally Jake had to tell Gary they would have to cut back some. They still ran the scam once in a while after that when Charlene went for groceries or had a doctor's appointment. Those times they upped the ante quite a bit to make up for the times they could not operate at all. For a while, Charlene got friendlier. Then, she was back to being an ice cave again when she caught Jake doing his trick with the pickup bumper. It seemed like she was not going to let him have any fun. Then he came up with the idea of carving tourists.

***

The flash looked like lightning had struck somewhere east of the fish pond. For one second the house, chicken coop, barn and trees cast sharp dark shadows. Instead of thunder following the flash there came a whir, snick. Bill pulled the developing photo from the front of the camera and tossed it on the table, then made lightning again.

Polaroids were useful if you needed to capture something quickly, the way it was, with no thought of prizes or publishing. Bill used this one to get some angles on the diorama of The Place, so he could compare it with the real thing.

Going back scared the hell out of him. He had not been there in close to thirty years. After they moved to Firth, Bill spent the first summer at The Place, living with cousins. Near it, actually, for The Place was no longer his. He tried fishing, horseback riding and exploring with Griff. It was not the same. He was now a visitor. Bill went back only once after that summer. Better to visit in his mind where ownership was still irrelevant.

He adapted to town life well, in spite of his longing. Not so Griff. Bill graduated from hiking and horses to a minibike. Now when he went adventuring, Griff stayed home. She greeted him wildly every time he returned, jumping and running and barking, even if it happened eleven times a day. Each return might signal a new adventure. They might once again set off on foot to conquer trees and corral poles together. Each time Griff got a quick pat on the head, or less.

Part of it was growing up, Bill thought. When cars and girls draw your attention, there is less room in life for a dog. Part of it was rejection. Bill could not explore with her, because he could not explore The Place. A lesser adventure would only remind him of the loss. Griff was such a part of that. He could barely stand to look at her.

Griff probably caught a dog disease, or succumbed to the ravages of age. He found her under the house one winter day, stiff and cold. Bill brought her out, wrapped her in a gunny sack, and borrowed the car from Mom. That was the last time he had visited The Place.

Bill heard the whoop upstairs through the open door to the family room.

"Hello? Hey, Bill?"

"I'm down here," he called, then immediately regretted it. The basement—especially this corner of the basement—was his. He always resented it when someone else entered that little world.

Pauline came bouncing down the wooden steps, making them thunder. He wondered how a hundred-pound woman could have such an impact.

"It's a go," she said, running into his arms. "It's a go, go, go!"

He automatically returned her hug and said, "That's great, honey. That's really great," all the time frantically trying to remember what the hell might be a "go." He supposed she had sold another house or helped a client get some permit or other.

She pulled back and held his waist at arm's length. "We're going to be rich!"

Bill gave her what he hoped was a convincing grin. "Yeah, I guess we are."

"Think about it. We'll be able to put in a pool, get a bigger hot tub. We can redecorate."

She suddenly brought her fingers up to her cheeks and gasped. "Oh wow! Screw redecorating. We can afford one of the view lots. Oh, Jesus, Bill, this is the big time!"

He held the grin while his mind continued to search.

Pauline's eyes narrowed. "Bill?"

"Yeah, babe?"

"You don't have the slightest fucking idea what I'm talking about, do you?'

"Uh, actually, no."

She stepped back and crossed her arms, giving him a scolding look. "Eagle Rock, dummy. I was at the P&Z meeting tonight. They approved it!"

He should want to share in his wife's joy, her victory. She had worked on the project for months. It was the first time Pauline had taken such a lead role in a development, and she had handled it well. He was proud of her for that. At least, he thought he should be proud of her.

"Approved it, huh? Any restrictions?"

"Nah. We got by all that. They even waved the river setback for a couple of the view lots."

"No problems with the Indians?"

"Well, they're not happy about it, but since when have Indians been happy about anything? They couldn't come up with the bones."

"Bones?"

"It was a 'burial ground,' remember? But they never could prove it."

He hesitated before asking the next question. "What about the eagles?"

"No sweat. We're going to build them a new roost tree further up river." Pauline shrugged dismissively. "Problem solved."

"You're going to build them a tree? How do you build a tree?"

"You use wood, I guess. Who cares?"

Bill ran his fingers along the plywood edge of his diorama platform, and asked, "So, what happens to the real roost tree?"

She shrugged. "Let's just say it won't block our view." She put her hand on his, one finger resting on a miniature road. "I really think we can swing it, honey. We tie up one view lot with savings, then build our dream house with the commissions I'll make off subdivision sales. What do you say?"

He watched as she gently rubbed her thumb across the back of his hand. His eyes followed her fingers onto the diorama road, then followed the road to where it intersected with the lane, then followed the lane to its terminus. His eyes rested there, recalling the day the airplane took the picture, the days when he swung in the swing, and climbed the corral with Griff. All those things took place in the backyard of his dream house.

"Bill?"

He turned and met her eyes.

"What do you think?"

With little enthusiasm he said, "I suppose we could swing it."

It had just occurred to him. Pauline had never seen The Place. And with that thought came a cold certainty. She never would.

***

Coyote watched from a grove of aspen as they ran lag bolts into the ties with a cordless drill. The whir of the tool sounded like the rattle of a pneumatic gun twisting lug nuts tight in a tire store. Two men worked on the edge of the trestle, 300 feet above the water, with the easy confidence of sun-browned steel workers walking the beams. They made it look easy slipping around the front of the tubular steel frame without fear, dancing along the edge of the thick ties with their heels over nothing.

Their confidence was calculated to calm eight others who watched and waited from very near the exact center of the abandoned trestle. Those eight were content to lift their chins from time to time to better view the meandering stream below. They shuffled and joked, sometimes laughing loud enough to hear the sound come sailing back from the rocks along the canyon wall. It was a hollow sound.

Each of them imagined they felt the light breeze sway the big timbers beneath their feet. Although the bridge had been engineered to hold locomotives and coal tenders without a tremble, they were certain they would be on it when the structure collapsed like a clever grid of toothpicks. They swallowed those fears in laughter and crude comments. Today was a day to vanquish fear. Those eight had already paid $85 apiece for the privilege of jumping off the structure they were terrified to stand on.

The Private watched as one installer strapped on a leather rigging and bravely pushed out, bouncing to test the strength of the frame. The trestle did not shake or sway or tremble. Something made the watcher grin. He needed sharper eyes to see something as tiny as a hair, so he shifted and took wing.

Larry Stone's mouth felt weathered inside; dry as the slivered timbers beneath his feet. It had to be a hundred degrees. He felt like he was standing inside the ice cream plant in Lorna Linda where he was a quality control inspector. Larry licked his lips as they strapped him into the harness. From the edge of his vision he saw the kid with the camcorder standing on the cliff to his left, eye welded to the viewfinder. Rhonda had refused to come. She was too frightened to watch. What a shame. At least he'd have it on video.

Gawd, what a rush it was going to be! Larry had opted for the Supreme package. It included a VHS tape of the event, a Certificate of Insanity and a Wethead t-shirt. You only got the shirt if your hair was really wet after the jump. The goal was to dip your locks in Bitch Creek on the initial bounce. The creek was only about 18 inches deep, so it required careful calculation. The owner of Bitchin' Bungees, an entrepreneurial enterprise neither sanctioned by the state nor approved by the railroad that still owned the trestle, was tapping the calculator keys right now. Larry hoped he didn't drop a decimal.

A shadow rippled across the railroad ties, dropping through and recovering in rapid succession. Larry looked up. The silhouette of a bird blocked the sun for an instant. "What the..? Holy shit! It's a vulture!"

The button pusher tipped his head back and held the pose for several chews of Juicy Fruit, then said, "Nah, it's just an owl."

Fun! The Private could see better now than with his own eyes. Sometimes you needed very good eyes to see his tricks.

The square black tubes met at right angles at critical junctures. Every weld was neat and flawless, looping along like practice penmanship O's. Following parallel to one, straight as a rail, was a thin, dark space. When the jumper leaned back, the space widened like a grin, then healed nearly shut again when he pulled himself forward. The grin appeared and disappeared several times before Larry finally took a deep, ragged breath and threw himself into space.

CHAPTER TWELVE

A quiet night in Idaho

In which Blaine learns about safe sex, Bill skates to a dead-end, the Wilsons take a wrong turn, Mary has a good sleep, and Frank does some moonlighting.

Blaine had won $150 in the Tri-West Lotto six months earlier. This here was even better than that. He had spotted the guy first thing on that last tour of the day. A skinny, bald guy with a big red mustache. Of course, there could be more than one guy who looked like that. He'd done a little test to make sure. Blaine asked where everyone was from, in a friendly kind of way. Then he'd asked the group how many of them were staying at the resort in Coeur d'Alene. As he expected over half the hands went up. One of those hands belonged to the skinny bald guy with the big red mustache.

All through the tour Blaine was distracted by him. He kept thinking how nice it would be to put an ingot through the front of his bald head. Every time Blaine looked up the guy was there, looking right back at him. Blaine would be explaining the operation of a machine or talking the numbers he knew by heart and there the man would be, smiling at him. It wasn't his imagination, either. The skinny bald guy with the big red mustache smiled at him like he knew something. Like he knew the look on Sally's face when she saw a tangle of red hair not everyone saw.

The man was talkative, too. He asked questions about everything. Especially about Blaine. He kept asking, and Blaine kept telling him, though it felt like every word he said was a confidence revealed. The little bastard knew things about his wife, and he was learning every secret Blaine had. And he was laughing about it all. Blaine had never seen anyone look so damn pleased with himself. Blaine wanted to break his nose on the spot and watch the blood soak into that stupid mustache. But he had to be civil. He was a tour guide.

Then the man asked another question: "Can we go down in the elevator?" Blaine got that question a lot. Everyone wanted to go down in the "elevator." His standard answer was it was not an elevator. Miners called it a lift. And, no, you couldn't go down. The shaft was over a mile deep, so liability was a real concern. They were always disappointed when they heard that answer, though most of them understood the company's position. The skinny bald guy with the red mustache was disappointed, too, until Blaine pulled him aside at the end of the tour.

***

Bill was surprised to see Mary skate up to where he had parked the Explorer.

"Hey, where's the Mustang?" he asked as she rolled up to his open door. He sat on the passenger side floor adjusting the buckle on his boot.

"It's in the car hospital," she said. "Didn't I tell you I got rear-ended the other day?"

"No, I guess not."

"Yeah, some jerk plowed into me at a stoplight."

"Were you hurt?"

"Nah. Didn't do Ol' Paint any good, though. Took out both taillights and wrecked the bumper. I won't get it back for at least a week."

"That's too bad," Bill said. "Are you going to need a ride to work?"

"No, I've got a rental. The guy's insurance company was really good about it." She wrinkled her nose. "I hate to drive it. It's a dippy little Toyota with an automatic. Besides, I don't live that far away."

Far enough he could insist on taking her home after they skated, Bill thought. With a little side trip, of course. He put his weight down on the skate and bent his knee, testing the fit. "Hey, I'm set. What are we waiting for?"

They skated down the block and into the exit of the parking garage, then quickly over to the elevator alcove where Bill pushed the button.

"We don't have to take the stairs?" Mary asked.

"Nah, I've got connections. Besides, I'm not good on stairs with skates on."

Mary laughed. The elevator took them down one flight to the basement of the garage. When they got into the tunnel, Mary said, "It's so quiet." The walls brought her whisper back to her.

"Won't be for long." Bill pushed off into the tunnel. The click of his strides was joined by the click of hers. They both built up speed on the seamless concrete until they were fairly flying.

'Whoa!" Bill shouted. "This is like glass!"

Mary came up next to him, gliding along easily with her hands clasped behind her back.

"You could do a hundred miles an hour in here," she said.

"I've told you a million times not to exaggerate."

Mary stuck her tongue out at him.

In a few seconds they were where the tunnel took a sharp left beneath the statehouse. Bill turned backward, forward, and backward again, finally coming to a stop in front of the doors that led to the basement of the Hall of Mirrors. Without the help of a big black dog, he executed the move perfectly this time. Mary heel-braked to a stop next to him.

"Let's stay out of the wing that goes to the Capitol," he said. "It's probably all right, but I'd just as soon not push our luck."

Bill could hardly believe he was here with this woman. Two weeks ago he wouldn't have dared take the minor risk of skating the tunnel alone. Although the chance of getting caught was small and the consequences hardly worth worrying about, Bill preferred to keep risk near zero. Now, skating on the sly with Mary, he felt no danger at all. His heart pumped, not from fear but from exhilaration. There was a higher risk now, wasn't there? A risk with consequences. He put that thought aside.

"You want to race?" Bill asked.

"Race? You'd kill me."

"Oh, come on, you're a great skater."

"I'm fine, but you're a bigger engine. I couldn't keep up."

He gave her a lectured puppy look. She sighed. "All right, I'll race you once, just to keep your overinflated male ego pumped."

"Perfect. Say when."

"When!" Mary was off like a quarter horse, near full speed in three strides.

"No fair!" Bill called after her, already pumping to catch up. In a few seconds he did catch, then pass her. He tucked lower and threw his arms out further, stretching his stride. One glance back told him she had given up. Mary rolled along 20 feet behind him, leaning forward with her hands on her knees. Bill skated faster, putting more distance between them. He reveled in the surge of power he felt in that moment, asking his muscles to take the extra coal and turn it into fire. He skated past the high school murals; saw the familiar drag racing scene and basketball game. He shot by the door to the parking garage where they had entered, and through a set of double doors in the tunnel beyond. Bill could not remember ever being in this part of the tunnel. He knew it connected to another state office building. Maybe two. No murals here. He strode on, forgetting Mary for the moment, devoting every thought to the joy of speed.

The tunnel branched off at a right angle ahead. He came up on it so fast he barely made the turn, then skidded and nearly fell when he saw the branch led nowhere. Funny, he thought, as he stood there panting, the tunnel didn't seem to have a purpose. The passage went back maybe forty feet and ended. There were no doors leading off either side. There wasn't even an overhead light, so the wall at the end of the tunnel was dark. It was not a gray wall, he saw. Bill leaned forward and squinted. Shapes seemed to swirl and form, then coalesce into something familiar. There was a mural of some kind on the far wall.

He pushed off and rolled forward until he was less than ten feet away. The light was terrible. It took a moment for his eyes to adjust. It was a painting of the big dunes at Bruneau. Bill grinned. He had stood on that spot, seen that perspective a dozen times. The sensuous sand rose and humped and flowed from one side of the painting to the other, in a gentle curve around moonlit lakes. The celestial reflection was an oblong smudge that shimmered across inky water at the foot of the dunes. Bill followed the reflection to its source, hanging like a bone china plate in a blue-black sky. Had this one been done by the art teacher? Its level of detail far surpassed the one-dimensional murals on the tunnel walls. The shading was remarkably realistic. The artist's strokes brought the bulges and ripples of sand to life. So much so he half expected to see a tiger beetle scurrying along, tracing a delicate track behind it with tiny, fragile legs.

Bill leaned closer. The moon was real. Well, realistic, at least. Delicate dabs of mottled gray on off-white portrayed the ethereal craters of its surface. It looked more like a tiny moon than a tiny representation of a moon. He felt he could put his fingers around it and heft the weight of that world like a softball heavy in his hand.

The painting was quiet. Bill frowned. Where had that thought come from? All paintings were quiet. Yet, this was the first he had seen that said so. It took quiet and added silence to it, like a scene from the vacuum of space. The mural pulled on him, a black hole of silence. He could almost step into it, feeling the sand grind into his wheels. Not hearing it. He would smell the sage and feel the day's heat radiate off the dunes. Yet, he would not hear the slither of a snake or the call of a red-tailed hawk or the shush of ubiquitous wind.

Bill felt the edge-of-a-cliff urge to let himself fall into the painting. It beckoned like a sandy siren. He detected movement. A ripple in the shimmering water or a silhouette disappearing over the lip of the dune. Bill felt the hair stand up on the back of his neck. He broke the artist's spell, turned and started skating. In six quick strides he was back in the main tunnel and...

"Bill!" He looked up to see Mary coming toward him. She bumped into him at a slow roll, grabbing him by his waist to avoid a fall. They scrambled together for a moment, then caught their balance. She kept one hand on his shoulder for support.

"I'm sorry," she said. "I must have been watching my feet. I didn't even see you."

"No, it was my fault. I should have watched where I was going." Bill felt his heart bumping bass against his ribs. He wondered how much of his excitement was from his odd encounter with the painting, and how much was from the touch of her hand, the nearness of her face.

Mary nodded over his shoulder. "I don't think I've seen that one before."

Reluctantly, Bill swung around to look down the tunnel at the mural. His heart caught. The painting rushed out of the darkness toward him like a runaway train. It slammed into focus five feet from his nose. There was no tunnel. There was only a flat expanse of wall in front of him between two support pillars.

"Hey, what's the matter? You look like you just saw Casper."

Painted between the pillars was the mural he had seen a moment before. Yet it was not the same. The scene was identical, a nighttime landscape of sand dunes, lakes and full moon. This painting was flat, lifeless and dreary. The subtleties of shading and nuances of stroke were gone. In places the crude paint had chipped to show cold gray concrete beneath. The quiet was missing. So was the power.

"Would you look at that," Mary said, pointing at the moon. It was a different, craterless moon. Someone had drawn a thick black chevron across the flat yellow face of it with a magic marker.

"I didn't do that," Bill said, shaking his head.

Mary raised an eyebrow. "Why would I think you did?"

For a few more minutes they continued to skate the tunnel. Mary skated beautifully; Bill listlessly. He could not get his mind off the painting. It had obviously been an optical illusion. His brain, short of oxygen from sprint skating, got the depth wrong. That was all. He only thought he turned a corner and skated into a dead-end passage. That had not happened. He had stopped in front of the mural and let his air-starved brain fill in some blanks with a reality that wasn't there. Vivid as it was, that had to be it. With every stride he became more certain that was the explanation. Weird. He couldn't remember ever hallucinating before.

After a while he let thoughts of the hallucination drift away, as he concentrated on the reality that was Mary Lewis.

***

The skinny bald guy with the big red mustache said, "My name's Lawrence." He stuck out his hand. After a second's hesitation, Blaine took it. He barely resisted crushing bones in his grip, bringing the guy squealing to his knees. Play nice, Blaine thought. Make it last.

"I really appreciate the private tour," Lawrence said, giving Blaine a conspiratorial look.

"No problem," Blaine said. "When you asked that question earlier, I got to thinking. I haven't been down the shaft myself in years. I'd like to do it again one more time, anyway."

They agreed to meet at 10 p.m. Blaine didn't want witnesses. He thought the guy might be suspicious of the late hour, but Lawrence seemed to think it was the most natural thing. What a dork.

"They don't use this much anymore, huh?" Lawrence said, as they approached the shaft.

"Not much," Blaine said, swinging back the chain link gate to the fenced area surrounding the skip.

"Are you sure it's safe? I always like to be safe."

"Yeah, it's safe. Don't worry about it," Blaine said, thinking the guy ought to be worrying a whole bunch.

Blaine gave Lawrence an after-you gesture, then stepped in and closed the skip gate behind them. He pressed the button to the first station. Two guys in a skip built for 12. It seemed a little empty.

"Wow, you can see the walls," Lawrence said, as the skip began to descend. The two-by-sixes that lined the shaft were clearly visible above the shoulder-high sides of the skip. "Are you going to turn on the light?" Lawrence asked. The light from the top station that filtered through the braces and guards above them was fading rapidly.

"No light, Lawrence. Miners always wore their own." Blaine saw the man smile in the flickering shadows. He had hoped to see a little glint of fear in his eyes. Oh well, that would come. "There'll be light at each station," Blaine said.

The rumble and creak of the cable was an old familiar song to Blaine. The smell of grease from the rusty mechanism above mixed with a hint of dust. The temperature dropped almost immediately.

"Kind of cold down here, isn't it?" Lawrence said. Blaine did not answer. Instead, he pressed the emergency stop with his thumb, then quickly punched the button to station two. The skip jolted, then descended again.

"What was that?" Lawrence said. It was too dark for Blaine to see the fear in his eyes. He knew it was there.

"Oh, don't worry about it. These old skips just do that once in a while. They hit a bad spot in the cable and give a little bounce."

It was an absolute lie. This was the newest skip in the mine. He chose it because most of the others required an operator from above. It had multiple safety systems. First, there was a thin little electric cable that followed the wall the length of the shaft. If you had a problem, you could reach out to that cable and hit one of the stop switches located all along it. The company was meticulous about maintenance and would never let "a bad spot" appear on a cable in the first place. Besides, if something happened to the cable the safety dogs would bite into the sides of the shaft and stop the skip right quick. Of course, there was no point in telling Lawrence any of this.

Blaine made the skip jerk a couple more times before they got to station one. He let the skip drift on by. Only one light marked the station at the entrance to the tunnel. Strange. He thought he saw a flash of light way back deep, almost like a reflecting pair of animal eyes. Blaine made the skip jump once, twice, then pressed the emergency button for real. They stopped twenty feet below station one, where the light was still strong enough to illuminate the skip.

"God, did you do that?" Lawrence asked.

"I stopped it."

"Oh, that's a relief." Lawrence looked a little pale. "I'm not sure I need to go much further."

"Had about all the fun you can stand?" Blaine asked. Lawrence nodded enthusiastically. "Well, we're not quite done yet." Blaine felt his lip curl looking at the pathetic little creep who was right now on the edge of a lesson. In a low voice Blaine said, "Drop your pants, Lawrence." He expected a puzzled look, a stammered question, righteous indignation.

Lawrence smiled. "You get right down to business, don't you?" He unbuckled his jeans and let them drop to the floor, then pushed a pair of red boxers down after them.

The easy compliance threw Blaine. He stood there for a few seconds, staring at the man's penis. The longer he stared the longer it got. Blaine reddened. This was the view Sally got.

The thought sickened him. By god, he was going to change that view forever.

Blaine shoved his fingers into his jeans pocket. Lawrence snickered and said, "Hey big boy, are you happy to see me or is that ..."

The skip bumped, then started to rise. What the hell? He must have hit the button with his elbow. Blaine fumbled in his pocket. Damn Levis. Seemed like they shrank every damn time Sally washed them nowadays.

Lawrence, with his pants around his ankles, shuffled forward. "Let me help you with that," he said, and pressed his hand to Blaine's fly. The skip continued to rise, lifting past station one and into the darkness above.

"What the fuck are you doing?"

Lawrence began to work on the silver dollar buckle of Blaine's belt. The skip stopped. He hadn't hit the button that time, he was sure, but Blaine didn't have time to think about it. The son of a bitch was trying to take off his pants.

"Hey!" Blaine yelled, pushing the man away. It dawned on him. "Jesus Christ, you're a fucking queer!"

He heard the strangest sound from above. It was like a pop, only not sharp enough to call it that. It was more of a poof. The skip began to drop. Station one went by in a flash. He saw a snapshot of Lawrence sitting on the floor with his hands behind him and his ridiculous penis pointing straight up. He looked more puzzled than frightened. Then, the station was behind them and they were in the dark again. Station two came and went in a flicker. He fought his panic and fumbled for the stop switch in the dark, then gave up and put his hand into the shaft. He felt a hundred splinters embed themselves in his palm. Someone screamed. There! Blaine felt the emergency wire. Almost at once his hand hit a switch.

Nothing. They fell faster. He hit another with the same result. The rushing air flapped Blaine's collar around his ears. What about the dogs? Jesus, he thought, what about the fucking dogs?!

***

Tips & Tricks from *The Private* newsletter

Hey, here's a good one from Sandpoint! You can call or write the Boise Booster Bureaucrats and tell them you're attending a convention out of state. Ask for anywhere from 50 to 300 brochures, so you can distribute them to participants. 'Course, you don't tell them it's a "convention" of garbage collectors!

If you have friends in other states who live in small towns write Letters To The Editor for them. If they send them to their local weekly paper, with their names on them, the paper will print 'em! Make sure the letter tells what an awful time your friends had in Idaho, and how unfriendly the people are.

***

It would come as some small surprise to the Wilsons there really was a lot to do in Firth, Idaho.

"Wow, can you imagine living in a place like this?" David Wilson observed the town from behind the wheel of his Lexus.

They would be surprised to know that boys the age of their Leonard, which was to say about 17, could fish, play tennis, hunt, play baseball, ride mountain bikes, play basketball, canoe, jump on a trampoline, swim, go horseback riding and chase girls, all within a mile of the center of town. In Firth, boys of Leonard's age could also take violin lessons, piano lessons, singing lessons and dance lessons. In Firth, they usually did not.

"They could put both city limit signs on the same post," said Pamela, who had looked up from her Triple A Trip Tick long enough to see Main Street. There was not much to see, especially in the dark. Firth's heyday had been in the 30s when it boasted an airport, a movie theater and its own newspaper. Now, to look at Main Street, one might think the town was in decline. No new building had risen to compete with Collet's bar, which scraped the sky fully two stories up, in forty years. Three or four had tumbled in on themselves and eventually become vacant lots. Several others were well down that ruinous road. Yet, the town's population had never been greater. It was now a bedroom community for the almost equally unknown towns of Blackfoot, Pocatello and Idaho Falls.

"Oh, look at this," David said, leaning over the wheel. "An actual traffic light!" Even taciturn Leonard laughed at that. The single lens light hung akilter from drooping wires across Main Street, flashing yellow to through traffic and red to the cross street in a dull routine that looked more a matter of habit than safety.

What the Wilsons did not know about Firth could crowd the shelves of the high school library. They did not know the football team took state three years in a row, back in the 70s. They did not know two brothers and a first cousin had enlisted together in '68 and never came home. They did not know the town had produced more MDs per capita (four) than any other in the state. They did not know they would die there.

The Wilsons, on their way to Yellowstone, had stopped for gas in Blackfoot, ten miles south of Firth. They planned to stay the night in Idaho Falls, 25 miles on up the interstate. It took great concentration to do so, but they got lost and ended up taking old highway 191 out of town instead of slipping back onto 1-15, the road they had used all the way from San Diego.

Firth was full of good kids with plenty to do. Still, they got bored. If they had cars they usually drove around, sometimes drag racing on the back roads outside of town, until they were low on gas. Then, they parked along Main Street, tailpipes pointed toward the railroad tracks, listening to music and talking about nothing until three a.m.

Chuck Hanson and Craig Conley were often found watching the traffic go by from Craig's jacked up '69 Olds 442, which had faded over the years from cherry red to chalky orange. Sometimes Chuck would say to Craig, in practiced sarcasm, "Golly gee, Craigo, here comes a semi. I don't think I can control my excitement." To which Craig might say, "Ah, that's nothin'. I was here one night when two semis came through at the same time." That was Chuck's cue to say, "No way! Two semis? Ya gotta be shittin' me, man." Usually the nights went pretty much like that. Usually.

The Wilsons knew only one thing about Idaho: It was where potatoes came from. They assumed potato fields were scattered all over just outside of town. They would have assumed that about Boise and Coeur d'Alene too. They happened to be right about Firth.

"Whoa! Tourist at one o'clock!" Craig said, sitting up straight in the shotgun seat.

"You sure?"

"Positive, man. You know anybody around here drives one of those babies? Besides, they're California plates."

"Yeah?" Chuck fired up the Olds' big V-8 and rapped the pipes. "All right!" He spun gravel onto the highway, pulling out a hundred feet behind the slow moving Lexus, and hit the brights.

"See! Told you, man."

"Hey, look." Chuck pointed across his dashboard, feeling the tassel from the mirror brush against his wrist. "It's a geek kid!"

Leonard squinted out the back window through horn rimmed glasses. Four headlights shot toward him. The car came close enough he could make out the grille through the glare. He knew he was being paranoid, but it looked like teeth.

"What's going on back there?" David Wilson wondered, frowning at his mirror. He picked up the speed a bit. The lights matched him. He flashed his own high beams to give them a clue. No response.

"Are you ready, man?" Chuck asked.

"I'm working on it, I'm working on it." Craig had twisted a number one baker into a piece of PVC pipe and was slamming it with the heel of his hand.

"Dad, they're still coming," Leonard said.

"I see them." Wilson put his foot down a little more firmly. The speed limit was 35. He thought he could risk 40. The head lights dropped back for a couple of seconds, then caught up almost immediately. He couldn't tell what kind of car it was. A junker of some sort. Well, it was capable of 40, obviously. He might have to risk a little more speed. A slight turn in the road included the bookend city limits sign Pamela had joked about. And here came the sign that allowed 55. Wilson reached over and turned on his radar detector. A warning beep would have been welcome at the moment, if it meant police were nearby. Frankly, he was a little concerned about the local delinquents who seemed to want to drive up his tailpipe.

"There!" Craig said. "It's in tighter than your asshole."

"Yeah, screw you." Chuck tromped the accelerator in response to a burst of speed from the Lexus. "Look at this. The guy thinks he can outrun us."

Doug Wilson was really not liking this. He had the Lexus up to 70. The headlights were still right on his bumper. He eyed his car phone and wondered if they had 911 service here in the outback.

"Bitchin'! Look how scared the geek looks." Chuck turned out his lights, dropped back a couple of car lengths, then flashed them on again as he floored it. "Whooie!"

"Dad!"

"I see them, I see them."

"Honey, you're going awfully fast already," said Pamela, putting one hand on the dashboard.

Wilson glanced in his mirror. He was going over 80 now, without any sign his tormentors were giving up. Maybe slowing way down would cause them to pass. Or, maybe, it would encourage them to run him off the road. Better not to risk it. "Hang on!" Wilson made his injectors fire.

"Asshole, there he goes again, just when I was ready." Craig pointed the PVC pipe out the passenger window.

"Don't worry about it, man. I can catch him." Chuck gave the Olds everything he could feed it. "I'll get up alongside him. Go for the geek!"

Over a hundred and they were still right there. Wait! They were passing. Maybe that was good. Jesus, maybe it was all they wanted all along.

"Dad, they've got a gun!"

The horrible car's front tire was even with the Lexus' back fender when Leonard shouted. His father reacted instantly. Wilson slammed on the brakes, confident the ABS would save them from a deadly skid. He thought the other car would rocket by. He thought he could turn around faster. He thought hell had been unleashed when the potato, intended for the back glass of the Lexus, came through his side window.

Not one of the engineers who designed the remarkable safety features of the Lexus had given a moment's thought to the need for protection against a potato gun.

Startled by an explosion of glass in his face, David Wilson jerked the wheel to the right at nearly a hundred miles an hour. The car became airborne as it left the road and vaulted a raised gravel driveway. A mailbox, cleverly crafted to look like a Holstein, came through the windshield and cut Pamela's life short before the airbag realized an accident was in progress. The Lexus did a flying twist and came down roof first against the far bank of the half-empty Government Canal. Water began to pour into what had been the car's interior.

The deputy's report would say, "Unsafe speed, driver error." Maybe the guy braked to avoid a jackrabbit. Since they did not see it, the officers made no connection between the wreckage and the spot of vomit a quarter mile up the road.

A coyote, scruffy and thin, trotted along the shoulder and stopped at the puddle. It tested the aroma with three short sniffs, then closed its eyes and breathed in deeply before lapping up the mess.

***

It had been too darn dry. Every day was in the 80s, at least. Some days pushed a hundred. The heat dried out cut alfalfa until it was thin and brittle. You needed a touch of moisture in it before it could be baled into decent cattle feed.

Frank closed the door on his F-350 and stood there and stretched for a minute. He yawned and shook his head. Getting kind of old for this late-night stuff, he told himself. He crawled between the fence wires and walked over to the first windrow. Frank picked up a handful of alfalfa and crushed it. Still a little dry, but the dew had plumped it up pretty well. He decided to bale.

***

When they tired of the illicit skating, Bill suggested they go to his house for a drink. There was an awkward moment when Mary asked how Pauline would react. He told her Pauline was away for the weekend. He thought she might refuse to come on those very grounds, but to his delight, she agreed to have "just one."

Bill made that "one" count. He sloshed together a vodka tonic for her that would have stopped a charging moose. His was a little lighter.

The polite host gave her a cursory tour of the house. He showed her the formal dining room they never used and the equally useful formal living room. She loved the kitchen with its southwestern motif. Mary was especially taken with the paper trim that covered the soffit across the cabinets. Cute little coyotes howled at cute little moons beneath cute little saguaro cacti. Bill had picked it out himself.

After they chatted for a few minutes in the kitchen, Bill said, "Say, there's something else I'd like to show you. Something kind of special to me." He narrowed his eyes and said in a stage whisper, "I have a secret life, you know."

"Okay." Mary laughed. "It sounds intriguing."

"Great. It's downstairs." He gestured toward her glass. "Let me fill that one more time while we're here."

"Oh, wow. I better not. I have to be careful with alcohol."

"Oh, come on. Just a little one." He grinned at her. "You might need a drink to bolster you for the upcoming experience." He put his fingers around her glass. After a moment's hesitation, she let it go.

Armed with fresh drinks they started down the stairs.

"You don't have a dungeon down here, do you?" Mary asked.

"Depends? Do you like dungeons?" Mary laughed. "Only if I'm in charge."

"Well, you'll be sorely disappointed, then. I'm in charge down here. But it's no dungeon."

He took her hand and led her barefoot across the concrete floor to the corner where the diorama stood on sawhorse legs.

"What do you think?"

He watched her eyes as they moved back and forth taking in the detail of The Place.

"It's fabulous," she said. "My god, did you do all this?"

"Yup. It's a model of the ranch where I grew up."

"Really? It's terrific. Where was it?"

"Oh, it's still there. We don't own it anymore, but it's still there. Over near Idaho Falls in a little valley on the Blackfoot River."

"And this was your home?" she asked, pointing to the miniature log structure in the middle of the diorama.

"That's just what it looked like." He reached into the wire basket next to his computer and pulled out the aerial of The Place. "See, this was taken in 1959."

She took the picture from him, holding it carefully along the edges.

"It's just like being in the same airplane," she said. "Look at that. There's the barn, and the house, and the outbuildings. There's the little lake. Even the corrals."

"I'm still working on it, but it's almost there." He stretched across the diorama and picked up the little barn. "See here, where the hole is on the back? There was a door there on the original, but I can't for the life of me remember just what it was like."

Mary examined the building. "It's so perfect. If you were two inches tall you could live there."

Bill chuckled. "Yeah. Too bad we're not two inches tall. We could go exploring together."

He gently set the barn back in place.

"You know," he said. "I'm planning to go back there sometime soon. I want to get another look at that barn door." He hesitated. "This is going to sound a little strange. In fact ... No, it's silly."

"What's silly? Tell me."

"Well, I was just thinking that I'd like you to see The Place. I'd like to show it to you."

Mary took a sip of her vodka tonic. "I'd love to see it sometime. If it's half as beautiful as your model, it must be really something." She ran her fingers delicately along the miniature gravel road that dipped and rose like a kiddie coaster across the backs of gentle hills. "Living in Boise, it's easy to forget there are still places like this left in Idaho."

Her fingers stroked the little roadway. Admired it. Loved it. Bill felt such a surge of emotions seeing that gentle touch he thought he might explode. He felt an ultimate affinity for this woman. Mary understood. She understood his every feeling. He knew he could trust her with his life just as she could trust him.

In that intimate moment, he nearly told her his deepest secret. It would be so easy standing together where they were. The flip of a switch; the keying of a password. But it could wait. There were other intimacies to reveal.

They climbed the stairs to the kitchen, where they talked away the night. Despite her objections, Bill kept topping off her drink. That she kept sipping was evidence to him her protests were only a polite social show. By 1 a.m. neither of them was in a condition to drive. Mary was barely in a condition to walk. He half-carried her to the bedroom, where they made slow, languid love. It was dream love for him. For her, too, he saw. She was deep in untroubled sleep when he rolled over and hit the pillow himself.

***

In the moonlight he ran the Baja with his trusty navigator beside him calling out the corners. "You've got a 45 degree right that slopes left, followed fast by a wild dip coming up," Mildred said, reading her notes by flashlight. "Then there's a series of slow second-gear switchbacks before we get an 85 mile-an-hour straight for seven tenths of a mile."

The little Ford was running fine. Frank had been around about four times, chugging out crisp new bales from the clattering machine behind him. Even in the bright moonlight he would have missed the man if he hadn't stepped in front of the fender lights. Frank stepped on the clutch and levered down the throttle.

The guy, who was wearing a dark blue robe, walked up to him quickly, stopping in front of the crawler's left rear wheel. He yelled something. Frank turned the key and killed the engine, leaving the lights still burning.

"Pardon me?" Frank said.

"What the hell do you think you're doing?" asked the man in the robe.

"I'm baling hay."

"At one o-fucking-clock in the morning?"

"It's when the dew is right," Frank answered. In the beam of his lights he saw the legs of a pair of red pajamas sticking out below the robe. It looked like the man might have slippers on.

"I'm sorry, did I wake you?"

"No shit you woke me! Me and everyone else in the fucking subdivision, I imagine."

The man's language should keep him awake saying prayers asking forgiveness, Frank thought.

"I'm sorry the noise disturbs you. I'll finish as quickly as I can."

"Finish!? You can finish in the morning, asshole."

"Too dry in the morning," Frank explained. "I can't bale then. I really will hurry, though." He turned the key back on and pressed the starter button with his thumb.

The man reached in front of Frank's knees and twisted the key. "I don't care what your fucking problem is, Farmer Brown, I need my sleep."

Frank stared at the man. His hair was stuck up in all directions and his eyes were wild.

"My name isn't Brown, mister. But I am a farmer. You're right about that. And a farmer has to farm when the time is right. A farmer can't wait because it's too hot or too cold or too dark. Now, if you'll excuse me, I have a crop to bring in."

He turned the key and pressed the button again. Again, the man reached across and turned the tractor off. This time he twisted the key like he was trying to remove it. Frank pushed the man away with his foot and started the tractor again. He put it in second and eased forward, expecting the man to jump out of his way. Instead, he made another lunge for the key. Frank blocked him with his knee. The man grabbed hold of Frank's shirtsleeve and pulled. Frank pulled back, but the man would not let go. The next thing Frank knew, the man had one leg over the axle of the tractor and was scrambling to climb up. He got both feet on the axle, and grabbed hold of the steering wheel with his free hand.

The man put his face in Frank's face and yelled. "You fucking farmer, I paid $50,000 for that lot and $150,000 for the house!"

He plunged his hand between Frank's legs and grabbed for the key. Frank shoved him away.

The man half-stood on the axle to catch his balance, wobbled, and fell backwards. Frank felt the left side of the tractor lift like it had just crossed an irrigation dike. He slammed on the brakes and killed the engine. The night was suddenly quiet enough for sleep.

In the moonlight he could see the form lying still behind the rear wheel of the little Ford. Frank brought his hands up to his cheeks.

"God save me," he whispered. "I'm going to jail for farming."

CHAPTER THIRTEEN

The shape he was and nothing more

In which Mary has third thoughts, Jake carves tourists, The Private does a good deed, Idaho has an explosive situation, Debbie gets the point, and Bill heads for The Dunes.

Sunday morning. His favorite time of the week. He liked nothing better than waking up at his leisure and spending a couple hours with coffee and toast and the pregnant Sunday paper. Until this morning. This morning he found something he liked better. He woke up next to the naked form of Mary Lewis. The paper could wait.

She lay sprawled next to him in his bed, a rumpled sheet pulled up nearly to her navel. Her raven hair flowed over her left shoulder and spread like a river delta on her pillow and across one breast. He wanted to touch her, to smooth his fingers over her skin and feel the soft, gentle curve of her waist. He wanted to kiss her tenderly on her neck, her breast, her tummy. He wanted to wake her and echo the lovemaking of the magical night before. Above all, he wanted to watch her. There had surely never been a more beautiful sight.

He could be content staring at her forever, oblivious of the up and down sun announcing the passing of endless days. No joy could be greater, he thought, until he saw her stir. Impossibly his spirits soared. This sculpture, this masterpiece next to him showed signs of transcendence. First, her unopened eyes squinted as if they were too sensitive for even the dim light in that gray room. Then, she slowly lifted and rolled her chin, licking her lips with the very tip of her tongue. One hand moved to her beautiful forehead which rippled into tiny furrows for a moment. Finally, she opened her eyes. She blinked and looked at the ceiling for a moment, then tilted her chin until it touched her chest and stared into the darkened room at the foot of the bed.

Lying beside her, propped up on one elbow, Bill watched the blossom unfold. He saw awareness seeping into her, one muscle at a time, until she was all there, with him in the wakened world.

Mary took in the room, the bed, her own naked body. Then, she quickly turned and looked straight into his face. Bill smiled broadly. If he were thinking about anything but that magic moment, he would have guessed the next moment would see her return his smile. And in the next, he might have kissed her. And in the next they would come together in a lover's embrace.

The moment of awareness came. Mary's face hardened. The masterpiece that was her became a sculpture of ice. She stared at him no longer than two seconds, then bolted from the bed. She stood there hugging herself, her eyes tracking the lay of the room, then grabbed a handful of clothing from the foot of the bed and stalked into the bathroom.

Stunned, Bill remained there next to the empty indentation her body had made in the bedding. He could smell the earthy perfume of her on the cooling sheets. From the bathroom he heard the muted gurgle of the toilet flushing. Then he stopped breathing, waiting to hear another familiar sound. He hoped to hear the spray of the shower against the tile stall. She might simply be embarrassed by the morning scents of one night's love. She might shower and dry herself with one of the big, fluffy towels Pauline preferred, then slip back between the sheets, warm and soft and fresh, ready to love him again.

He did not hear the shower. Some rustling came from the bathroom, and finally a short, sharp zip. Mary opened the door and stepped into the bedroom, more or less dressed. She bent down and grabbed a bra, stuffing it into her back pocket.

In an edgy voice, she said, "Where are my shoes?" She bent again, recovering first one sock, then another.

Bill sat up. "You didn't have shoes. Just your skates." He swung his legs over the edge of the bed.

"Stay right there!" she said, pointing a finger that skewered him to the spot.

"Mary, what's wrong?"

She bent one leg up like a crane and began to pull on her sock. "What's wrong? You sit there in that ... that bed, and ask me what's wrong?"

Bill turned to look at the bed, as if it really held some answer. It was a common bed, a king-size mattress, with king-size sheets and three king-size pillows scattered across the rumpled bedding. The only thing wrong with it, from his perspective, was its emptiness. He slowly shook his head..

"I don't understand."

Mary had worked both socks onto her feet. She kicked Bill's shirt out of the way, and bent to pick up something else.

"Do you understand these?" She held up a pair of black lace panties. "I was wearing these last night."

Bill frowned at her. What was making her so angry?

"I don't remember taking them off," she said.

He gave her a halfhearted grin. "Mary, you probably don't remember a lot of things. You were kind of blasted."

"Who took them off?" She shouted it.

Before he could answer, she yanked the bra from her back pocket.

"And who took this off, Clark? Was it elves, maybe?"

"Well, it's hard to remember the exact sequence. We were making love, after all. I don't remember all the details that led up to it."

"You don't?" Mary asked. "You don't remember details? Do you remember giving me maybe one little drink somewhere along the line? Maybe even more than one? My head feels like it's going to explode."

"We had some drinks, sure."

"Who took them off, Clark?" she asked again, holding up her underclothes.

"Look, Mary ... "

"Who took them off?"

"Okay, okay. I did, all right? What's wrong with that? It's not like I raped you."

Mary closed her eyes and tilted her head back. She took in a long slow breath, then released it.

"I know when I've been raped, Clark." She folded her arms and looked at the floor. Evenly, she said, "I've had some experience with that."

She had been raped? The revelation struck him to the core. That someone could hurt her in the worst of ways left him speechless. He wanted to comfort her, to say soothing words that would make it all right. He wanted to take her in his arms and cuddle her, protecting her from the world. But, had he heard right? Was she accusing him of rape, too?

"Mary, no. It wasn't like that. We were having a good time. One thing led to another. You enjoyed it, too."

"Did I?" she said, sarcastically. "I'll have to take your word for it. I don't remember a thing after about the fourth drink."

"Hey, come on. I didn't force you to drink. I didn't poor vodka and tonic down your throat."

Mary looked away. She said nothing for a few heartbeats.

"I know I share some blame. I should have known better than to take the first drink. It almost always leads to trouble for me. That's why I rarely drink at all. I should have known better than to come back here with you." Gesturing toward the bed, she said, "Hell, I should have known better than to think having a friendship with a man might not lead to this, just once." She stuffed her bra and panties into the pockets of her shorts. "Goodbye, Clark."

"Wait, don't go," Bill said. "We need to talk about this."

"No. We don't need to talk," she said, quietly. "I know you think you're innocent. I'll never change your mind about that. Maybe you are innocent, in a way. Maybe I'm the guilty one. I don't care who's right and who's wrong. I just don't want to break up a marriage."

"You're not breaking us up. Pauline and I are on the rocks, anyway. It wouldn't have lasted even if you hadn't come along."

"I didn't 'come along.' I've been living my life for years without even knowing you existed, Clark. I plan to live the rest of it as if you didn't."

She slipped out the door and slammed it behind her. Bill sat there on the edge of the bed. A few minutes later he heard his front door close, then he heard the familiar click and rumble of tiny wheels rolling down his driveway fast, then faster.

***

The rifle crack echoed in the canyon, taking the center stage of sound from the churning Payette River for one second. Jake leaned his Winchester against a crosscut round and got to his feet. He dusted off the back of his jeans and walked across the lot to retrieve his latest creations. Good shot, this one. He always tried for the exact center of the forehead, right between and just above the eyes. The slug was off to the left a little and about an inch high on the first one. Not perfection, just art. The other one was about the same, high and to the left.

Jake grabbed the tiny tourists by their necks and carried them back to the shop. These two would sell right away, he figured. Sometimes they split a little and almost ruined the effect he was looking for. Once in a while, one would split right down the middle, spoiling the whole dang carving: Half an hour's work right down the drain.

He set the wooden tourists down next to three others on the front row. Behind them were rows of squirrels, eagles, owls and deer, along with a few jumping fish. There was still a demand for those, but the goofy tourists were definitely the hot item. Eighty-five bucks for a fat, buck toothed, big-eared wooden man in Bermuda shorts with two cameras hanging from his neck. The tourists ate 'em up, especially the ones with the genuine thirty-ought-six slug in their forehead. Jesus people were stupid, Jake thought. They didn't even know when you were making fun of them.

"Maybe I ought to try hanging one from under the eaves," Jake said to Charlene. She was fanning herself beneath the ramada during a lull between customers. "You know, with a hangman's noose around their scrawny little necks."

Charlene shook her head in exasperation. "You always got to push it, don't you," she said.

"Push what? They like this shit."

Charlene sat on a bale of straw, leaning back on her hands. She turned her head and gazed down river for a few seconds. "Can't argue that," she said. "They like it, and it is shit."

They'd had this conversation before. It was the one where she told him how he was wasting his talent, and where he told her there wasn't no talent to it. He had the conversation pretty well memorized for life, so Jake ignored her and walked back to his shop to get another tourist.

There was one left. He would put a slug in it, then knock off for lunch. Some days he stayed with Charlene to keep her company. She was in a pissy mood today. He would make the climb to the ponderosa instead.

Jake plopped the tourist down in the target zone and kicked some gravel under it so it stood up straight. Crap, he thought. There was already a hairline crack in the forehead of this one. He considered letting it live. There was still a market for tourists without holes. Then decided to risk it. He liked shooting them more than anything. Carving tourists was not any more fun than carving squirrels, really. Oh, he got a little kick out of seeing if he could make each one more stupid than the last, but that was hard to do. You could only do so much stupid. Shooting them was the real fun. He loved getting their whole head in his scope, seeing their goofy expressions looking right at him, then squeezing off a shot. Usually the impact knocked them over. Once in a while they would rock back and forth like a bowling pin about to go down, then settle right back in their original spot. He liked that the best because he could see the hole happen. One second their foreheads were as smooth as an oak table top; the next pow!, they were knotty pine.

Jake liked to shoot sitting down with his elbows propped on his knees. He wrapped his wrist through the strap of the ought-six in that familiar way that almost made it a part of his arm. Then he closed his left eye, sighted in, breathed out and held it, then squeeeeezed one off. It was better than sex. Hell, it practically was sex for him lately. Charlene carried her art criticism to the bedroom most of the time.

One more tourist, then lunch. Jake hunkered down into position and put his eye up close to the scope. There was that familiar goofy grin he loved to hate. You couldn't see the crack at all. Maybe it would be all right. He adjusted his aim a tad, compensating for the little breeze that probably threw him off a few minutes earlier. He released his breath and held it. Squeeeeze. Crack. A different crack this time.

"Son of a bitch," Jake muttered. "Fucker split." He eased the rifle down a fraction and saw two perfect halves lying on the gravel like someone with a big damn splitting wedge had pounded them apart.

Jake stood up slapping his jeans and cursing. From behind him Charlene called, "Serves you right. Should've made a squirrel."

"Yeah, yeah," he said. He picked up his rifle and started back to the shop. After taking a few steps he glanced in the direction of the ruined carving and stopped. Something was not right. He brought the rifle up to his shoulder and looked through the scope. Upriver a quarter mile he saw a little station wagon parked in the dirt on the point a little ways off the highway. Sometimes people fished there, though Jake never could understand why. The fishing was lousy in that spot. Two people were there now, just below the station wagon on the sloping bank of the river. What were they doing? He watched for a few seconds, then lowered the rifle.

Jake leaned the ought-six up against the side of the building and hurried into his shop. He had a dusty old pair of army surplus binoculars sitting up on the back of his bench. He grabbed them and swiped at the lenses with the tail of his t-shirt, then stepped to where he could see the river and the road above it. He closed his left eye—never could make a damn pair of binoculars work with both eyes open—and focused in on the people up stream. A middle aged woman dressed in polyester slacks was scrambling up the bank toward the car. California plates, he noticed. Just below her a man was sprawled out on the bank, one foot in the water. A fishing pole lay next to him. An Igloo cooler sat near his feet. Off to one side Jake saw a crumpled hat lying in the gravel. He made himself look at each of those items for a few seconds as if they mattered in some way. Finally, he focused on the man himself. The binocs were a powerful old pair. Even with the trembling of his hands he saw it clearly. Unless the guy was Hindu, he had a hole in his forehead. Dead center.

Jake let the binoculars drop in the dirt. He stood there staring at the scene up river. After a moment he shuffled around like some mechanical thing and stared at the tools hung over his workbench. He saw a line of screwdrivers stuck in pegboard, saws and clamps hung from hooks, the painted outline of a missing hammer, and pliers in their proper place. His favorite Stihl was sitting on the work top. Beneath the bench was the big McCulloch, just gathering dust. What had it been, two years? Three? Jake horsed the saw out and checked the tank. Empty, like it was supposed to be. He slopped a quart of gas in it, then headed across the road and up the hill toward the lone Ponderosa. This time, he forgot his lunch.

***

Bev Williams could not believe her luck. She had gone into Ontario, Oregon for her shopping to avoid the sales tax, like she always did. Like always she had picked up half a dozen lottery tickets with the money she figured she had saved, and like always that was a waste of time. Bev had dropped a dozen eggs in the parking lot trying to get her groceries into the car while she was keeping track of Nicholas, who was two. She was only able to save three of them. Then, on the way back into Idaho, as she crossed the bridge over the Snake River, her right front tire blew.

Her Escort rocked like a grenade had hit it every time a semi blasted by, which they did about every six seconds, none of them stopping to help her either, thank you very much. Bev had wrestled with the jack until she had the flat tire far enough off the ground to remove it. Then she actually tried taking the wheel off and discovered that it just spun in circles when she twisted a lug nut. At that point she stalked around the car to make sure the emergency brake was set and put the transmission in gear. When she got to the driver's door another truck came by, pulling a tornado behind it. She made herself thin against the side of the car and felt the hem of her dress flap up against her neck. Bev heard the long blast of an air horn and felt another gust from hell.

"Bastards," she spat. "I hope they got themselves a show."

She quickly opened the door and slid inside. Bev made a quick swipe at her itchy nose with one finger, then looked at her hands. They were covered in road grime from the tire. Bev cocked the mirror and saw a half mustache etched across one side of her lip.

"Fuck!"

"Momma? What's fuck?"

She turned and gave Nicholas the imitation of a smile. "Nothing sweetie, Mom's just having a bad day."

"I hep?"

"No, I don't think you can help me. I have to do this myself, I guess."

"Hep?"

Bev put the shifter into second, checked her outside mirror and opened the door. "Hep?" she heard Nicholas say, just before she stepped out onto the interstate again.

Bev was cranking the fourth and last lug nut when the man walked up. Maybe she did not see him because she was concentrating so hard her eyes were squeezed shut. The man wore a green field jacket, which Bev would have noticed as completely out of place on a 90 degree day. If she had seen him.

Nicholas, meanwhile, had worked his way out of the straps and buckles on the car seat, chanting "Hep, hep, hep," practically the whole time. The rear door would have presented a problem for him normally, because he was not a big boy, yet. This time, he barely touched the lever and the door swung open, thanks to the way the car was tilted by the jack. Nicholas scrambled down onto the pavement and stood there.

"Mom? Hep?" He had taken two steps toward the center line when the man picked him up. A semi zoomed by oblivious to anything but schedules.

The rush of wind and big noise scared Nicholas quiet, not to mention the fact he had been picked up and lifted into the sky.

"It's okay little people," the man said. "You don't want to walk on this trail."

Nicholas stared at the man and realized he had never seen him before. Instantly he started to cry.

"Hey, hey you're safe." The man made a face for Nicholas that made him laugh. It was a furry face. Then the man put him back in the car. All four doors locked when he nodded at the child. Bev would be furious in a few minutes when she found she was locked out. The man made another face—a rabbit this time—and waved bye-bye, then walked down the road, whistling. Bev did not hear the tune, but she could not get it out of her head for days. Something by the B-52s.

A hundred feet toward Oregon, the man put one hand on the bridge railing and jumped over the edge, landing in the sloping gravel. He slipped under the bridge and began to work, oblivious to the thunder of traffic above his head. Nicholas would have liked to hep him. He loved Play Dough.

This stuff was fun, too. The man worked it between his fingers and watched it squish out, then started pushing it in the crack between the top of one upright support and the cross support of the concrete decking. He put a good wad of it in there, and packed more of it all along the angle of one side. It looked okay. This was a new thing. Interesting. He had not bothered to learn everything about it.

He began packing the stuff into the cracks at the top of the other two supports. By the time he got to the third one he thought he was an expert. He could make his fingers small and shove it way back in there. Fun!

The next thing was not as much fun. He had a silver thing that looked like a reed cut down to the size of a little people's littlest finger. The string in his pocket was supposed to go inside that, then he was supposed to set the string on fire. Seemed silly. He liked that.

He poked the silver thing into the soft stuff. It wiggled where he put it first, so he moved it into the crack on top of the support. He frowned at what was happening there. Sometimes, when a big loud thing came over the bridge, the weight of it pushed down on the squishy stuff and squished some of it out. He thought it was probably important that the silver thing not get squished out, so he wedged it in there real tight.

Something was coming on the bridge. It sounded big. He jumped down and stepped out to where he might see. It was a BIG Loud Thing, okay. That would be a good test to see if the silver thing stayed in the squishy stuff. The BIG Loud Thing pulled some Big Yellow Thing behind it. As it came across the part of the bridge where he had worked, Coyote leaned down to where he could see the squishy stuff and the silver thing. So far so good. He straightened to get a look at the BIG Loud Thing and...

He was in the water. How did he get in the water? He was standing on the shore looking at the BIG Loud Thing, looking at the bridge, and now he was in the water. Other things were falling in the water around him: big things and little things. The water was splashing all around him, yet he did not hear the sound. That was a new thing. The BIG Loud Thing was falling in the water, too. For some reason the Big Yellow Thing was now pulling the BIG Loud Thing, and it wanted to be in the water. And here was another new thing. He was having a hard time floating in the river because his legs would not work. And another new thing, he was surrounded by snakes. No, wait. The snakes were coming from him. Snakes and snakes and snakes were coming out of him where his legs were supposed to be. Then he understood, and laughed and laughed. The joke was on him. He had killed himself. It had been a long time since that had happened.

***

Subscribing to *The Private* was a whim. Debbie remembered being in a dark mood over the sale of the homestead when she saw the little ad: "Tired of tourists and traffic? Sick of Californians and crowding? Do you yearn for yesterday's Idaho?" She sent in her $14. As soon as the letter was irretrievable she regretted sending it. What a foolish waste of money. Charlie would tease her about it, she just knew it.

The first issue of the newsletter had come the week after. By that time she had forgotten about it. Charlie had picked up the mail and tossed it on the kitchen table without even looking at it. She saw one corner of the masthead peeking out of the stack. It was just three quarters of the chevron. Enough to jog her memory. Debbie slipped it out of the pile of ads and bills and hid the newsletter temporarily in the back of the knife drawer.

A week and a day later, she remembered it was there. The dark mood that made her subscribe was back, and blacker. When she reached into the drawer to retrieve it, the blackest thought she ever had made her hesitate, her hand hanging for a moment over the handle of Charlie's best carving knife. She imagined it buried to its heel in Bill Baker's chest. The thought tantalized, then repulsed her in quick succession. She grabbed the newsletter and yanked it out, catching the heel of her hand on the tip of the knife. It was a tiny cut; didn't even need a Band-Aid.

She read the horror stories from readers and the clips picked up from papers around the state. She read about favorite fishing holes trampled and trashed, and good farmland being sold to developers. She read the tips section. It was as mean as she felt. She read about Idahoans being priced out of recreation in their own backyard. She read, then reread a story about a protest being organized at Bruneau Dunes State Park. Debbie checked her calendar, and read the story again.

***

Bill had his backpack, dome tent, sleeping bag and hi tech air pad rolled up in the back of the Explorer, ready for the overnight at Bruneau. He planned to get there about six, check in with the park manager, then hike for 15 minutes to the picture point where he would stay the night. He figured his chance of getting any sleep was about nil.

Interstate 84 between Boise and Mountain Home covered only 37 miles. It was the longest 37 miles in the state. Even someone who loved every square inch of Idaho, as Bill Clark did, had to admit there were more scenic drives. A trained eye could spot the bones of shield volcanoes hidden beneath a few inches of topsoil, cheatgrass and sagebrush on either side of the road. Looking toward the horizon, that eye could imagine where the ancient lakes, Bruneau and Idaho, had lapped up on the gentle shores of what were now respectable mountains. That eye could spot Sinker Butte in the distance to the south, and contemplate the massacre that took place not far away, or remember how the Owyhee Mountains to the southwest were named for Hawaiian natives who were lost there on a fur trapping expedition. By the time that thinking was done, with a little thinking about the Snake River Birds of Prey area and the Oregon Trail thrown in to keep from getting bored, there would be about three hours of thinking time left before the Mountain Home city limits sign. Or so it seemed. Bill had thought all those thoughts so many times he could turn his head in a one hundred and eighty degree sweep a couple of miles outside of Boise and just tick the trivia off, a, b, c, d. There. Done.

Now, with the Road That Never Ends before him, Bill had plenty of time to think, as well as time to avoid thinking about some things. Mary Lewis dominated his thoughts, though he valiantly tried driving her out of his mind by listening to the B-52s on CD. Bill felt like someone had taken an ice cream scoop to his insides, scraping out the last little bit of good stuff and leaving only the container. That night, when he thought she understood him, wanted him, loved him, he felt transcendence. He was becoming the man he always wanted to be, and she was the catalyst. Their night of lovemaking had given him wings to soar away. His dreams were made Manifest. Then came the morning. Her misunderstanding left him an empty chrysalis, the shape he was and nothing more.

It was a misunderstanding; some miscommunication that could be explained away. If she would only listen. She thought he had raped her, for god sakes! Didn't rape imply intent? He had not intended rape, therefore it could not be rape.

Couldn't she understand that? And, he hadn't forced her. She had not resisted in any way, that he could remember. Of course, he had been drinking too. He remembered little of it himself, beyond the sense of joy he felt having her in his arms, the sense of Destiny.

She had been raped before. That someone would do that to her—really do it to her—repelled him. If he knew who it was he would kill them for what they did. He loved her that much.

The B-52s were getting on his nerves, telling him over and over "You better change the state of mind you're in." He stabbed the stop button, switching the sound from CD to radio.

The local news was ending. The announcer, sounding almost breathless, said, "Repeating our top story, an explosion rocked southwestern Idaho this afternoon, disrupting traffic on the major route entering the state. At 2:45 p.m. the east bound lanes of the 1-84 bridge over the Snake River near Ontario, Oregon were destroyed by a bomb. A truck driver on the bridge at the time was injured when he lost control of his rig and rolled into the median. He was taken by Life Flite to St. Alphonsus hospital in Boise where he is in serious condition at this hour. Police believe someone else, perhaps the bomber, was also seriously injured in the blast, though they are not releasing details. Calls to this station have credited the anti-tourism, anti-growth group Private Idaho for the explosion." There was a promise of further details as the story developed.

A semi blasted its horn as it flew by him. Bill looked at his speedometer. The needle drifted just under 30. He pulled over into the emergency lane and stopped, killing the engine. He sat there feeling the Explorer rock every time a vehicle passed. Looking out on the desert that was once the bottom of an ocean-sized lake, Bill Clark's mind chased the familiar. Sagebrush. Very common in southern Idaho. Pollinates in the fall. Big cause of hay fever. Cheatgrass. Some people called it

June grass, because it was green for a couple of weeks about then before turning a gray brown for the rest of the year. It was an accidental import from Europe where they had used it as cover on sod-roofed homes. A big fire hazard every summer when lightning struck. Red-tailed hawk. A common raptor... Twenty minutes later he wiped his trembling hands on the legs of his jeans and started the engine.

CHAPTER FOURTEEN

The sorrow he saw

In which Bill walks in the shadows, Debbie sees another sign, Jo Beth plays chauffeur, and the sun comes up over the mountain.

Setting up the tent took less than five minutes. Unrolling his sleeping bag and mat consumed a minute more. He lingered over his ham sandwich and Coke, killing a half hour. The sun was planning to hang around for another hour and a half. After that, it would be only seven more hours until sunrise. Seven hours in the sleepless dark with himself for company. Bill Clark wanted another companion.

He had his camera with him ready for tomorrow's sunrise to turn the dunes into shadow-carved sculptures of themselves. He toyed with the idea of dragging out his gear and taking a few evening shots, then discarded the thought. True, he might get some interesting shadows on sand ripples, or clever composition with animal tracks. He was on the wrong side of the dunes to get good evening panoramics. It wasn't worth the hike to change that. The sky was cloudless, so there wasn't any chance of a decent sunset. Besides, he did not have the energy to take the Nikon from its case, set up the tripod and fuss about sand getting into everything. He barely had energy to sit.

So he sat, tuning around the dial on his portable radio trying to catch more news of the explosion. He heard the story seven times on network newscasts. He listened hard to every take on the incident without learning anything new. One thing new. Traffic was now being routed around the bridge in a sixty-mile detour. They expected to turn the westbound lanes into a temporary, two-way stretch sometime Monday.

Each story mentioned that Private Idaho had taken credit for the blast. Bill kept listening for word that a chevron had been found painted somewhere nearby. That word never came. Without the chevron, he held hope the bomber was an opportunist in a misguided effort to gain notoriety. That hope thinned, then popped like a soap bubble when NBC began calling Private Idaho a terrorist group.

Bill pulled the earpiece out and let the radio drop to the floor of his tent, oblivious to the insect noises that now came from the tiny speaker. Crickets outside the tent nearly drowned it out, chirping a background blanket of sound that was the pulse of the desert at night. He lay back on his sleeping bag and closed his eyes. Flashes of red and roiling smoke appeared on the back of his lids the moment he did. His eyes snapped open. The sun was half an hour over the far side of the horizon, so he could see stars fading forth through the net window at his feet. He concentrated on those tiny points of light to drive out the images his mind kept fighting for him to see. He wished upon the stars. He wished he were upon them.

One refuge had never failed him. Whenever the stress of living in the present proved too much, Bill Clark took a trip to the past. He would find that familiar boy and his faithful dog walking beneath the towering cottonwoods on their way to explore the tangled grove they called The Jungle, or join them for a swim in the cool smooth waters of the Blackfoot River, or locate The Place in a time before That Time.

So he went back, as he had a dozen times a day for more than thirty years. Staring at the stars, he searched for one time of comfort among the many. Only one time came. He started down that memory path, then stopped and looked for another. It kept coming back. He searched his mind for memories of straw stack forts and dirt bank cities. He looked again for the rocket ship in a grain of wheat and the speedboat in a walnut shell. He sought the feel of hard-packed dirt beneath balloon tires and the smell of dust kicked up by a lizard that had just lost its tail. Nothing would come to him. Nothing but that day in fifth grade. He knew that memory well enough to never visit. Tonight, it was the only one he had. Finally, with every other door closing, he opened that one. Even there was better than here.

Mrs. Aikens was marveling over art at the front of the room. She shared magazine prints of The Blue Boy and The Harvest with children more interested in the backs of their own hands. Billy Clark was especially concerned about his hands. He had a real problem. It started with the rocket ships in his ballpoint pen. Every retractable pen had a fleet of them, if you knew where to look. First, you took the pen apart. The pointy part where you put your fingers made a good one, shaped like a bullet. The top half of the pen was almost the same shape, and it had the clip which was a natural cabin for the pilots in Billy's eyes. The real rockets were inside. After you took off the spring, the refill made kind of a goofy rocket, a little too long and thin. Okay, for a transport or a cargo ship. The clicker was the best. It made an inch-long rocket Flash Gordon would be proud to ride. The long, narrow body flared out at the bottom into a series of teeth that made perfect landing fins. Better yet, it had a booster, like the Mercury missions, nested inside where the flames came out. That squatty little ship always had four stubby fins. It could be an alien vessel in a pinch.

Today, the troop transport had turned on him. Somehow, it leaked ink all over his hands. It might have been rocket fuel or oil for the Mars colony on another day, but Billy was in school. And in trouble. Mrs. Aikens had warned him more than once to quit playing with his pen. Now, there he sat with the evidence of his crime in plain view, wondering what to do.

When Mrs. Baird, their neighbor from across the field, knocked on the door he thought he was in luck. Billy waited until the teacher's back was turned to crumple a sheet of composition paper between his hands, wiping the worst of it off. When Mrs. Aikens turned and called his name he thought it was all over. But no, she wanted him to go with Mrs. Baird. Saved! He hid his hands behind his binder and made his escape.

Billy was so relieved to miss the lecture, so happy he was not on his way to the principal's office that he did not think to ask why Mrs. Baird was taking him home. He did not ask when she told him the story from when she was in school about how she had gotten in trouble for chasing a ball across new grass. He did not ask when she talked about how wonderful the weather was and wasn't it nice they would get a third crop of hay this year. He did not wonder why Mrs. Baird, who had never spoken more than five words to him at once was now talking like they had been fast friends forever.

He did not wonder as they drove the seven miles of rural roads from the elementary school to the mailbox at the top of the hill. When Mrs. Baird quit talking that last quarter mile as they drove down the dirt lane to his house he did not wonder. And when he saw his mother kneel at the end of the walk and grab him in her arms he only wondered one thing. Why was she saying "Daddy" when they always called him Pop?

Bill closed his eyes tight. When he opened them again, the stars were a blur. He fumbled for the earphone, letting the tinny, distant sound be his guide. Better to listen to someone else's thoughts about Congress or the Mets than his own.

Sometime later he fell asleep. He did not remember turning off the radio. No sound came from it when he woke abruptly at 3:00 a.m. It was the absence of sound that awakened him. The crickets were quiet. So quiet they might have been on another planet.

Bill closed his eyes and tried to drift back to sleep. He tried to concentrate on nothing, a commodity in great supply both inside and outside the tent. Looking at his lids he felt like he was floating in space, a vacuum where crickets used sign language. The feeling of nothingness around him was so intense he had to open his eyes. The absence was true only for sound. The inside of his tent was so bright he might have been camped beneath a streetlight.

Bill threw back the sleeping bag and sat up. Maybe sleep would come if he would go pee. He slipped on his boots, letting the laces dangle, then unzipped the inner and outer flaps just enough to let him crawl from his tiny tent like a pupating insect. Outside he stood and stretched, looking up at the moon. The reflection its full face sent back to him was so bright he shaded his sleep-widened eyes for a moment.

Fifty feet away he found a sagebrush that looked thirsty. The trickle of water soaked silently into the sand. Bill started to walk back to his tent. He looked up and saw the dunes. An instant thrill of deja vu coursed through him. The bright white moon hung over the smooth curves of the rolling mountains of sand like an audition for an Ansel Adams print. Like a mural on a wall.

He felt the hair prickle on the back of his neck. After a few seconds he took a deep breath and smiled. What did he expect this scene to look like? The mural in the tunnel had been painted by someone who had stood about here to sketch the scene. Or, maybe they took a photo from this point, as a dozen travel writers would in three hours. It made about as much sense to be frightened by the Eiffel Tower upon seeing it and realizing it looked just like all those pictures.

Something moved. Bill caught it out of the corner of his eye. Or was it a trick of the moonlight? No, there it was again. Something in the gully where two small dunes met a hundred feet away. Some kind of animal. Bill looked hard to make it out. It was in shadow, but he thought he could see it moving his way. Yes. It was a coyote, coming right up the draw toward him. Bill stood perfectly still so as not to frighten it. The animal trotted toward him, its gray fur barely visible against the creamy sand in the moonlight. It looked right at him and kept on trotting.

It had to see him. He was standing in full moonlight. It kept on coming. Bill thought about waving an arm to make sure he had been seen. He was reluctant to do so. You did not often get this close to wildlife. The coyote stopped about ten feet away. It stood there a second next to the bush where Bill had peed, then lifted its leg and did the same. When it finished the coyote stared at him for a moment, winked, then turned and trotted back the way he had come.

A cool breeze kicked up, combing through the hairs on Bill's arms.

It had winked. Probably just sand in its eye, but it had winked. Bill had never been so close to a wild coyote in his life. They were wary creatures, primed to run at the slightest sign of danger. Maybe they winked all the time when you got close, how did he know? Curious, he walked over to where the animal had marked, hoping to get some better measure of its size by the tracks it left. He knelt in the moonlight, then dropped to his hands and knees. There were no tracks. He crawled slowly forward feeling the soft sand. A stinkbug, out on some early errand, stalked in front of him, leaving behind a fragile sketch of its path.

Bill got up and went back to the sagebrush. Kneeling down he breathed in deep through his nose, expecting the acrid smell of coyote urine. Nothing. Hesitantly, he bent and felt the surface for moisture. The sand was dry. It could not be dry. He peed here himself not three minutes ago. Bill felt all around the roots of the bush, then touched the sand around its neighbors. His own tracks led right to the first sagebrush and stopped. He checked, and checked again until the first gray smudge of dawn began to fade the stars in the east.

***

Debbie Bennett Anderson tapped the top of her alarm at 4 am. Next to her Charlie muttered something and turned over. This was the perfect time for her to do the same. Their bedroom was dark as a mine shaft. A little breezed came in off the desert through the window, sending a shiver across her shoulders. It was the perfect time to scoot back down into the bed and pull the covers up to her neck. Dawn would come no matter where she was.

She threw the covers back and searched for slippers with her toes. If dawn came while she was still in bed it would mean she had given up. Going to the dunes to stand around carrying a sign wasn't much, but it was something. She hoped it would make her feel a little less helpless.

***

Gawd, that disc jockey was so predictable. Every morning for a week the same song was playing when she hit the snooze button on her radio. Mary tapped it to silence and lay there a few seconds trying to decide if another ten minutes was worth getting jolted awake twice. She looked at the digital readout: 4:01. Oh yeah, this wasn't just another normal day at the office. She jumped out of bed and headed for the shower with the earworm from that miserable song writhing around in her head. "Where do I go from here to a better state than this?"

***

Jo Beth jockeyed the rented stretch van around the circle and under the portico. She could have had someone else drive them to the dunes. Would have, under normal circumstances. After the opening night dinner disaster, she was making sure there were no more mistakes. If that meant driving for an hour and half with a dozen photographers with the morning grumps, so be it. Their first impression of Idaho was flawed. Their last impression, and lasting impression, had to be perfect.

***

The catering crew pulled up to the edge of the parking lot at 5 am. Bill was glad to be their first customer, accepting a hot cup of White Cloud. Watching them scurry to set up folding tables was good medicine for the morning. The crunch their shoes made when they walked, the clatter of utensils, the slam of the van door, were all familiar sounds. He could hold the coffee cup in his hands and enjoy the heat. When he spoke, they answered. After his strange, restless night, Bill felt reality creeping back. When he saw the first carload of protestors pull up, he remembered that reality was not all good.

***

She felt a little silly carrying the sign, like some fifty-something hippy. She had never done anything remotely like it before. Debbie thought her inexperience must show in the crudely lettered placard, if not in her face. Her sign read, "Take your $$ to Disneyland." It seemed like a cutting statement when she put it down in Magic Marker the night before. Now, she was embarrassed to show it. Next to the others she saw, it was piffle. One had a vulgar drawing of a fat man on his back with an apple in his mouth. The caption was, "Take a Tourist to Lunch!" Another said, "Tourists: No License, No Limit." Several signs chimed in with "Idaho for Idahoans." There were three or four with bull's eyes superimposed over the hated word. And, somewhere on nearly every sign, was a private's chevron.

***

Watching the small crowd gathering across the way made his heart sink. Some of them looked a little ragged, like sleeping in their clothes was a normal thing. Many had arrived in battered pickups and smoke-belching station wagons. They brought with them gritty little children who shoved and shouted, oblivious to the threats of severe punishment their parents doled out like breath mints. Several dogs ferociously defended empty pickup beds from children and other yapping dogs. These are my people, Bill thought. My people.

***

Jo Beth usually loved the sight of a news van. Her presence at an event was often enough to assure they showed up in force. As one reporter told her, she gave good "bite." The van she followed into the park was likely to bite her back. This time, the protestors were the draw. In her mind she started rehearsing short pithy lines for the folks at home.

***

They started chanting as soon as the travel writers pulled up. "Idaho for Idahoans! Idaho for Idahoans!" It was largely a waste of time, Bill thought. Channel three didn't have their camera unpacked and five was just pulling in. The noise made the travel writers nervous. They sipped their coffee and munched on breakfast croissants, joking with each other about their warm reception. Jo Beth was doing her best to distract them, but several had already fired off a few shots of the protestors.

Someone from Parks and Recreation had rounded up four-wheelers for each of the writers, courtesy of local dealers. One might also say, courtesy of The Guv. They were parked in three neat rows beyond the caterer's tables.

"Clark!" Jo Beth shouted. She strode toward him. "Let's get this moving before that bunch of assholes gets the bright idea of throwing themselves in front of the ATVs or something."

"Will do. The sun will be up in another 15 minutes anyway."

Already the sky was white in the east. In the west the moon was huge, just above the horizon. In a few more minutes the brightening sky would start to wash it out. Bill gave the signal to a ranger to start the engines.

***

He could hear them if he chose to. Watching them through the lens was good enough. Coyote looked at them one at a time trying to choose.

***

Debbie felt a little better about being there. The men and women who got out of the big van did not look like any of her friends. They wore khaki trousers with lots of pockets, or neatly hemmed shorts, or polo shirts, or sandals. There wasn't a pair of Levis among them. Levis and boots and plaid shirts were everywhere on her side of the lot. Someone smiled at her and asked where she was from. They meant what town, of course. Since she wasn't from a town, she had hesitated, then said, "Idaho." They had all laughed and shook her hand and said things like "right on." It puzzled her a little that she was suddenly so accepted. But she liked it. And the chanting had warmed her up.

***

Bill stood next to the ATV he would use to guide the group back to the site. Even with the protestors catcalling them, some of the writers were reluctant to leave the coffee. They were straggling to their machines when another car pulled up. It was a new Toyota sedan. Bill spotted the Alamo sticker on the bumper when it parked. Not a great place for a tourist, he thought. Then he saw the woman get out of the car. A tourist only in the statistical sense, 50 miles from home. It was Mary Lewis.

***

The woman with the long black hair could have gone either way, Debbie thought. She wore Levis and a cotton shirt, but she also had on hiking boots. The woman closed the car door. Debbie found herself thinking, walk this way, walk this way. When the woman set out toward the writers Debbie felt an inexplicable sense of loss.

***

Someone new. He had not made up his mind yet, and now there was someone new to think about. He sighed a burdensome sigh and carefully moved the scope. Coyote had to hurry now. In a moment he would see the sun coming over the mountain. He had to choose. The new one had long black hair that made him smile. And shrug.

***

She stopped walking when she saw him. In the dim predawn light he could barely see her eyes. He wanted so much to see forgiveness there. To see love. He was even ready for hate. The last thing he expected was the sorrow he saw.

Mary dropped to the ground like an empty set of clothes.

***

Debbie heard the rifle crack and saw the woman fall. Others around her froze, or dropped to the ground. One man, one of the others, ran to the fallen woman. Debbie let her sign fall and began to move fast.

***

"Mary."

Someone was calling her from far away.

"Oh, Ma-ry."

She could not answer because she was down there in the dirt.

"Ma-ry Looo-is."

The voice was sing-songy, like a little child's. It sounded strange and familiar at once.

"Mary, Mary, Mary."

She looked away. The voice was next to her on all sides.

"Looks like I killed you a little, Mary."

She saw her body there in the dirt and said, "Looks like you killed me a lot."

That made Coyote laugh.

***

Debbie ran up to the woman. The man knelt in the sand next to the fallen woman, doing nothing but holding a strand of her hair in his fingers. She was about to scream at him to help her for god sakes. Then she caught the smell. A wild, coppery smell. The sun coming over the mountain crept across the woman's face. Debbie quickly turned and put a hand to her mouth.

***

Jo Beth crouched behind the catering van with three travel writers. No one was in any hurry to move until they were certain the shooting had stopped. Someone said they'd seen a woman get hit. She didn't know if that was true or not, but she had definitely heard a shot. Sons of bitches were going to make them late. She felt the first rays of the morning sun warming the back of her neck. She turned her head to see it rise.

"Oh, great! That just tears it. They've completely ruined the shoot."

The big dune, centerpiece of the desert panorama she had envisioned on the cover of Conde Nast Traveler, had a blemish on the side facing the sun. Someone had stomped an enormous symbol into the sand overnight, the shadow creating a perfect chevron.

CHAPTER FIFTEEN

His Own Private Idaho

In which Bill has a private moment

He barely recognized the countryside around Blackfoot. There were far fewer fields than he remembered and far, far more houses. He expected that. It still depressed him. He was preparing himself for the worst when he came to the point of the bench that pushed out into the Snake River Plain like a finger, forming a tiny valley between itself and the foothills a mile away across the Blackfoot River. The paved road turned to gravel there, as it always had.

He drove over the tip of the bench and rounded the corner in his Explorer. There was the valley where he had spent the best years of his life. The Blackfoot River meandered through the center of it, nudging first this way then that, like a curious child. The few spots where tall trees stood along its banks marked the farmyards and houses of the valley. Low red willows were the rule for most of its length. And how long was the valley? Maybe three or four miles. Smaller than he remembered. He expected that, too. For three years he had been looking at this scene in miniature. That the original was three-quarter size now did not diminish it.

The road followed the gentle ups and downs of the little hills extending from the bench and into the valley. With his window down, Bill drove slowly, listening to the pop and crunch of the gravel beneath his tires. The adults used to complain about the size of the rocks. The county had dredged them straight from a dried up river bed and put them down without bothering with a crusher. The too-big rocks spoke to him now in a familiar shushing voice. They scooted away, parting before his tires and shifted against each other, scolding him for staying away so long.

A part of him noted the new homes. He passed three. Most of him looked right through them. The fields looked much the same, and he could already see the jumbled green tops of the big trees in The Jungle at the far end of the valley.

When he came to the head of the lane, he stopped by the mailbox. Was it the same? Surely over the years a snowplow or neighborhood delinquent with a cherry bomb would have taken out the original. It looked the same. He decided to think it was.

From where he sat he could let the lane lead his eyes down the hill and along the trees to the house. The Place. He could. And he could not. To even look that way yet was almost impossible. To drive down the lane, get out of the Explorer and go knock on the door was unthinkable. He needed to approach it slowly, obliquely.

Bill dropped the lever into drive and rolled down the road and across the cattle guard, where he pulled over. He got out and began to follow the fence line down the hill. On foot, he felt he could absorb it all better. Slowly. He saw glimpses of buildings through the trees—trees his great grandmother had planted. Slowly he walked along a fence his father built. Pop planted cedar posts he had cut and peeled and treated himself. Bill stopped next to one, a twisted branch barely straight enough for the duty. He broke off a sliver and inhaled the sweet, spicy aroma. He could picture Pop digging holes by hand every few feet to set the cedar posts. He saw him holding them up straight with one hand, kicking a few inches of dirt in the hole, then tamping the dirt with his homemade tamping pole.

Forty, maybe fifty years this fence had stood. Bill wondered what mark of his would remain that long. What mark could he be proud of? Private Idaho would be at least a footnote in history books for many years, right alongside the 1905 assassination of Governor Steunenberg. That he had not pulled a trigger, had not placed a bomb was no comfort to him. He knew those actions flowed from his words as surely as the Blackfoot flowed from mountain springs, gathering runoff as it went, forming a river big enough to cut canyons before it retired to meander through this little valley. He could not say when he lost control, or if he ever really had it. Could he have prevented Mary's death? That question was his constant companion now.

He continued to walk down the fence line until he came to the one-lane dirt road that hugged the bottom of the bench. From there, he could stoop down and get an almost full view of The Place from beneath the branches of the trees. He remained erect. For several minutes he stood there with The Place obscured. He stood and looked through that veil of leaves, imagining nothing had changed. Nothing would change, he knew, if he turned around and went away. It would remain forever constant in his mind.

He remembered that Sunday morning when Mary was still asleep beside him. With no close second it was the best moment of his life. How many times had he yearned to go back to that moment, to capture it and hold it unchanged forever? This moment was like that, and this time the decision was his. Mary had awakened. That was beyond his control. But this moment was truly his.

It occurred to Bill that any freshman English major could tell him the answer: You cannot go home again. He smiled at the thought, and nearly accepted it. Then he crossed the road and ducked under the trees.

The Place stood 200 feet away, not smaller than he remembered, but larger. He folded his hands on top of one of Pop's posts and rested his chin there. It took him a long time to see the little log house hidden inside the big one, but it was there. Covered with steel siding now, it looked like a small addition to the main house; like it was being swallowed whole by a behemoth. The monster rose three stories, its glass-walled front giving unobstructed views of the pond to the north. It must have been 3,600 square feet. As big as the house in Boise he once shared with Pauline.

Bill tried to remember what the log house had looked like. When he looked back at The Place from a skiff while poling the pond, what exactly had he seen? Now, without the diorama, he could not picture the Idaho of his youth.

There was another missing piece in his mind's jigsaw puzzle. The barn. He had once intended to come to see the door, to perfect the miniature barn on the diorama. That door would remain forever gaping. The barn was gone.

The chicken coop was no longer there and the wooden outbuildings were missing. If it weren't for the big boxelder tree in the back yard he might wonder if this were even the right place. The park was still there, with the windbreak Pop had planted still protecting it. He thought he recognized sections of the old corral he and Griff had balanced on. Everything else had changed. There were trees missing, and new ones in their place. New, mature trees. Shiny metal buildings stood where the tractor shed had been. Even the lane was reconfigured, wrapping now around the other side of the house. Why, he could not imagine.

Then the dogs began barking. Dogs, barking at him on his own...

Bill began walking the fence line again. There was one more place he wanted to see. It was a place that might be the same. He walked alongside the pastures below the house, along another familiar windbreak, and by another grove of trees planted by his great grandmother. These were not doing well. Over half showed naked white snags at the top. Rotting logs spoke of those that had fallen years before.

A shallow gully drained the pasture closest to the river. He stepped into the willows and ducked their clothes-grabbing branches. Almost as if they recognized him, the willows let him slip through as easily as he had as a kid. He squatted on the edge of the gully, half-hidden still by foliage. There was no trace of the tree that had once been his airplane, his bridge, his rocket ship. He had not expected there would be even a branch after all these years. He had expected to be alone.

This was the place where once he could think and dream. It was the place of renewal. It was his most private place those years ago. Now someone was there. His jaw tightened.

A boy, about ten, knelt in the bottom of the gully, oblivious to Bill. Dressed in T-shirt, tennis shoes and jeans, he concentrated on the scene spread out before him. The boy had made a little farm down there with a metal barn, an assortment of tractors and trucks, plastic animals of all kinds and sticks laid out for fences. He was making enthusiastic engine sounds while rolling a pickup along in the dirt.

Bill sat on his haunches quietly watching him. He watched as the boy opened a stick gate for his cows, then dragged a toy cultivator in the dirt making tiny dusty rows. Bill watched him make his little world for a long while, then slowly backed away through the willows.

With his hands in his pockets he followed the fence line back past his great grandmother's grove, past the barking dogs, past The Place. When he got to the dirt road, he turned and looked through the obscuring branches one last time and knew the freshmen were wrong. They did not even have the right question. The question was, can you ever leave it?

EPILOGUE

Get out of the state you're in

"Look at that," Mark Angel said, as they crested the hill. "There's the Snake River, which means that's Oregon on the other side, which means we'll be only one state away from... " He let it hang there for a second. As if they'd practiced it for months, his wife, Rita, and daughter, Heather, chimed in with, "California!"

John Todd stared out the window.

"It will be so good to get back to where there's decent shopping," Rita said.

"To where people know how to drive," said Mark.

"To where there's an ocean!" Heather said.

John stared at the sagebrush in the distance and remembered the weekend he went camping in the Owyhees.

"Oh, and where the wind doesn't always blow," said Rita.

"Where people don't dress like dorks," Heather said.

"Yeah, and to where the TV news comes on at eleven," said Mark.

John Todd stared at a passing pasture and remembered the first time he went horseback riding with Erica.

"Seafood! Remember seafood?" asked Mark.

"And dinner theater," said Rita. "Gawd, entertainment of any kind in fact."

"Rock bands!" said Heather.

John Todd stared at the approaching river and remembered rafting on the Payette with the scout troop Robert had talked him into joining. They'd gone fishing five times and seen Hells Canyon, too.

"The Sunday Times that weighs ten pounds!" said Mark.

"Places that are open all night," Rita added.

"Malls, and malls, and malls," said Heather.

John Todd stared at the visitor center going by on the hill. He watched as it disappeared, then quickly turned to catch it again in the rear window. They were crossing the Snake River into Oregon on the one span of bridge that remained open.

"They still haven't got that fixed," Mark said.

"Yeah. Who cares?" said Heather. "This one still gets us out of the stupid state."

"Wait!" John Todd said. "Turn around!"

"Turn around? What are you talking about?" Mark asked.

John Todd put his fingers in his pocket and felt the smooth surface of his favorite Idaho souvenir.

"Just turn around. Please? Just for a minute. I've got something I can give back."

Afterward, 1995

The third ghost

This book is about an Idaho that isn't. It is the description of a future phantom. Idahoans will notice some geographic details that seem akilter and histories more a shadow of the real thing. This is a parallel state of mind.

As I write this, another summer season is on those of us in the tourism industry. We anxiously watch the monthly numbers. Will they be higher this year? If they are lower, is that because last year's numbers were so high? If so, is it a blip or is it a trend?

The people at the real Idaho Department of Commerce watch those numbers. Unlike their fictional counterparts, they do so with deep concern over what those numbers could portend. They know you can love a place to death. Idaho is fortunate to have people who care about our quality of life serving in key positions of travel promotion and economic development. They are 180 degrees from Jo Beth Crowder. I purposely wrote her character, and the other Commerce characters, against type. Clearly stated, these are not real people. They are not like the real people who hold those jobs.

I believe this disclaimer is necessary because the very elements portrayed in this book do exist in the real Idaho. I would not have written the book if I did not think so.

There will be people who are convinced I am advocating violence, because I portrayed it. There may be people who misunderstand so completely they emulate some anti-tourist, anti-growth actions depicted in the book. That is a risk every writer takes. I could not have told the story without illustrating the radical reactions to change people sometimes have. That does not mean I condone them.

How serious is the threat of over-reaction? Serious as a bullet. As I was completing the first draft of this novel my brother, Kent Just, who was the Executive Director of the Twin Falls Chamber of Commerce, came to work one morning to find bullet holes in his office window. Anti-growth notes were found in connection with the incident and a similar one a few days later.

As the book was going to press, those conducting recreation surveys in Boise County were being harassed by locals against tourism, even as a whitewater put-in on the South Fork of the Payette River was being repeatedly vandalized. In Eagle, Idaho a couple narrowly escaped injury as the result of vandalism pointedly aimed at new highway construction. Days earlier, such vandalism was being promoted locally in an anonymous flier.

People have legitimate concerns about growth and tourism in Idaho. Tourism industry professionals recognize that, and they address those concerns every day. They shift use by de-marketing areas, they educate travelers about the fragility of natural resources, and they emphasize activities that help sustain our quality of life. Doing otherwise would ruin Idaho and it would ruin the tourism industry. Without that quality of life, travelers would simply quit coming.

I am optimistic Idaho will rationally meet the challenge of being discovered. This book is merely Dickens' third ghost. It is a future that does not have to be.

Afterward, 2013

Nearly 20 years after writing *Keeping Private Idaho*, and 150 years after my family moved to Idaho Territory, I am happy to report the xenophobia depicted in the book and described in the first afterword has largely gone away. The tourists continued to come. Idaho's population continued to grow, sometimes dramatically. Many of those new residents came from California. It is not uncommon to hear some mild grousing about that. But, in the end, who came blame someone for falling in love with this state? And, who came blame someone for wanting to keep it their own private Idaho?

www.ingramcontent.com/pod-product-compliance
Lightning Source LLC
Chambersburg PA
CBHW021002120726
47905CB00009B/2820